Graven Images

Callie Cassidy Mysteries, Book 6

Lori Roberts Herbst

Editor: Lisa Mathews, Kill Your Darlings Editing Services

Cover Designer: Molly Burton, Cozy Cover Designs

ISBN-13: 979-8-9903-698-0-1 (ebook); 979-8-9903698-1-8 (paperback)

Become a Subscriber

Lori Roberts Herbst's subscribers get access to free prequel short stories, as well as updates, news, and giveaways.

Subscribers are always the first to hear about new books and publications.

See the back of the book for details on how to sign up!

The Callie Cassidy Mystery Series

Chapter One

A soft breeze wafted through the aspen trees, sending dangling golden leaves into a frenzied dance beneath the glinting sunlight. The scent of pine drifted on the wind. I turned my face upward and smiled at the warmth of the autumn sun as it broke through the low-hanging fog. My golden retriever, Woody, lay curled at my feet, his leash coiled on the ground. Woody's adopted brother, an orange tabby cat named Carl, purred from the confines of the pet carrier strapped across my back. Around my neck, my camera hung on its strap, offering a familiar sense of comfort.

I sighed in contentment, thinking I'd need to add this to my ever-growing list of happy places.

If I mentioned that to anyone else, though, I was certain to be the recipient of befuddled stares. After all, I was surrounded by dead people.

Nevertheless, the Western Pioneer Cemetery, nestled as it was into a valley of the Colorado Rockies, provided a sense of peace and serenity. The rugged old tombstones jutted from the surrounding buffalo grass. Overhead, a canopy of trees offered the dearly departed a bounty of shade. Dating back to the late 1800s, the cemetery offered a fitting resting place to hundreds of former Rock Creek Villagers.

"Callie, let's get this show on the road." My mother's voice wrenched me from my reverie. "I'm not getting any younger, darling."

I winced. Not the most appropriate words for a seventy-year-old to utter to her forty-six-year-old daughter as they both stood in a cemetery. The mischievous lilt in her voice told me she knew it, too.

"Coming." I glanced at Woody snoozing on a patch of grass and decided against grabbing his leash and tugging him along behind me. Dogs were permitted in the cemetery only if constrained, but I'd never been much of a rule follower. Besides, Woody was well-behaved, and I'd keep an eye on him. In fact, I wriggled the cat carrier off my back and placed it on the ground next to the dog. Carl emitted a tiny groan before curling up for a nap of his own.

I headed toward Mom, who crouched beside an aged tombstone. Dressed in loose-fitting jeans and a green quilted pullover, her trim figure made me almost envious. Her silver hair was styled into a bob, and her porcelain skin glowed with pleasure. I couldn't help but smile at her enthusiasm. For the past few years, Maggie Cassidy had become something of a hobby jumper. She'd tried her hand at knitting, cake decorating, scrapbooking, and jigsaw puzzles. Now she was immersing herself in the oddest pursuit of all: grave rubbing.

Not grave *robbing*, which I thought I'd heard when she first spoke of her new pastime. No, this hobby didn't require a shovel and the dark of night, but rather rice paper, rubbing wax, a spray bottle filled with clean water, a soft brush—and tombstones.

A few days ago, in a lecture worthy of her high school English teacher years, Mom had explained to me that the purpose of grave rubbing was the creation of a permanent historical record. Over the span of years, weather elements such as sun, snow, and wind pounded burial markers, eroding the inscribed names, dates, and messages. Even with the best of care, the monuments would be eventually reduced to mounds of stone with nothing left to memorialize the people housed beneath them. Grave rubbing helped to preserve their time on Earth.

Mom's interest in grave rubbing had been sparked by the woman standing beside her—Mrs. Barney, the librarian at Rock Creek Village High School since my days as a student there. Though decades had passed since then, she still appeared youthful, with just a smattering of wrinkles lining her otherwise smooth face.

The librarian was writing a book about the village's past. After reading an early draft, Mom had provided me with an unsolicited—though admittedly interesting—history lesson, straight from the manuscript. It's how I'd learned Western Pioneer Cemetery was one of the oldest burial grounds in the state and that Rock Creek Village's earliest settlers rested here. Mrs. Barney was a descendent of those residents and wanted to document their history.

"You should be in these photos, too," I said, gesturing to her now.

"Oh, no, no, no," she said, waving her hands. "I'm just writing the book. This part is your mother's department."

Mom made a clucking noise. "Nonsense, Glenda. This is your ancestor. You must be in the photos. Besides, it would help me if you held the paper as I rubbed."

I grinned. When Maggie Cassidy used that tone of voice, there was no sense arguing. Mrs. Barney obediently dropped to her knees on the soft grass, took the thin paper from Mom and pulled it tight across the face of the marker.

I positioned myself behind the tombstone to capture the women's faces as they began the process. Mom's expression was one of deep concentration, while Mrs. Barney's bordered on reverence. The diffused light of the sun peeked through the fog, highlighting the stone's texture.

After a half dozen shots, I made my way around the grave and aimed the lens over the women's shoulders. Mom rubbed the bar of blue wax slowly and carefully across the paper, and the words etched into the stone began to reveal themselves. "Here lies Ezra Pendleton..."

It was like watching a photo come to life in the darkroom. When the dates appeared on the paper, Mrs. Barney drew a breath. "I just realized Ezra was my age when he died."

Mom rocked back and studied the paper. "Yes, I suppose that's true. Of course, people didn't live as long in those days."

"They didn't have access to the same level of health care and medicine we do now," I added. "Mrs. Barney, you'll probably outlive your...what...great great grandfather?...by fifty years."

She looked up at me and smiled. "Callie, I've asked you many times to call me Glenda. It's been thirty years since you were a student browsing the shelves of my library. And for your information, you left out a great. There should be three of them. Ezra was my great grandmother's grandfather and among Rock Creek Village's earliest settlers. Colorado wasn't even a state when he moved here in 1865."

"Wow," I said, doing the math in my head. "He was only twenty-five then."

"Hard to fathom, isn't it? I sometimes imagine what it must have been like. Those brutal winters living in log cabins built by hand. No central heat. No grocery stores. No roads. No cars, for heaven's sake. I complain when my internet connection takes too long. Thinking of his life makes me feel...I don't know, soft."

I understood what she meant, of course, but she was comparing apples and oranges. Each generation faced challenges of its own. For example, Mrs. Barney's ancestors couldn't fathom the concept of artificial intelligence, identity theft, or cyber fraud.

Still, I reflected on my townhome's central heating and air conditioning and knew I wouldn't want to trade places with those old timers.

As I scrolled through my photos, trying to decide if I had enough, a sudden stiff breeze blew through the cemetery. A flurry of movement caught my peripheral vision, and I lifted my gaze.

An elderly man charged up the path, looking like a cross between Ichabod Crane of Sleepy Hollow fame and the Wicked Witch of the West—except not nearly as friendly. His approach triggered an unwelcome jolt of adrenaline.

The man ground to a halt next to Woody and Carl, dropped the toolbag he was carrying, and pointed a bony finger at the creatures.

"I'll thank you to get these animals out of my cemetery."

Chapter Two

I half expected him to follow with, "I'll get you, my pretty, and your dog and cat, too." Instead, he stomped a well-worn boot, sending up a swirl of dust.

The tall, gaunt man was Cedric Fallow, who had served as cemetery caretaker for as long as I could remember. At seventy muscular pounds, Woody could have knocked the man over with a swish of his furry tail, but that wasn't my pup's nature. Instead, he flattened his ears and ducked his head, appearing intimidated. Crouched low, the dog whined and scooted backward. Then he shot a glance at Carl, who issued a hiss from within his carrier. Woody slunk over to the cat, grabbed the carrier's shoulder strap in his teeth, and dragged the contraption to safety.

I hurried toward them and wriggled the carrier onto my back. I grabbed Woody's leash and gave him a reassuring pat.

Mr. Fallow grunted. "Miss Cassidy, I must insist—"

"Ms," I said.

His face creased. "What's that?"

"I go by Ms. Cassidy, not Miss. Differentiating between a married and an unmarried woman is archaic. There's no—"

The caretaker waved off my lecture on cultural evolution. "I don't give a rat's keister what you go by. You need to get those beasts out of my cemetery. Otherwise, I'll contact animal services and have it done for you."

Before I could respond, Mom planted herself between us.

"Cedric, what's gotten into you, scaring a couple of sweet, innocent creatures that way?"

From his position on my back, Carl issued a yowl. If I had the ability to interpret catspeak, I'm certain his words would have consisted of the four-letter kind. Not exactly the poster cat for sweet and innocent.

I turned my attention back to Mr. Fallow. The man looked every day of his seventy-plus years. His stringy gray hair hung to his shoulders, thin enough that patches of pale scalp glistened through it. Yellow-toned skin stretched tight across his face, giving him a skeletal appearance. I marveled that he still managed this entire cemetery on his own.

Then I noticed the ropy muscles of his arms and the defiant lift of his chin as he stared down his beak nose at my mother.

"Those animals have no business on these grounds, Maggie," he said. "Neither do you, for that matter—desecrating my tombstones with your...whatever it is." He pointed to the rubbing wax in Mom's hand.

He widened his stance and crossed his arms, as if challenging her to a duel. I stifled a smirk. Foolish man, to take on my mother.

Predictably, Mom's eyes narrowed. "Cedric," she began. Her voice was low and even. I wondered if Mr.

Fallow realized he'd entered the eye of the storm. "I know you are aware that dogs are permitted in the cemetery—"

"It's a ridiculous rule," he sputtered. "Besides which, they're only allowed if they're restrained. This dog's leash was lying untended on the ground. What if the brute—"

Mom held up her hand. "I will not allow you to insult my granddog. He is a sweet, well-disciplined creature." I may have cringed at that characterization, but I let it pass. Poetic license and all.

"He's much better behaved than many humans I know," Mrs. Barney added pointedly.

"Rules are rules," Mr. Fallow said, but I could see the wind leaving his sails. He'd lost this battle before it began.

Mom rolled back her shoulders. "And as for my grave rubbing..." She held up the wax and gestured to the tombstone. "I completed a class on how to conduct the process without damaging the stone, and I presented you with a notarized statement of the Chamber of Commerce's permission to proceed. Remember?"

Mr. Farrow nodded glumly. "My memory is fully intact."

"Then I'm not sure why you're making a fuss. These rubbings, along with Mrs. Barney's book, are likely to draw attention to this place, which you've tended to so well all these years."

Ah, the catch-more-flies-with-honey strategy. Well-played, Mom. Well-played.

Mr. Fallow's fingers curled into fists. "I don't want attention. I don't want looky loos here, trampling the grounds. My residents deserve a proper rest. I've spent my life caring for them, and I don't want them disturbed by so-called history buffs who want a...what do they call 'em? Selfie."

He stared at my camera. "Sheesh, old man," I mumbled.

His nostrils flared. "What did you say?"

My eyes widened. "Leash. I'll hold Woody's leash. I'm sorry I wasn't more conscientious. It won't happen again."

Mom nodded. "There, you see? All is well. As for the cemetery, our only goal is documenting the history of the town. You've lived here a long time, Cedric. I'd think you'd want that, too."

He took a deep breath and looked over his shoulder toward the tree-lined path. When he spoke again, his voice carried an ominous tone. "Bad things happen when the living encroach on places where the dead rest. I can already sense a change here. Mark my words, nothing good will come of your intrusion."

He lifted his heavy toolbag with ease. After one more glance down the path, he strode past us to the little cottage that served as his home. He climbed the steps to the wooden porch and faced us. "I'll be watching you."

Woody whimpered. Carl squirmed in his carrier. Mr. Fallow trudged inside, slamming the door so hard the windows shook. A curtain shimmied, and we saw him peering out at us.

I shuddered. "Crazy old man."

My mother pivoted, her face stern. "Callahan Maureen Cassidy, don't let me hear you talk like that. Cedric Fallow has given his life to the service of this place. He deserves our respect."

I lifted my hands, surprised at her response. Hadn't she spent the last few minutes reading him the riot act herself? "Sorry. I guess I'm a little shaken up."

Her expression softened. "I get it, darling. It just bothers me when I hear someone writing off an older person as crazy, or rambling, or demented. Cedric Fallow is passionate about this cemetery, and he feels a kinship with the souls in his care. In many ways, it's an admirable trait."

What she said made sense. I marveled again at the tough, compassionate woman who was my mother. Tenderness swelled in my chest. Maggie Cassidy was getting older, too. I'd never write her off—and I'd never allow anyone else to, either.

She looked at Mrs. Barney and gestured to the tombstone. "Ready to get to it, Glenda?"

They both sneaked a peek at the cottage. The curtain fluttered again, and Mrs. Barney smiled. "Wouldn't want to keep our audience waiting," she said.

I touched my camera. "Ladies, I took plenty of good rubbing photos. I'm going to head deeper into the grounds to shoot the rest of the graves on Mrs. Barney...er, Glenda's...list. It's a perfect day for it. The fog and mist give the place an...ambience." Spooky factor, I almost said, but I didn't want Mom to think I was being insensitive again.

I pulled out a folded page of notebook paper. "Shouldn't take me more than half an hour."

Mom nodded. "Perfect. We're planning on completing two more rubbings this morning. We'll meet you here when we're done."

I turned toward the path and waved over my shoulder. "See you in a bit."

"Don't let go of that leash, darling," Mom warned. "I have a feeling there are eyes everywhere."

I peered down the path and up to the branches of the trees. Spooky factor, indeed.

Chapter Three

As I traipsed down the path, a ray of sunshine pierced the fog, all but erasing the eerie atmosphere. That bright beam from above reminded me of something my therapist said—even on the darkest of days, the sun and the blue sky still exist.

The loop of Woody's leash dangled from my wrist as he cantered a few steps ahead. Carl floundered about in the carrier on my back, no doubt indulging in his morning grooming session. The cemetery stretched across a space so large it seemed carved from the landscape. With its untamed grasses and tall white aspens, there was a wildness about the place. But beneath that feral layer rested a sense of order and meaning. The place appeared nurtured. The gravestones lining the trail stood proud, weathered but clean, old but not forgotten. I pictured Cedric Fallow trudging this path every day, week after week, year after year, stretching back to...who knew when? Finally, I began to appreciate the fervor of his devotion.

I scanned the names on the stones as I passed and paused to consult Glenda's hand-drawn map. I was searching for Zachary Pendleton's marker, and it should be...a few more steps...

I held Woody back with a tug on his leash. "Hang on, fella. We're here." The dog plopped down and stretched out on the path, completely at ease. I glanced around to make sure Mr. Fallow wasn't lurking, then slid the leash off my wrist and the carrier off my back. "What happens in the graveyard stays in the graveyard," I whispered. Woody grinned at me, tongue lolling, and Carl emitted an appreciative meow.

Crouching, I studied Zachary's tombstone. Beneath the name, his birth and death dates were etched into the stone: July 31, 1862-July 1, 1904. Not quite forty-two-years old when he died. Younger than me, in fact. But as we'd discussed earlier, longevity wasn't to be expected in those days. Not in the rugged wilderness of nineteenth century Colorado. I brushed a clump of dirt off the worn stone, lifted the camera to my eye, focused, and snapped the shutter.

A few shots later, I got to my feet, satisfied. The cracking of my knees reminded me I hadn't attended class at my friend Summer Simmons' Yoga Delight studio in far too long. I vowed to remedy that this week. Not only was the practice good for my body, I'd discovered, much to my surprise, that what everyone had been trying to tell me was true—Summer's yoga and meditation classes helped stabilize and even elevate my mood.

I chuckled. Who was this new Callie Cassidy? A few years ago, I'd been a go-getting, hard-nosed investigative photojournalist. If someone had told me back then I'd be strolling through a cemetery shooting photos of old graves while pondering the benefits of yoga and meditation, I'd have called them crazy.

Turns out, I'd been the crazy one, burning myself out

documenting the worst of human nature, when here, in the place I'd been raised, the better side of life had been patiently waiting for me.

As I stepped back onto the trail, ready to head to the next site, a puff of wind blew through the trees like the exhalation of a god. The breeze swirled the mist. A flurry of leaves gave up their tenuous hold and spiraled downward, settling across the graves. I had the sudden sense I wasn't alone, that other presences hovered nearby. I looked around, half expecting Mr. Fallow to leap out from behind a stone and scold me for disregarding his rules. But no one was there...except...Could I be sensing lingering souls, detached from their bodies but unwilling to leave them behind? Were ghosts floating among the trunks of the aspens, watching as I snapped photos?

I chided myself. Silly woman, letting a cemetery get to you—and in the light of day, too. The people here were long since dead and buried. I didn't know exactly what I believed about an afterlife, but I certainly didn't think people who died over a hundred years ago haunted the place where their bodies were interred. Nope. I didn't believe that at all.

Then Woody scrambled to his feet, his ears perked and the hair rising along the scruff of his neck. In his carrier, Carl's tail shot straight up. I cocked my head and listened to the sound that had roused their interest. Amidst the shuddering of the wind came a high-pitched keening. I held my breath and waited. There it was again. A cry, almost a moan, undulating from the shadow of the trees. The third time I heard it, I recognized it. It was the sound of an animal in pain.

Carl emitted a plaintive yowl. Woody took a step toward the wail. I snatched up his leash, halting him in his tracks. Autumn meant mating season, when elk made their way to lower ground to rut. Could this baying sound be an elk who'd been injured in his quest? The last thing I wanted was for my well-meaning golden retriever to entangle himself with a wounded bull elk. I knew who'd win that battle, and it wouldn't be my sweet pup.

I took a step backward, quickly lifting Carl's carrier back across my shoulders. Having grown up in Rock Creek Village, I was accustomed to sightings of wildlife, but that didn't diminish my trepidation at the prospect of an elk encounter. My every instinct screamed at me to run, but my rational side told me that was the wrong choice. I needed to keep Woody and Carl quiet and slowly back away. After all, an injured animal probably wanted even less to do with me than I with him. He'd simply limp off and leave me here quivering. At least, that's what I tried to convince myself.

As I murmured unnecessary shushes at the dog and cat, who'd grown still on their own, I heard the moan again. When I turned toward the sound, I spotted movement some twenty yards away. I squinted as a figure made its way out of the trees.

I saw then it wasn't an injured animal—not the four-legged kind, anyway. Before me stood a woman in a gauzy white dress that hung to her ankles. Her long, gray hair framed a delicate, wrinkled face so pale it almost seemed translucent. A breeze swirled her hair and her dress. I had the fanciful notion she might levitate and flutter away.

She looked like one of the souls I'd been contemplating before—a ghost who had risen from her grave.

Except for one thing.

A splotch of red painted the scalp beneath her billowing hair. It took me only a moment to identify it. After all, it wasn't the first time I'd seen blood.

Chapter Four

The woman reached out with trembling, blood-smeared fingers. Her otherworldly wailing did nothing to dissuade me from the notion that she might be a ghost.

Except the blood was real, very real.

"I was too late." She crumpled to her knees and wept. "Too late."

"Too late for what?" She looked at me through her tears but didn't respond.

My pulse pounding in my ears, I took a tentative step toward her. Woody had no such hesitation. Tugging on the leash, he dragged me toward the woman, sat beside her, and nuzzled her hand with his nose.

Her demeanor transformed. After a few seconds, she ceased crying. She gazed at the dog and stroked his soft fur.

I winced. Her bloody hands meant that fur would need a thorough scrubbing later.

Still, the tenderness of the tableau was enough to prod me from my paralysis. I knelt beside Woody and the woman. She stared at me with blank eyes.

"You're bleeding," I said. "Would it be okay if I checked your scalp?"

She made no response but didn't seem inclined to bite me if I tried. I released Woody's leash, and he snuggled closer to her as I parted her hair and examined the laceration on the crest of her forehead. Blood oozed from it but didn't gush. The injury didn't appear serious.

Still, it needed attention. I patted the dog's flank. "Woody, go get Mom."

He gave the woman's arm a soft lick, then stood and galloped up the trail, dragging his leash behind him. Mr. Fallow was going to have a conniption fit.

Once I'd shrugged off the cat carrier and settled it on the ground, I checked the woman's pulse. Strong and steady. I put a hand on her cheek. Warm, not clammy. She was younger than I'd first thought—only a couple of years older than Mom, I guessed. I sat beside her, trying my best to replace Woody's comforting presence. "Help is coming."

She nodded, which encouraged me to keep talking. "I'm Callie Cassidy. I live here. Rock Creek Village, I mean, not the cemetery."

She looked me in the eye but didn't speak. "What's your name?" I asked.

Her mouth opened and closed, and she touched her forehead. "I...I don't know."

I lifted my eyebrows. Had her head injury been severe enough to cause memory loss? Had she perhaps lain unconscious in the cemetery before emerging from the trees like an angel?

She trailed a hand across her face, as if trying to paint an internal picture of herself. "I don't know what happened or where I am. I don't even know who I am. I can't...I can't remember anything."

Suddenly, her head jerked up. Her breathing quickened, and she struggled to stand.

"I think it's best if you stay seated," I said, but the woman wasn't having it. She pushed up onto her knees. When I saw there was no talking her out of it, I rose and helped her up, keeping an arm around her. As soon as she was steady on her feet, she touched her head again and stared at the blood on her hand.

"You have a wound on your scalp," I repeated. "Do you have any idea how it happened?"

She shook her head too hard and winced at the pain. "I told you, I remember nothing."

Her eyes darted away almost guiltily, which gave me pause. Did she recall more than she was telling me? As a former investigative photojournalist, my knee-jerk reaction was to shift into interrogation mode. From Carl's commanding meow, I knew he agreed. But then we heard footsteps. The woman quivered, and I tightened my arm around her shoulder. "Don't be alarmed. It's just the dog, back with my mother."

Sure enough, Woody appeared first. Mom hurried along behind, followed by Mrs. Barney and...uh oh. Cedric Fallow trailed in their wake. I cringed at the sight of Woody's leash dragging through the dirt. Mr. Fallow didn't seem the type to make allowances for exigent circumstances. I quickly returned Carl's carrier to my back, so at least the old man couldn't reprimand me for the cat.

Before he could start in on me, I snatched up Woody's leash, turned to Mom, and gestured toward the woman.

"She's bleeding from the scalp. Says she has no memory of what happened. Couldn't even tell me her name."

My mother gently examined the wound. Then she brushed back the hair hanging across the woman's pale gray eyes, studied her for a moment, and gasped. "Vivian? Is that you?"

Mr. Fallow, who'd been preoccupied with glowering at Woody, startled. When he turned to inspect the woman, his face registered his recognition. I didn't think he seemed happy about it. "Vivian. We all thought you were dead."

The woman...Vivian...sagged against my mother, who shot a sharp look at Mr. Fallow. He thrust his hands in his pockets. Mom gave the woman an apologetic smile. "Please forgive Cedric's insensitivity. It's just that this is..." She took a deep breath. "Well, suffice it to say, many people are going to be astonished to see you."

The turn of events baffled me. I glanced at Mrs. Barney. She shrugged, also at a loss. I tapped Mom's shoulder and put my lips near her ear. "Who is Vivian?"

Mom frowned. "We need to get your father here. Right away. I left my phone in the car, so you'll need to call him. Tell him where we are and that Vivian is here. He'll know who I'm talking about." Her eyes darted to the tombstones lining the path. "Be sure to tell him she's alive."

"Okay. But shouldn't we call an ambulance?"

"Her injury seems minor."

"But Mom, there's apparently memory loss. I think—"

She nodded. "Yes, of course. Call the paramedics. Then your father."

I stepped aside, pulled my phone from my pocket, and pressed 9. Before I could get to 1, Carl screeched, and Woody howled. My head shot up as Woody took off down the trail in the direction from which Vivian had appeared.

"What's wrong?" Mom asked. Vivian's eyes widened in panic.

Mr. Fallow shook a finger at me. "Get that beast under control!"

I bristled at his tone, but my worry superseded my irritation. What had gotten into the dog? I shouted after him. "Woody! Come back here, right now!"

Woody hesitated long enough for a backward glance then continued toward the interior of the cemetery. A moment later, he disappeared into a copse of trees. I took off after him, running as fast as my middle-aged legs would carry me—which admittedly wasn't lightning speed, especially with Carl bouncing in the carrier on my back, shrieking what I could only interpret as language worthy of a salty sailor.

As soon as I rounded the bend, it was as if I'd entered a movie set. The fog hung low, giving the place an ethereal atmosphere. The leaves rendered the shadows darker. Even the sound seemed muted. Tombstones rose from the ground like a crooked grin.

Though I'd only gone twenty yards, I'd sprinted the distance, and now I experienced a hitch in my ribs. When I stopped to catch my breath, Carl protested with a derisive meow. Through the mesh of his carrier, he clawed at my neck.

"Look, cat, I'm doing the best I can. I'm not as young as I used to be, and you're heavier than you used to be. Carrying you around is no picnic."

Carl squawked at the insult. Then we heard Woody bark. I squinted into the mist and spotted a patch of gold. There he stood, at the curve of the path, not much farther ahead.

I puckered my lips and whistled. The dog didn't move. I called out to him, offering treats. No response, so I changed tactics. "Get over here right now, you naughty dog, or I'll tell Sam never again to offer you dinner scraps!"

Woody looked at me but otherwise didn't budge.

I cocked my head. He was as fixated as a hunting dog with a duck in his sights. A shiver of apprehension coursed through me as I moved toward him. This behavior was out of character for my playful, easy-going dog. Something had gripped his attention, and he wasn't leaving until he showed me whatever it was.

My adrenaline had been pumping nonstop for the past fifteen minutes, but now the level ratcheted up even higher. I wondered if a person could overdose on the hormone. Blood pressure had never been an issue for me, but now, my heart pumped so fast I felt every beat.

As I edged toward the dog, I saw that he was standing sentinel at one of the newer graves. The marker was whiter than the others, and the dirt mound fresher. Woody gave me an apologetic wag and a small whine.

"What do we have here?" I murmured. Carl scrambled and hissed in the carrier until I pivoted so he could get a look. George Corwin, according to the name on the marker. Ah, yes. Mr. Corwin, a long-time but reclusive resident of Rock Creek Village who had died a few weeks ago. I hadn't known the man, but my parents had been friends with him years back. They'd gone to his funeral and mentioned that only a few others had attended. A sad ending to a life, I remember thinking.

I scooped up Woody's leash. "I'm not sure what brought you here, pup, but you've paid your respects. Time to head back and figure out who this Vivian woman is."

I tugged on the leash, but Woody dug his paws into the dirt. "What is with you today?" I asked. He lifted his nose toward the tombstone.

Then I saw it. On the upper left corner of the granite, a dark patch. I bent in and studied it.

"Blood," I said. Carl meowed. Woody seemed to nod.

I took a step back. Vivian had come from this part of the cemetery. She must have fallen and struck her head on the gravestone. Perhaps she'd lost consciousness, explaining her fuzzy memory.

"Good boy," I said, giving Woody a pat. "One mystery solved. Now, let's go back so we can figure out what the woman was doing at George Corwin's grave."

I took a few steps toward the path, but Woody still wouldn't move. There was something more the dog was trying to communicate.

I took a step forward. Craning my neck, I spotted the object of his attention.

Behind the gravestone lay a running shoe. An ankle. A hairy but well-formed calf.

Woody's nose nudged my leg. Gathering my resolve, I rounded the grave.

My eyes followed the calf to the thigh, then to the torso. Up the torso and to the head. I inhaled sharply as I recognized the man.

I surmised he was dead based on the pallor of his skin and his glazed, unblinking eyes.

And, of course, there was the pickaxe jammed into the side of his neck.

Chapter Five

For a moment, time froze. The air ceased circulating. The leaves stopped falling. Even Woody and Carl seemed to hold their breath.

I held a hand in front of the man's open mouth. No breath.

I dropped my eyes, paying a moment's respect at the man's passing, as I always did at a death scene.

Then, as was also my habit at a death scene, I lifted my camera and started snapping the shutter. I knew I needed to summon the police, but taking a few seconds to document the scene wouldn't hurt the man—and it might even help nab his killer.

Along with running shoes, the dead man wore jogging shorts and a tank top. Near his open mouth, I spotted a small sliver of wood. Beside his hand, a lone pinecone. Scattered aspen leaves rested on his body—just a few, though, meaning he hadn't been here long.

I'd shot a half dozen photos before the sound of footsteps interrupted me. Mr. Fallow hurried toward me, fire in his eyes. I held up a hand to ward off the inevitable blitz.

"Mr. Fallow, you can reprimand me later. Right now, there's something more important we need to focus on. Woody made a terrible discovery."

I pointed at the tombstone. The caretaker narrowed his watery eyes. "George Corwin's grave? Did the dog know him or something?"

"What? No." I took a breath. "Brace yourself, Mr. Fallow. Someone is dead."

He folded his arms. "I don't think this is an appropriate time for jokes, Miss Cassidy." He emphasized Miss and stared at me in a challenge.

"No, I mean…well, take a look."

I pointed again. Mr. Fallow frowned but took a step toward the tombstone. Woody and I moved back to give him room to pass. He noticed the blood on the grave marker and tsked in irritation, shooting me an accusatory glare that implied I'd been gallivanting through the cemetery dripping bags of blood onto his precious graves.

I tilted my head toward the tombstone. He took another step and spotted the feet. His gaze, as mine had, traveled from the feet to the body. The moment he noticed the pickaxe in the man's neck, he stiffened. "This is horrible," he said.

"I agree. We need to—"

"This grave has been sullied."

My brow furrowed. Mr. Fallow had just observed a dead body with a pickaxe protruding from the neck, and his primary concern was the tombstone?

"Mr. Fallow, a man is dead."

He sighed. "I've seen dead bodies before, young lady. So have you, from what I'm told."

"But this is…you must…we need to…"

"We'll need to summon the police, I suppose." He

sighed again. "More people trampling the graves and disturbing my residents."

I shook my head in wonder and scanned the trees for a hidden camera. Was I being pranked? Had I unwittingly been cast in some dark comedy? "Mr. Fallow, I'm not sure you're grasping the situation. Look at this man. There's a pickaxe in his neck."

"Mattock."

"What?"

"It's not a pickaxe. It's a mattock. I use it to break up roots and weeds around the graves."

"Well, then, there's a mattock in the man's neck. I doubt he stumbled and fell on it. Someone murdered this man. So yes, we need to summon the police."

I pulled my phone from my pocket and pressed 9-1-1. Nothing.

He grunted. "You're too deep in the cemetery. No service here. And thank goodness for that, since my residents deserve peace. You'll have to go closer to the entrance to contact them. I'll wait here with George."

"His name's not George," I began before realizing he meant the buried dead man rather than the freshly dead one. I puffed out my cheeks, unsure whether leaving him here with the body constituted proper protocol. But he seemed as adamant about not budging as Woody had earlier. "Okay," I said at last. "Don't touch anything. The police won't want the crime scene disturbed."

He lifted his hands in exasperation. "I may be old, *Miss* Cassidy, but I'm not stupid."

"I didn't mean to imply—"

"Just go," he said, turning back to gaze at George Corwin's grave. "George and I would like a moment to ourselves before the circus comes to town."

I headed up the path, wondering about the strange

caretaker who'd spent his life ministering to the resting places of the dead. Did such a job change a person, or did only a certain type sign up for such a job? Either way, Mr. Fallow was an odd duck.

But I didn't have time to contemplate the complexities of the caretaker's personality. There were other things to consider—such as who'd killed the man lying behind George Corwin's grave.

From the opening in the trees, I could see that Mom had led the woman back to the cemetery's entrance. She stood with her arm around Vivian's shoulders, as Mrs. Barney hovered nearby. How was I going to break this news? The old woman already seemed fragile—would the report of a dead body further fracture her tenuous grasp on sanity?

Then again, perhaps the woman already knew. She'd come from that direction, after all. Had she seen the dead man as she'd traversed the cemetery? I'd sensed something off about her...maybe that was it.

When I stopped in front of the women, I studied Vivian's face. Beneath the veneer of frailty lay a steeliness that suggested toughness. My gut told me she might not be as delicate as she appeared.

At any rate, I had little choice. I needed to call the police, and Vivian deserved to hear why.

I locked eyes with Mom. "There's been...an incident."

Her jaw tightened. She'd been the wife of a police chief most of her life and was skilled at handling bad news. I tilted my head toward the trees. "There's a...a dead body in there. One that doesn't belong, that is. I have to call the police."

Mom exhaled. "Tell them to send an ambulance, too." She glanced at Vivian and Mrs. Barney. "Glenda, will you take Vivian to the cottage to wait? I saw a bench on the porch, and I think she should get her off her feet. Perhaps you could go inside and get her a glass of water. I'm sure Cedric wouldn't mind."

I wasn't quite as certain of Mr. Fallow's hospitality, but better to ask forgiveness than permission.

Mrs. Barney pressed a gentle hand to Vivian's back, and Vivian allowed herself to be led away. Woody glanced up at me, silently asking permission to accompany the women. I gave him a smile and a nod, and he trotted after them.

I lifted my phone and pressed 9-1-1, putting the call on speaker. When the emergency operator answered, I said, "I need to report a dead body in the Western Pioneer Cemetery."

There was a long pause. "A dead body in the cemetery?"

I scrunched up my face. "Yes, but this one doesn't belong here. Well, I guess technically he does now, but he's not, like, buried or anything."

Another pause. "Is this Callie Cassidy?"

"How did you know?"

"You're on our frequent caller list." My mother sighed, and the operator continued. "So anyway, about this body…"

"Yes, well, he was lying behind a tombstone with a pickaxe…or rather, a mattock…in his neck."

"Okaaayyy. You're certain he's dead?"

"I'm sure. Mr. Fallow is with him now."

"The caretaker?"

"Yes. He was with my mom and Mrs. Barney and me when we were trying to help the ghost lady."

"Ghost lady?"

I visualized the operator shaking her head in confusion. I was muddying the waters by offering too many details.

"The point is, there's a dead body here, and I believe he was murdered. We need the police. Also, the ghost lady sustained a head wound, so we need an ambulance, too."

"I've dispatched officers and EMTs. Ten-minute ETA. Have someone meet them at the entrance. I also contacted Detectives Sanchez and Clarke. They'll be there shortly as well. For the record, did you recognize the dead man?"

I glanced at Mom. "I did. His name is Eugene Murray."

Chapter Six

Mom raised her eyebrows. I told the operator I was hanging up, heard her object, but disconnected anyway. Carl rustled around in his carrier making angry ack ack ack noises. I slipped the contraption off my back, unzipped it, and lifted him out. He squirmed into a comfortable position in my arms, ready to listen.

"Eugene Murray," Mom repeated. "Oh, my."

We stood silently for a moment, contemplating the repercussions. Eugene—or Gene, as he preferred to be called—was a member of a minor Las Vegas mob family. About a year ago, he'd hooked up with Lydia Fredericks, the mother of my best friend, Tonya Stephens. The two of them had been visiting Rock Creek Village frequently, much to Tonya's chagrin.

"This is going to be sticky," Mom said.

I couldn't argue with that. I'd been friends with Tonya since we were in junior high school, and her relationship with her mother had always been tumultuous. Lydia's interests veered less toward motherhood and more toward amassing wealth via a series of sugar daddies. Since Tonya's engagement and subsequent wedding, she and Lydia had been attempting to forge a more harmonious connection, thus Lydia's regular visits. Her newest beau, Gene, who was at least thirty years younger than she, tagged along. Tonya mostly ignored the man's presence, but her husband, David Parisi, found it more difficult. He couldn't stand Gene and could barely be civil to him—a surprise, since David liked almost everyone.

The image of Gene lying on the ground with a sharp metal tool implanted in his carotid artery flashed into my mind. I lifted my eyes to the sky, trying to erase the picture. The fog had burned off, and the sun glittered through the trees. Mom laced her arm through mine, and I rested my head on her shoulder. "Are you okay, Angelface?" she asked. The pet name she'd given me at birth comforted me.

"I'm fine. Well, not fine, exactly. Finding Gene...it was a shock. But it's not the first time I've discovered a dead body."

"Don't I know it," she muttered.

I ignored her comment and looked at the cottage. "What's the story with this Vivian person?"

"I'll explain everything, darling—after we've contacted your father."

She held out her hand, and I passed over my phone. She poked the screen and held it to her ear. I moved closer so I could overhear both sides of the conversation. The phone rang twice, and my father answered. I heard his cheerful greeting before Mom cut him off. "Butch, I need to tell you something, and I want you to prepare yourself."

"Are you all right?"

"I'm fine, sweetheart. It's not about me. It's...Vivian Corwin. She turned up here at the cemetery, where I'm doing my grave rubbing. Butch, she's alive."

There was silence for a few moments as my father processed the information. I used the time to assemble the few tidbits I'd gathered. Mom had referred to the woman as Vivian Corwin. I'd just been at George Corwin's grave. The two of them were about the same age. His sister, maybe? Or had they once been married?

Finally, my father's voice came across the line. "I'll be right there."

He hung up. Concern etched my mother's face. I placed my hand on her arm. "Mom, tell me what's going on. Who is Vivian?"

Mom cast a glance at the cottage where Mrs. Barney and Vivian sat side by side on the bench. Woody lay in front of them with his head on Vivian's feet. Mom turned her back to them and kept her voice low. "She's a ghost, Callie. From forty years ago."

I shuddered. "Care to elaborate?"

"It's a complicated story. For the sake of time, I'll give you a condensed version. Vivian Corwin came to Rock Creek Village back in the early eighties when she was about thirty. She was cordial, funny, kind. A bit of an enigma, though, as if some other life simmered inside her. She never talked much about herself or her past. Still, I took to her right away. And so did George."

"I don't remember her at all, and I hardly remember George. When you told me he passed away, it took me a while to place him. He suffered from some degenerative disease, right? Used a wheelchair?"

"He was diagnosed with a form of muscular dystrophy in his late twenties. But even before that, he was a bit of an introvert. An accountant. Spent most of his time in his own head. He worked out of an office in his house, keeping the books for people and businesses here in the village and around the county. He and your father were friendly—

played chess regularly. When Vivian moved to town and needed a job, your dad mentioned that George was looking for a secretary. We introduced them, and George hired her on the spot."

"I'm guessing their relationship progressed from there."

She nodded. "Rather quickly, in fact. Within six months, the two of them announced their marriage. They'd driven to Pine Haven and had the justice of the peace perform the ceremony."

"A whirlwind romance," I said.

"Almost like a fairy tale. The four of us became good friends. We ate dinner and played cards a couple of times a month. You probably don't remember much about them because we almost always went to their house. It was just easier for George that way, with his wheelchair and all." Her eyes glazed as she remembered the past. "The two of them were so happy together. I'd never seen George smile so much. We had a lot of laughs. And then..."

She trailed off and shot another look at Vivian. "She disappeared." Mom snapped her fingers. "Just like that."

"Disappeared?"

"George called your father at the police station to report that she'd gone missing. The two of us went to their house, along with Frank, who'd joined the force by then. Vivian had taken a few things from the house—clothing, toiletries, her contact lenses. But she'd left her purse and wallet behind."

"Taking her things indicates she left willingly, doesn't it?"

"I'd agree with you, if not for the purse. Why would she leave her bank cards? Her ID?" Mom shook her head. "Your father and Frank did everything in their power to find her. Twelve-hour days, sometimes sixteen. They contacted police departments all over the state and posted flyers everywhere. This was pre-internet, so it meant a lot of footwork. They never turned up a single clue."

"I assume they looked hard at George, right?" I asked. "The spouse is usually the first suspect in a disappearance."

"They investigated George. Of course they did. But there was no evidence indicating his involvement. Still, that didn't stop tongues from wagging around the village. Lots of whispers that Vivian was dead and that George had something to do with it. Your father tried to put a stop to the rumor-mongering, but...well, you know how it goes in a small town."

I did indeed, having been run through the gossip mill myself a few times since I'd moved back. "How did George handle it?"

Mom's eyes filled with tears. "The poor man was devastated. Blamed himself. Kept saying Viv must not have wanted to be saddled with his condition and all the future care he'd require. We tried to tell him that wasn't true, that something else must have happened, but...well, he was never the same. He turned into a total recluse. He managed to maintain his business, but that was about it. The only people he allowed in his home were his medical caregivers and a housekeeper. No matter how much your father and I tried, he refused to see us."

I bit my lip. "What a terrible story. Why don't I remember any of it?"

"You were young when it happened. After the dust settled, your father didn't talk about it much. He considered it his worst failure. The cloud George lived under the rest of his life...it weighed heavily on Butch. It didn't help that there was never any sign of Vivian. No bank accounts, no driver's license, nothing. It was as if she'd fallen off the face of the earth." She looked at Vivian sitting on the porch. "Until today."

"Now everyone will know George didn't kill his wife," I said.

"Yes. George will be vindicated. Just too late to matter."

I sighed. Vivian's return may have created more mysteries than it solved. Where had she been all those years? Why had she come back only after her husband's death? How had she been injured?

And who had killed Eugene?

Chapter Seven

We heard the all-too-familiar sound of sirens, followed by car doors slamming and footsteps pounding. Detective Raul Sanchez and Detective Lynn Clarke appeared first, followed by two Rock Creek Village EMTs. Two uniformed police officers brought up the rear.

I responded with a shrug to Raul's *What, again?* look and pointed toward the cottage. "The injured woman is up there." One of the EMTs headed that direction. Lynn conferred with her partner, then jogged off after the paramedic. The other medic hung back, awaiting instructions.

"Where's the body?" Raul barked.

"I'll take you," I said. I handed Carl to Mom, ignoring his squeals of protest at being left behind, then led the way down the path, with Raul and the officers close behind. As we walked, I filled him in on Vivian's appearance, her wound, and her memory loss. He took it all in without a word.

A minute later, we arrived at George Corwin's grave. Mr. Fallow stood there with his hands folded in front of him like an irritable butler. Raul trod past him through the tall grass and leaned over the body. After a quick look, he stepped back and gestured to the medic to make the final determination. We watched as the EMT tapped and poked and listened. It didn't take long for him to confirm what we already knew. "Dead."

"How long?" Raul asked.

"I'd guess a couple of hours, but the coroner will be more specific. I'll call him." He checked his phone and shook his head. "No service. Back in a flash."

He loped up the trail. Raul laced his hands behind his back so as not to contaminate evidence as he studied the body. He turned to the two officers. "Okay, it's a crime scene. Go call forensics and get everything you need to set up."

They left, and Mr. Fallow groaned. "I don't want those people trampling the grave."

"Can't be helped, sir. We have a murder on our hands." I marveled at his patient tone. Why was I never the recipient of such forbearance?

Raul pointed to Eugene's neck. "Does that pickaxe belong to you?"

"Mattock," Mr. Fallow responded.

"What?"

Mr. Fallow heaved a long-suffering sigh. "It's not a pickaxe. It's a mattock. And yes, it belongs to me. To the cemetery, that is. See the inscription on the handle? WPC —Western Pioneer Cemetery. It's one of the tools I use to keep this place in order."

"How did it end up here?"

"In the man's neck? I have no idea."

Raul closed his eyes, and the corner of my mouth quirked up. Here was the Raul I'd come to know and love. After a ten count, he opened his eyes and smiled indulgently. "What I meant was, how accessible was the tool? Would someone have had to retrieve it from a toolshed, or was it lying nearby?"

Mr. Fallow squared his shoulders. "Young man, I do not leave my tools strewn about."

"Can you recall the last time you used this particular tool?"

Mr. Fallow tapped his chin. "Early this morning. I was working on a headstone across the way. Mr. Parson, an early-1900s resident. Weeds have taken root, and I..." He hesitated, and his face paled.

"Sir?" Raul prompted.

"I...just remembered. As I was tending to Mr. Parson's stone, I recalled that Mrs. Smythe's family was planning a visit this afternoon. I wanted her headstone pristine, so I grabbed my toolbag and headed over. But..." His voice caught. "I may have left my digging tools with Mr. Parson. So reckless of me." He rubbed a gnarled hand across his forehead.

I felt a stirring of skepticism. Was Mr. Fallow truly flustered by his own negligence, or did he just want us to think so? Ah, the perils of a suspicious nature.

"Where is Mr. Parson's grave?" Raul asked.

Mr. Fallow pointed again. "Just over there. Toward the road."

"And the grave you went to tend?"

"Mrs. Smythe. She's up the path in that direction." Mr. Fallow pointed to a winding trail forking off the main path.

"How long were you there?"

"I spent half an hour cleaning Mrs. Smythe's stone. I was almost finished when I heard a noise." His embarrassment, whether real or feigned, dissolved as he stared daggers at me. "A barking dog, disturbing our serenity."

I cringed, recalling that Woody had at one point

spotted a chipmunk and emitted a single playful bark before remembering his manners. I was sure Mr. Fallow's "residents" hadn't minded. In fact, they probably enjoyed a glimpse into the energy of a life they'd left behind. If I were an occupant of the cemetery, I'd tire of perpetual tranquility. Give me a dog frolicking with a chipmunk any day.

Raul cleared his throat. "So, you went to the cemetery entrance to deal with Ms. Cassidy's dog. Then what?"

"I saw everyone gathered around Vivian. She was standing there as if she'd been raised from the dead. There was some blood..." He tapped his forehead... "but otherwise, she looked...almost spiritual. As if she belonged among my residents."

"What happened after you saw Vivian?" Raul asked.

Mr. Fallow folded his arms. "That blasted dog took off. I keep telling everyone animals should not be permitted in this place, but no one listens. We cannot allow irresponsible pet owners to bring their uncontrollable dogs onto the premises."

I opened my mouth, ready to defend Woody—and myself—but Raul gave me a side eye and continued his interview. "What did you do when the dog ran off?"

Mr. Fallow tugged the end of his shirt. After one last glower in my direction, he turned his focus to Raul. "I followed Miss Cassidy down the trail..."

"Ms.," I interjected, unable to restrain myself.

Raul sighed. Mr. Fallow ignored me. "I found her at George Corwin's grave. She pointed out the body."

"Did you recognize the man?"

Mr. Fallow shook his head. "Never saw him before. Unless someone comes to visit the deceased, I wouldn't know them. I don't get out much."

Maybe you should, I thought. The man had spent

decades interred in his own graveyard. What must that do to a person's psyche?

The two officers returned, carrying supplies. One of them situated the bag near the grave and addressed Raul. "Detective Clarke said to tell you the ambulance is transporting the injured woman to Pine Haven Hospital, and she's riding along. She'll be in touch as soon as she knows something."

Raul instructed the officer to accompany Mr. Fallow back to his cottage. The old man bristled. "I'll stay here to supervise. I don't want strangers plodding around willy nilly."

"I understand your concern, sir, but I must insist that you vacate the area. I assure you, we will treat the place with the utmost respect."

"Humph. I highly doubt that." Mr. Fallow stalked off ahead of the officer, muttering to himself.

"I get the idea he was putting a curse on your family," I said to Raul.

"Wouldn't be the first."

Raul called over the other officer and issued a few instructions to pass along when the crime scene techs arrived. "If you find a wallet or a phone on him, bag them."

As he continued talking, the sunlight dappled across his olive skin and glittered like flecks of gold in his thick, black hair. Similar gold flecks appeared in his brown eyes. A perpetual dark stubble blanketed his cheeks and chin. His chest and biceps strained against his burgundy button-down shirt. I sometimes took for granted how gorgeous the man was. There was nothing romantic between us and never would be—not in this lifetime, anyway. For one thing, Raul was ten years my junior and more like a younger brother than a love interest. More importantly, we were both involved in serious relationships. I was smitten with my new-old boyfriend Sam, and if Raul's partnership with Detective Lynn Clarke hadn't already transcended a professional union, it was on the verge.

Still, a girl couldn't help but notice.

"Make sure they take a sample of the blood on the corner of the headstone," he concluded. The officer nodded, and Raul and I stepped away.

"Do you think it's Murray's blood on the headstone?" he asked me.

I shrugged. "I wondered the same thing. But did you see the wound on Vivian Corwin's forehead? The blood could just as easily be hers."

He gave me a skeptical look. "You're saying Vivian Corwin and Eugene Murray engaged in a brawl at George Corwin's grave? And Vivian... what?... banged her head, but had the fortitude to grab a pickaxe..."

"Mattock," I said.

He rolled his eyes. "Whatever. Then she swung it into Murray's neck and conveniently lost her memory?"

I made a face. "Sounds farfetched when you put it that way. If that scenario is too bizarre for your taste, how do you explain things?"

He chewed his lip as he pondered. "I don't like to speculate until I gather the facts. But I will say this: we've had our eye on Eugene Murray for a while now. He was a smarmy character."

"Smarmy?" I chuckled. "Is that a word they teach in detective school?"

He huffed. "How much do you know about the guy?"

I considered his question. Gene had been dating Lydia for a while now. On the few occasions I'd been around him, he'd come across as a mobster wannabe who talked the talk but had little in the way of substance. I figured he wouldn't be playing the role of Lydia's boy-toy much longer. In fact, Tonya recently mentioned that Lydia was tiring of him. *He's facing extinction, like all the other pseudo stepdads,* she'd said.

In hindsight, her word choice might have been chillingly foreboding.

I told all this to Raul. "I'm afraid that's not much in the way of insight," I concluded.

When the first officer returned to assist his partner, Raul and I headed back up the path.

"Why have you had Gene in your sights?" I asked.

Raul frowned. "This isn't for public release." Predictably, he was warning me against sharing information with Tonya, the owner and editor-in-chief of the *Rock Creek Gazette*. I guessed he wouldn't want me spilling it to the village's new reporter, Monika Schiff, either—even though she'd played an instrumental role in solving a recent crime.

I made a zip-my-lips motion. Raul smirked but started talking. "As I'm sure you know, Eugene Murray hails from a Vegas crime family. The Murrays used to be powerful, but they're small-time now. The FBI doesn't even pay them much attention. They run several legitimate businesses but dabble in a few illegal ventures. Still, Eugene's father is the patriarch. And Eugene has been showing up in the village quite a bit—"

"I assumed he was tagging along with Lydia while she tried to make amends with Tonya. You're saying there's more to his visits?"

"We believe he's been cultivating a few friendships of his own."

"Trying to establish a foothold?" I asked. "Here in tiny Rock Creek Village?"

"It's easier to launder illicit cash in an out-of-the-way location. Or so I've been told."

"So, Eugene is attempting to recruit local businesses? To what, impress his father?"

"The Murrays aren't the Waltons," Raul said. "In the Murray family, they eat their young. If a member isn't producing, he could be, well, expelled."

Ugh. An interesting speculation—one that wouldn't bode well for Lydia, and by extension, Tonya.

"The investigation is in its early stages," he said. "And Eugene's death ups the ante."

"Gambling puns?"

He smiled. "Too soon?"

As we walked in silence, I considered the ramifications of murder and mobs and money-laundering schemes. A thought occurred to me, and I swiveled to face Raul. "What about Vivian?"

"What about her?"

"Is it just a coincidence that a woman missing forty years returns to town the same day and in the same place as a man is killed?"

He lifted his eyebrows. "Stranger things have happened."

I wasn't big on coincidences, and despite his seeming nonchalance, Raul wasn't either. There had to be a connection. But I wasn't seeing it. Not yet.

I exhaled. "Well, one way or the other, someone has to notify Lydia."

"Gee, wish I'd thought of that."

"Just saying, I'll go tell her if it would help you out."

He made a face. "Thanks for the offer, but after we learned *smarmy* in detective school, they taught us that a professional should handle notifications."

"I'd be happy to tag along," I said, wheedling. "I'm her daughter's friend. My presence might soften the blow."

"I'm not sure I want the blow softened."

It took me a second to comprehend his meaning. "Wait, are you implying that Lydia might be a suspect?"

"Can't rule her out."

"She's seventy years old! Besides, the most strenuous thing I've ever seen her do is lift a glass to her lips. I can't picture her ambling into a cemetery in her stilettos, swinging a mattock into her much-younger paramour's neck, then tromping through the dirt back to Tonya's house. That's crazy."

"You're probably right. But as I said before, stranger things have happened."

We arrived at the cemetery entrance then. Mr. Fallow stood with his arms crossed and his signature scowl. I peered past him to where Mom had taken Vivian's spot on the bench next to Mrs. Barney, with Woody and Carl curled up between their feet. On the steps stood former Rock Creek Village Chief of Police Butch Cassidy, who also happened to be my father.

At least, the man standing there resembled my father—if he'd aged ten years since yesterday.

Dad stared into the distance, his shoulders slumped and his hands in his pockets. His lips were tight and his face pale. Almost as if he'd seen...

A ghost.

Chapter Eight

I hurried toward the cottage. Mom scooped Carl into her arms and descended the porch stairs. The rest of the group gathered around.

"Your mother tells me you found Vivian Corwin injured in the cemetery," Dad said. My heart constricted at the worry choking his voice.

I nodded. "Her injury doesn't appear serious. She doesn't remember anything, though. Not even her name. She wasn't carrying any identification, so if Mom hadn't recognized her, we wouldn't even know who she is."

Mom handed Carl to me and snaked her arm through Dad's. "She's back, Butch. After forty years. I can't believe it."

My father stared into the distance, and I was struck as always by his Paul Newman good looks. Back in Charlie Cassidy's teenage years, when *Butch Cassidy and the Sundance Kid* was released, his resemblance to the actor had encouraged his friends to start calling him Butch. The nickname had stuck and eventually led to Dad's pet name for his only daughter—Sundance.

He roused himself from his thoughts. "I need to get to the hospital and talk to Vivian. Find out where she's been all these years."

"That's not a good idea, Chief," Raul interjected. "As soon as the doctors treat her, we'll need to interview her. You shouldn't talk to her until we're done."

Dad bristled. "Where's Frank?"

I raised my eyebrows. I could see where Dad was going with that question, and I figured Raul could, too. Dad and Frank Laramie, who took the mantle of Chief of Police when Dad retired, had worked together for decades and were still the closest of friends. Dad was counting on Frank to loop him in on the investigation.

To his credit, Raul didn't respond defensively. In fact, he seemed almost sympathetic. He understood no cops wanted unsolved cases haunting them over the course of their lives. Still, no matter how much he might empathize, Raul's obligation was to the current case and its victims, not to my father.

"Frank's been attending a conference in Boulder. We've apprised him of the situation, and he's on his way back to the village. But he'd tell you the same thing, Chief: let the doctors do their job. Let us do our job. You can talk to Vivian Corwin when it's appropriate."

Mom took my father's hand in hers and squeezed his fingers. "Butch, we have to think about what's best for Vivian. We don't want to jeopardize her welfare. Not after all this time."

Dad took a long, shuddering breath. When he exhaled, every part of him appeared to deflate. I'd never seen him like this.

He looked toward the path leading into the trees, toward the place where he'd attended a burial a few weeks earlier. "Poor George," he said. "He died without knowing his wife was still alive."

"Perhaps he knows, sweetheart," Mom said. "Perhaps he finally has all the answers."

Dad considered this and nodded. I was pleased to see some color returning to his cheeks. He looked at Raul with renewed vigor. "You win, Sanchez. I won't talk to Vivian until you give me the green light. But I'm going to the hospital. That's non-negotiable. I won't leave until I've spoken to her. So don't think about stringing me along."

"Never, Chief." Raul stuck out his hand, and Dad shook it.

Then Dad turned to Mom. "I'm going over now."

"I'll go with you," she said. "Glenda gave me a lift this morning, so I don't have my car to worry about."

"I'll be right behind you," I said.

Dad smiled wryly. Raul sighed. My mother cleared her throat. "What?" I asked. "I saw her first. I'm invested in this."

"Yes, darling, we're not questioning your...investment, as you call it. Just your appearance. Perhaps it would be a good idea to go home and clean up. Otherwise, hospital personnel might strap you onto a gurney and examine you for injuries."

My eyes dropped to my shirt, splotched with blood. Grime covered my beige tennies. Even my socks were dirty. I looked like a serial killer who'd come to the cemetery to bury the evidence.

"Guess I should change clothes."

"And maybe have a quick shower." Mom ran a finger down Carl's spine, earning a soft purr. Then she scratched behind Woody's ears. "Besides, you'll need to take these boys home. Unless, of course, you plan to leave them in Cedric's care."

Mr. Fallow scowled, and I grabbed Woody's leash.

We headed toward the parking lot—except for Mr. Fallow, who clenched his jaw and stared down the path. I figured he wouldn't rest until the crime scene techs had exited the premises.

Mrs. Barney said a few consoling words to my mother before getting into her car and driving away. My parents settled into Dad's truck and pulled out of the parking lot. I tucked the creatures into the back seat of my red Honda Civic. As I reached for the driver's door handle, I felt a hand on my shoulder and turned to see Raul standing beside me. "Remember, Callie, we need to keep this between us."

I shook my head. "That's not how things work in this village, Raul. Word will get around. I'm sure it already has."

"But the details need to stay private. Especially regarding Eugene Murray's business exploits. Don't make me regret confiding in you."

"You can trust me, Raul. You know me."

The corners of his mouth curled up. "Yeah. I know you, Callie."

I couldn't tell if he was being sincere or cynical.

As I DROVE through the village toward my townhouse, I played my voicemails. First came a message from Tonya: "Heard there was something going on at the cemetery. Weren't you headed there this morning? Call me."

On its heels came her second message: "Rumor has it you found a body. Call me ASAP."

I debated whether to return her call and let her know Raul was on his way. But I recalled his admonition and decided against it. I didn't want to shake his trust in me. Besides, Raul would be there soon enough, and he'd answer Tonya's questions.

The next message brought Monika's voice through the car's speakers. "Hey, Callie. I'm hearing gossip, and it involves you. Shocker. Don't ignore your favorite reporter. The pen is mightier than the sword. Call me."

I smiled at her reference, thinking back a few months to a mystery—and a murder—Monika and I had worked together to solve. The stories she'd written about the events had earned her national accolades. I'd half expected her to abandon us for the greener journalistic pastures of a big-city newspaper, but she'd chosen to remain in Rock Creek Village. "More big stories here than New York or Washington, D.C.," she'd said. Unfortunately, she wasn't far off the mark.

I made a mental note to call her later but figured I wouldn't have to. The woman was an excellent reporter. She'd ferret out the necessary information and would probably be at the hospital before me.

I couldn't help but grin as I listened to my next message. The voice of my friend and self-appointed protector, Mrs. Finney, trilled through the speakers, complete with her faux British accent. "Callahan, dear, I'm calling regarding the recent circumstances at the cemetery. Details are sketchy. I anticipate your presence at the coffee shop to offer a report. Don't dally, dear."

As I listened to the fumbling noises of her disconnecting, I pictured the seventy-something woman standing behind the counter of her ironically named Rocky Mountain High coffee shop. Her stocky figure would be adorned by her favorite violet apron, which she claimed set off her curly, purple-tinted hair. I wondered idly if she was still going by Mrs. Finney now that she was a married woman.

She and her paramour, Mr. Purdy, had eloped after one of their recent ice dancing competitions. Was Mrs. Finney now Mrs. Purdy? I doubted it. Like Tonya, she didn't seem inclined to take her husband's name.

Besides, had she ever been Mrs. Finney at all? Despite my best efforts—and Monika's top-notch research skills—we'd yet to turn up any significant background information on the woman. The only thing I knew for certain was that she'd once been a CIA agent, as had her new husband. The name Mrs. Finney was likely an alias, but whenever I pressed her on the point, her eyes sparkled, and her lips curled into an enigmatic grin. She enjoyed watching me spin my wheels.

When the next message began playing, my gut clenched. It wasn't the caller's voice, which belonged to my boyfriend, Sam Petrie. It was what he had to say—a simple, "Where are you?"

I smacked my forehead with my palm as I pulled into the alley behind my townhouse and eased beneath my carport. I'd forgotten all about the brunch he'd planned—the one that included his parents.

Chapter Nine

I scrambled out of the car and steered the creatures into the house. "I blew it." Woody licked my hand for moral support. Carl meowed in disdain over the drama of human relationships.

"You don't get it," I said to the cat. Sam's parents, whom I hadn't seen in over a quarter of a century, had flown in from Florida last night, and the four of us were supposed to meet for brunch at a fancy restaurant in Valley Ridge.

A half hour ago.

With trembling fingers, I pressed Sam's smiling face on my speed dial. "Callie?" His voice was tense. "Where are you? We've been worried."

"I'm so, so sorry, Sam. There was...well, an incident at the cemetery. It's...big. Murder big."

"Murder? Are you all right?"

"I'm okay. But Eugene Murray isn't. I found him dead in the cemetery with a mattock in his neck, and...well, it's all too much to go into right now."

There was a long silence. "I guess this means you're not coming," he said at last.

I glanced at my watch. "I'm covered in blood and dirt, so I'll need a shower. Give me a half hour. Forty-five minutes, tops."

He paused, and I could hear the chatter of restaurant patrons in the background. "Don't worry about it. We've already been here a while. I think we need to go ahead and eat." His voice was tight with disappointment.

"Sam, I'm so sorry—"

"You said that already." He exhaled. "It's not your fault. Dead bodies just seem to seek you out."

I winced. He wasn't wrong. "Now your parents are going to think even worse of me."

"I'll explain what happened. They'll understand."

I doubted that, but there wasn't much I could do about it.

"I'll make it up to them—and you, I promise. I love you, Sam."

"Love you, too."

I tossed my phone onto the kitchen counter and bellowed in frustration. Sam's gentle response only compounded my guilt. But I agreed with him that this wasn't my fault. When I'd gone to the cemetery this morning to shoot photos for Mrs. Barney's book, I'd expected to complete the task with plenty of time to spare to make it to the mountain-view spot he'd chosen for my big reunion with his parents. How was I to know a ghost from the past would turn up, and then a dead man?

Still, I knew how much this brunch date had meant to Sam. I hadn't seen his parents in person since just after I'd graduated high school, when I'd left the village—and my boyfriend—to pursue a career in journalism. At first, Sam and I had promised not to let the distance come between us. We vowed our romance would survive.

Of course, things rarely work out that way. No matter how sincerely they're made, teenage promises tend to float into the sky like embers from a fire, drifting away on the breeze of the future. Sam and I spoke on the phone often those first months. Later, after I made new college friends and immersed myself in the Austin, Texas, culture and lifestyle, I grew too busy to take those calls. Finally, when I returned to the village for a few weeks the summer after my freshman year, I broke it off.

Sam was heartbroken. And it was his parents, along with Tonya, who'd been forced to pick up the pieces.

Sam had since forgiven me—so much so that he was willing to take another chance on us. But his parents were another matter, as parents so often are. And I got it. Though I'd never been a mom, I could imagine how difficult it must be to forgive someone who hurt your kid.

I pictured Sam returning to the brunch table now and telling his parents I wouldn't be coming. Lila would shoot a knowing look at Conrad, who'd shake his head sadly. They had probably predicted this reboot relationship would fizzle and were already girding themselves for a fresh bout of Sam's pain.

I squared my shoulders, determined to prove them wrong. I'd told Sam I'd make it up to him, and I intended to. I wasn't sure how, not yet, but I'd figure it out.

After my visit to the hospital.

I headed upstairs for a shower, shaking my head in frustration. I'd believed Sam and I were on a quiet, stress-free path these days. But evidently, old Will Shakespeare had been right: the course of true love never did run smooth.

I FILLED PET BOWLS, scratched furry heads and backs, and promised the creatures I'd return soon. Then I headed off for Pine Haven Hospital, the closest major facility and a half hour's drive through a craggy mountain pass. I tried calling Tonya on my way out of town, assuming Raul had broken the news of Gene's death by now, but she didn't answer. Knowing I'd lose service once I entered the mountains, I didn't bother leaving a message. We'd be talking soon, I was certain.

Traffic was light on the two-lane road. I rolled down my window and let in the cool mountain air and the scent of pine. The earlier fog had cleared, and the sun beamed through the trees, speckling the asphalt. I kept an eye on the surrounding terrain, and sure enough, I soon spotted a herd of elk grazing in a nearby meadow. Autumn offered prime wildlife viewing in the Rockies, as animals made their way into the valley for the winter. The gorgeous scenery occupied my attention for the entire drive, and I noted the tension leaving my shoulders. I didn't fixate on relationship woes or murder and mayhem for all of twenty-five minutes.

That mental calm evaporated the moment I pulled into the hospital parking lot. As soon as I put the car in park, the floodgates around my brain reopened. What had happened to Vivian in the cemetery? Why had she disappeared all those years ago? And most important—who killed Gene?

Entering the lobby, I located Mom and Dad sitting side by side. Lynn sat across from them, tapping away at her phone. I settled in next to the detective.

"I thought you'd be with Vivian," I said to her.

"Doc sent her for a CT scan," she replied, barely looking up.

"Have you spoken to her? Did she tell you what happened?"

Lynn finished her text and tucked the phone into her pocket. "She still can't remember anything. Only knows her name because Maggie told her."

I scrunched up my face. How do you investigate if the only player left alive has no recollection of events—or even who she is? "So, what's next?"

Lynn shrugged. "I'm hoping the doctor can give us a timeline on when—or if—her memory might return. In the meantime, we're sending in a sample of the blood on her hands for testing to see if it's hers."

"Are you thinking it might be Gene's? Can you picture that frail old lady attacking and killing a physically fit younger man? Seems implausible."

"Stranger things have happened," she said, echoing Raul's earlier words. "We have to cover all the bases."

The doctor came through the door marked ER then, and we stood as he approached. He straightened his stethoscope and consulted his clipboard. "Scan was negative. No concussion. No brain bleed. She has some nasty bumps and bruises, but she'll mend. We'll be moving her to a room for the night, but we should be able to release her tomorrow."

"Has her memory returned?" Lynn asked.

"Not yet."

Lynn shook her head. "I'm confused. If there's no brain injury, why can't she remember anything?"

The doctor frowned. "Things like this are always a bit of a mystery. Medical issues aren't always predictable. The scan showed a slight bit of swelling. Pair that with shock and trauma, and it's not out of the ordinary to experience temporary amnesia. I'm hoping rest and fluids will kick start her memory by tomorrow. If not, we'll arrange for a neurologist."

"She'll stay in the hospital until then?" Mom asked.

His eyes traveled to my mother. "No. If she's well enough physically, we'll need to discharge her, regardless of her mental state. We can't allocate hospital beds for patients who don't need them."

I grimaced. As always, it all came down to money. Here was an old woman who hadn't arrived with an insurance card. The hospital wasn't sure they'd get paid. Guess we should count our lucky stars that the doctor had ordered any tests at all. If not for the police presence, they might have already discharged Vivian.

"But she has nowhere to go," I said.

Mom glanced at Dad. "She'll stay with us."

Dad nodded. "In our guest room."

He didn't even want her in one of the lodge rooms. My father had lost this woman once, and he wasn't about to let it happen again.

"That's very generous of you," Lynn said. "I'll discuss it with Chief Laramie and Detective Sanchez. In the meantime, I've sent for an officer to sit outside her door until she's released."

The doctor nodded, as if the Pine Haven Hospital entertained police guards on a regular basis, but I was surprised. A police guard? Did Lynn believe Vivian was in danger? I hadn't considered that prospect. Would it be safe for my parents to make her their roommate?

"I'd like to speak to Ms. Corwin now," Lynn said to the doctor.

He cleared his throat. "Well, here's the thing. I told Ms. Corwin a detective was waiting to speak with her, but she said the only person she'd talk to was Maggie, the nice woman who said she knew her from the past." His eyes shifted to my mother. "I assume you're Maggie?"

"I am," Mom affirmed.

The doctor glanced nervously at Lynn, who pulled herself to full height and crossed her arms. "Why don't both of you come with me? Perhaps Ms. Corwin will agree to speak to you then."

Lynn nodded curtly. Mom pursed her lips. "I'd like my husband and daughter to join us, too."

The doctor shook his head. "Hospital policy states only two visitors per patient in the ER."

"Just him, then," I said, laying a hand on my father's arm. "He's the former Rock Creek Village Chief of Police and has knowledge of Vivian's case."

Tucking his clipboard under his arm, the doctor tightened his jaw. "Rules are rules. Two visitors."

Lynn turned impatiently to Mom. "Maggie, I need to get in there."

Dad patted Mom's shoulder. "You go ahead. Use your charms on her. You'll get more answers out of her than I could, anyway."

Lynn had advanced to the ER door and waited as the doctor used his keycard to open it. Mom headed in after them, shooting one last look over her shoulder before she disappeared down the hall.

Chapter Ten

My father sank into the chair, looking forlorn. I sat across from him and rested my elbows on my knees. "Dad, what happened all those years ago? Mom told me some of it, but not the details."

He ran a hand through his hair. "It's a long story, Sundance. Vivian was—"

Just then, the front doors slid open. We glanced toward them, surprised to see Pinky entering, looking frantic.

Michael "Pinky" Pinkerton owned Pinkerton's Place, Rock Creek Village's local grocery store. He'd been a fixture in the village since I was a child. I figured he must be eighty by now, but he was fit, strong, and mentally sharp. If the two of us were to arm wrestle, there was no doubt in my mind he'd take me in seconds.

Pinky noticed us and stalked over. His hands balled into fists at his sides. His bald head gleamed beneath the fluorescent lights. He reminded me of an older version of Popeye.

I rose. "Pinky, what—?"

He looked past me at my father. "Where is she, Butch?"

Dad's brow creased. "You mean Vivian Corwin?"

Pinky huffed. "Well, I'm not talking about Marilyn Monroe. Of course I mean Vivian. She's here, isn't she?"

"Why don't you take a seat?" I said. "Let's talk."

"I need to see her," he said through gritted teeth.

"They won't let you," Dad said. "Only two visitors at a time, and Maggie's already back there, along with Detective Clarke."

"She's going to be okay," I added. "They did a CT scan—"

He didn't bother to hear me out. Storming past us, he marched toward the ER door. Dad and I looked at each other and trotted after him. The nurse at the front desk called out, "You can't go back there."

Considering the security keypad beside the door, I didn't figure Pinky would be able to gain entry anyway. But when a man in scrubs barreled through the door, Pinky grabbed it and scuttled through. Dad and I wedged ourselves inside on his heels. I risked a glance over my shoulder as the nurse picked up the phone—contacting security, no doubt.

The lights buzzed overhead, and the odor of antiseptic assaulted my nostrils. Without breaking stride, Pinky marched down the narrow corridor. Thin curtains separated the beds, and when Pinky came across any that were closed, he peered through the slit. Dad and I trailed him, uncertain what else to do.

Soon, Mom's voice sounded from one of the procedure areas. Pinky hurried over and pulled back the curtain. I glanced toward the ER door. Still no sign of security, but it wouldn't be long.

In the meantime, we had an irate detective to contend with.

Lynn's brow furrowed at the sight of a crazed-looking Pinky. Out of instinct, her hand dropped to her hip, skimming the holster positioned there and the badge on her belt. I felt like I was watching a scene from a TV cop show. Pinky noticed, too, but didn't take so much as a step back.

My eyes fixed on Vivian sitting in the narrow bed wearing in a thin gown. She looked even paler than she had at the cemetery. Though startled by the flurry of activity, she didn't appear frightened. In fact, did I notice a flicker of recognition when she spotted Pinky? Surely she'd known him when she lived in the village. Maybe her memory was returning.

Then the flicker abated, and her eyes once again went blank.

I glanced at my father, whose face might compete with Vivian's in a paleness contest. I realized this was the first glimpse he'd had of her in forty years.

Lynn stepped between Pinky and Vivian and planted her feet. "Mr. Pinkerton, why are you here?"

He craned his neck to see past her. "I need to talk to Vivian. Make sure she's safe."

Lynn touched her holster again. "I assure you, she's well-protected. You need to leave." Her eyes traveled to Dad and me. "All of you. Go. Now."

Behind us, the ER door opened, and a hefty, middle-aged security guard strode our direction. Lynn held up her badge. "Detective Lynn Clarke. I'll handle this, sir."

The man puffed out his chest. "Too many visitors. Some of you gotta get out."

"I understand," Lynn said. "I'll see to it."

He narrowed his eyes, and I could sense his quandary. On the one hand, Lynn was obviously a detective—gun, badge, the whole kit and caboodle. On the other hand, she was a woman. A good-looking one, at that. Should he be taking his orders from an attractive female?

She apparently assessed the situation the same way I did. After an irritated sigh, she spoke in an authoritative voice. "As I said, sir, I'll take care of it. You're free to return to your duties."

He blinked. Lynn raised a perfectly plucked eyebrow and tightened her lips. After a moment's pause, the guard huffed, hitched up his pants, and trudged away.

Lynn turned back to Pinky. "Mr. Pinkerton, I'll say this one more time. You need to leave the ER. You're welcome to wait in the lobby. I'll come out as soon as possible to answer any questions I can."

He ignored Lynn's instructions and gazed at Vivian. His demeanor softened, and he addressed her with tenderness. "What are you doing here, Viv?"

Her hand fluttered to her chest. "I...I'm sorry. I don't know who you are."

When he took a step toward Vivian's bed, Lynn didn't stop him. I figured she'd decided to watch the scene play out.

Pinky paused a few feet away and held out a tentative hand, as if approaching a frightened animal. "Vivian, it's me. Michael. Michael Pinkerton. We're...old friends."

She looked at him blankly. His eyes glistened. "You shouldn't be here, Viv."

Her gaze traveled across his face as if she were reading a map to an unknown destination. Then she closed her eyes and pressed her head back against the thin pillow. "I'm very tired."

Mom moved closer to the bed and looked around the group. "That's enough for now. Vivian has been through an ordeal. She needs to rest."

Lynn placed a hand on Pinky's shoulder. "Mr. Pinkerton—"

He spun to face her, his expression fierce. "Why can't the police just leave the poor woman in peace?"

Lynn drew back and squared her shoulders. "I'm investigating a crime, Mr. Pinkerton, and I won't tolerate your interference."

"Crime? If you're referring to that man's death in the cemetery, you can't possibly think Vivian is responsible." I looked at Vivian in the bed, her eyes glazed. Pinky was right. It was hard to fathom her as a killer.

Lynn didn't flinch, though. "Whatever I might think, I'm not discussing it with you. I need you to—"

"If you're suggesting Vivian killed Eugene Murray, you are dead wrong."

I cringed at his word choice. I feared Lynn was on the verge of losing it, so I put a hand on Pinky's arm. "Pinky, we need to go. Let Detective Clarke do her job."

He shook me off. "I'm telling you, Vivian didn't do it." He stood ramrod straight, his jaw tight. "I know because I did it. I killed Eugene Murray."

Chapter Eleven

It was as if a vacuum had sucked the air from the room. Vivian's eyes flew open, and her hands clenched on top of the sheet. Mom laid a comforting hand on her shoulder. Dad's brows drew together. Lynn's lips tightened as she stared at Pinky in frustration.

"Mr. Pinkerton, offering a false confession constitutes a criminal act. I could charge you with perjury and obstruction of justice. Now, I'm going to pretend I didn't hear what you said. But you need to leave these premises at once. I'm through messing around."

Dad grasped Pinky's shoulder. "Come on, man. You're not doing anyone any good. Let's go."

"I'm not leaving until I'm in handcuffs." Pinky held out his wrists and glared at Lynn. "Do your job, Detective."

I rarely observed Detective Lynn Clarke appear uncertain, but she did then. Her eyes flicked to Dad, who gave her a small shrug. *Your call.* She looked back at Pinky and sighed. "All right, Mr. Pinkerton. Have it your way."

At that moment, chaos descended with the ferocity of

an erupting volcano. Vivian's doctor approached, unhappy at the sight of a small crowd gathered in Vivian's tiny cubicle. The front desk nurse rushed through the emergency room door, dragging the security guard behind her. A wide-eyed uniformed officer followed them.

By this time, a few patients had opened their privacy curtains, hoping to get a glimpse of the ruckus. One twenty-something with a bloody bandage across the bridge of his nose held up his phone to record the incident. I nudged Lynn and pointed his direction.

"Stop filming, sir," she said sternly. "The hospital does not permit the use of video." She swept her gaze across the others. "All of you, please close your curtains."

The front desk nurse hurried toward the wannabe filmmaker, hustled him into his bed, and pulled the curtain tight. The rest of the patients complied with Lynn's directive. Even if they couldn't see what was happening, though, it wouldn't stop them from eavesdropping. We needed to get this situation under control before it ended up on the evening news.

The doctor folded his arms. "What is going on here? Never mind. I just want everyone out. Now." He pointed to the door, then moved to Vivian's side and took her wrist in his fingers, checking her pulse.

Lynn said a few words to the uniformed officer, who moved into position outside Vivian's curtained cubby and stood at attention.

My eyes drifted to Vivian. Her shoulders were slumped and her eyes clouded. She'd remained stoic throughout the ordeal, but it was taking a toll. Mom noticed, too, and lifted her chin in a gesture I recognized all too well. She wasn't about to leave her friend's side. She took Vivian's hand in hers. "Doctor, Viv is scared. She needs a friend. I'd like to stay with her."

Dad stood behind my mother and placed his hands on her shoulders. "Me, too."

The doctor opened his mouth to object, but the determination on my parents' faces stopped him. "That's fine. Only two visitors, though. And when we're ready to move Ms. Corwin to her room, you'll need to wait in the lobby."

Lynn put a hand on Pinky's elbow and guided him down the hall, with the security guard strutting beside them as if he'd taken the man into custody himself. Pinky wrenched around to get one last look at Vivian. I told my parents to keep me posted, then, alongside the nurse, made my way to the exit. In the lobby, the security guard disappeared into his tiny office. The nurse went back to her station, settling an evil eye on me. I wasn't sure what I'd done to anger her, but I paid her no heed. It wasn't the first evil eye I'd ever received. I thought of Sam's parents and concluded it probably wouldn't be the last.

Lynn released Pinky's arm and regarded him with curiosity. I stayed as still as possible, hoping to keep off Lynn's radar so I could continue listening.

"Why are you doing this, Mr. Pinkerton?" Lynn asked.

"It's not what I'm doing, young lady. It's what I did. I confessed to murdering Eugene Murray. You have no choice but to arrest me."

Lynn narrowed her eyes. "How was he killed?"

Pinky's brows knit together. "What?"

"If you killed the man, you must know how you did it. So, tell me. How did he die?"

Pinky appeared momentarily flummoxed, then he tightened his jaw. "I don't want to talk about that. All you need to know is that I did it."

"Why did you kill him?" Lynn asked.

Pinky shook his head. "I said I'm done talking, Detective. Just put the cuffs on me and take me to the station."

Lynn hesitated, then sighed. "So be it, Mr. Pinkerton. I'll take you in. No handcuffs, though. You're not under arrest."

"But—"

Lynn held up a hand. "It won't do you any good to argue. I have serious doubts as to the veracity of your confession. And there's currently nothing tangible linking you to the murder. I'll take you to the station, where Detective Sanchez and I will interview you and investigate your claim. But unless something concrete turns up, we will not be arresting you. Not today."

Pinky stared at the doors leading to the emergency room. "Maybe not yet. But you will, if I have to get the media involved to make it happen."

He strode toward the hospital doors. Lynn shot me a befuddled look, then trailed after him.

Outside, Lynn settled Pinky in the back of her police-issued SUV, got behind the wheel, and headed toward Rock Creek Village. As I watched them drive away, my mind tussled with Pinky's confession. The man had clearly been in a state of panic when he arrived at the hospital. I remembered the look of raw emotion on his face when he saw Vivian. What was the link between them? Could Pinky have killed for her?

I got in my car and took a moment to compose myself. Thoughts of Sam and the brunch I'd missed flitted into my mind. Sam had handled it with his usual good nature, but I still needed to extend an olive branch to his parents.

I texted him. *On my way back from Pine Haven. Can I stop by to visit your folks?*

Three telltale dots appeared. A moment later: *We're going to Boulder. Think I told you about that, didn't I?*

I cringed. Yes, he'd mentioned he was taking Conrad and Lila to tour Elyse's college campus. Another fumble on my part.

You did. Sorry. Chaotic day. How about tomorrow? Breakfast?

I drummed my fingers against the steering wheel as I awaited his response. *They're spending the day with friends tomorrow.*

I chewed my bottom lip. This reunion meant a lot to my boyfriend. I'd missed the opportunity he'd created. Now it was up to me to devise a plan for our get together. An idea began to blossom in my mind.

How about a picnic Wednesday? We'll take them to Moraine Lake. Beautiful this time of year. I'll arrange everything.

A long pause. Then: *You sure? I don't want to mention it if it's going to fall through.*

I realized he didn't mean to take a jab at me, but ouch. I was tempted to reply, *Well, I can't promise there won't be another murder.* Instead, I typed, *I'm sure. I'll take care of everything. It'll be great.*

In that case, let's do it.

I worried I may have overpromised when I'd used the word "great." At this point, I'd settle for a step in the right direction. But for Sam's sake, I'd do everything in my power to make it all transpire smoothly.

BEFORE I PULLED out of the lot, I dialed Tonya's number. She picked up on the first ring. "There you are, sugarplum," she said, using the nickname she'd bestowed on me in junior high school. "I was wondering when you'd call." She tried to keep her tone light, but I could hear the worry.

"Raul notified Lydia, I assume?"

"Oh, yes. Mommy dearest faked a few tears and took to her bed, but I don't think she's any the worse for wear. I, on the other hand…"

"Taking it hard? Hmm. Not sure I believe that. As I recall, you wanted the man out of your mother's life from the get-go."

"Hush," she said. "If you talk like that, it'll be me Raul interrogates next." She sighed. "Anyway, Callahan, not liking the man doesn't mean I wished him dead. Besides, I have…additional concerns."

My eyebrow quirked. "Such as?"

"I'd rather not get into it on the phone."

"Want me to stop by?" I asked.

"Can't. I'm at the office. Paper goes to press this afternoon, so I'm tied up."

I wrinkled my nose. "Are you covering today's events?"

"Too late for that, at least in the print version. Monika is writing up a basic story for the online version, but it won't consist of much. So far, no one's talking. It'll be tomorrow before we get anything more thorough. Unless you're willing to go on the record…"

"Raul would skin me alive," I said.

"Figured as much. Anyway, Phil's taking over editorial oversight on the story. Conflict of interest for me, you know. He and Monika are huddled together devising a plan of action. In the meantime, I'm in charge of heavy-hitting matters such as the Garden Club meeting."

I gave her a sympathetic chuckle. "Will you have the flower vetting done by happy hour? If so, I know a place we can drink for free."

She snorted. "I hope you're not referring to your kitchen and that cheap boxed stuff."

"Hey! I resent that. No boxes in my fridge. I've long since graduated to cheap bottled wine. But to answer your question, I was thinking of the Knotty Pine..."

She rewarded me with a squeal. "Mulled wine and those delicious hors d'oeuvres. My mouth is watering."

"Five o'clock?"

"Perfect," she said.

"Should I invite the girlfriend group? Or would that be an overload of moral support?"

"I'd like that. Fortification through wine and friendship. Nothing beats it."

I smiled, then had a thought. "Um...will Lydia be joining us?"

"Nope. She's not invited. I'll stop by the house to check on her before I come, but I need to talk without her. Know what I mean?"

"Absolutely." For as long as I'd known her, Tonya's relationship with her mother had been contentious. When they handed out Maternal Instinct, Lydia was standing in the I Need a Man line instead. As soon as Tonya graduated from high school, Lydia had bailed in search of her next husband. She'd since been through four of them...or was it five?

"Okay, girlfriend, get that paper to bed. Talk to you in a few hours."

"Can't wait."

She disconnected, and I scrolled through my list of contacts and touched Summer's number.

Time to rally the troops.

Chapter Twelve

Once I'd organized the evening with the girlfriend group, I set off on the half-hour trek back to Rock Creek Village. I glanced at the clock on the dashboard. Two in the afternoon. Had it only been six hours since I'd first spotted Vivian emerging from the trees in the cemetery? It felt more like a week. I was exhausted and considered heading home to snuggle up for a nap with the creatures.

But I felt the synapses in my brain firing and realized a nap was not to be. My racing thoughts would never let me rest. After a couple of mugs of Knotty Pine's signature mulled wine, perhaps, but not yet.

What should I do between now and happy hour? Sam was in Boulder, unavailable to serve as my sounding board. Mom and Dad were occupied at the hospital. Sundance Studio, the photography gallery I'd opened a couple of years ago, was closed on Mondays. There was always work to do, of course—photos to print, canvases to order, bills to pay. But I wasn't in the mood. The itch in my brain illuminated my genuine desire. I wanted to investigate.

I didn't regret abandoning my successful career as a big-city photojournalist for the more laid-back pursuits of landscape and wildlife photographer in my mountainside village, but I couldn't deny that I sometimes missed the rush of deadlines and the drama of a crime scene. Still, I'd experienced my share of adrenaline-pumping scenarios here since I'd moved back. Now, it seemed, I faced another one.

My mind drifted across the day's events, from my first sighting of Vivian through Pinky's strange confession. I realized how little I knew about the man. As much as small-town residents tout our sense of community, we often pigeonhole our residents into easy-to-explain descriptors. Fran from Quicker Liquor was the town gossip. Chamber of Commerce president Willie Wright was the haughty realtor who craved status. Steakhouse proprietor Ken Pearly was the hard-working restauranteur. And Pinky took on the role of gruff grocer. But there was more to them than those labels suggested. Beneath the stereotype, Michael Pinkerton was a man with feelings, longings, desires—and a past. What lurked inside him that would trigger a confession to a murder I simply couldn't believe he'd committed?

I pondered why I was so reluctant to view Pinky as Gene's killer. The plain truth was that I liked the man. Pinky and I had formed a tenuous bond during another murder case in Rock Creek Village, and I'd glimpsed his compassionate heart and dedication to justice. My gut told me he wasn't a murderer.

Still, my gut had been wrong before.

I wondered how Lynn and Raul were faring with Pinky's interview. Only one way to find out. Next stop: the Rock Creek Village Police Department.

I PULLED into a parking space near Town Hall, where city offices, including the police station, were housed. Before I entered, I took a moment to check my phone for messages. One from Monika and three—count 'em, three—from Mrs. Finney. Though I'd face the women's wrath later, I didn't take the time to respond.

Inside, I found the two detectives talking with their boss in the lobby. Frank waved me over and draped a lean arm around my shoulders. "Figured you'd turn up sooner rather than later. How's Butch holding up?"

"Same as you, I expect. From what I'm told, the two of you spearheaded the search for Vivian Corwin all those years ago. I imagine you're experiencing the same shock as my dad."

Frank was quiet for a moment, focusing on a past the rest of us couldn't see. It occurred to me that he looked a bit worn around the edges. He was a few years younger than my father, and with his long, lean stature, he wasn't anywhere in the vicinity of geriatric. But the years in law enforcement—especially the past few—had carved their effects on his craggy face. Worry lines circled his mouth, and deep trenches crisscrossed his forehead. The gray in his hair far overshadowed the brown.

He pinched the bridge of his nose. "Yeah, Vivian showing up when she did—like she did—it gave me a jolt. But the past is the past. Right now, we have other concerns. Someone murdered Eugene Murray, and Michael Pinkerton is trying to persuade us it was him."

"You're not convinced?" I asked.

"Nope," Frank said. "I consider myself a pretty reliable human lie detector, and Pinky's confession sends my needle off the chart."

Raul nodded. "He's gotta be covering for someone."

"Vivian?" I asked.

"That'd be my guess," Lynn said. "You saw how frantic he was at the hospital. When he caught sight of her in the emergency room, he was like a papa bear protecting his cub."

Frank stroked his chin. "Still, the man did confess. Even if he's lying, we need to find proof. I'm going to round up a few officers to canvass the village. I imagine it won't take long to find someone who gives Pinky an alibi." He gave my shoulder a quick squeeze. "Tell Butch I'll be in touch."

As Frank ambled away, Raul huffed. "Waste of resources."

"Chief's right, though," Lynn said. "We can't release Pinky until we're sure he's not guilty."

"I'm already sure," Raul said. Lynn opened her mouth to object, but he waved her off. "I get what you're saying. It just irks me that Michael Pinkerton is consuming resources better spent hunting the actual killer."

"Any ideas who that might be?" I ventured. I needed to tread cautiously. Raul and I had successfully consulted several times in the past, but sometimes he could be...well, territorial when it came to sharing information with me.

This time, though, he appeared to harbor no such misgivings. "Eugene Murray wasn't Mr. Clean," he said. "You know about his family. As I mentioned earlier, we already had him in our sights regarding possible shady dealings in the village."

"The Murrays aren't a crime family of legendary proportions," I said. "I'm told they're third tier, if that. Not exactly the Gambinos."

"Third-tier crime families still engage in illegal activities," Raul said. "And they still accumulate enemies."

It was a solid point. "I can't believe Tonya's mother got mixed up with them," I said. "Speaking of Lydia, how did she handle the news of Gene's death?"

"She appeared suitably upset," Raul said cryptically.

I narrowed my eyes. "Wait a minute. You're not thinking Lydia is a suspect, are you?"

"Right now, everyone's a suspect." He shrugged. "You might have done it, for all we know. You were in the cemetery, after all."

The corner of Lynn's mouth twitched, and she glanced at her watch. "We should get back in there before the food arrives."

"Food?" I asked.

Raul rolled his eyes. "Mrs. Finney called to tell us she's sending over a meal for Pinky. She warned us not to deprive the man of sustenance."

I stared at him in astonishment. "How did she know he'd confessed?"

"We figured you told her," Lynn said.

I shook my head. "Wasn't me."

"Must be one of the listening devices she's installed throughout the town," Raul said.

Lynn nodded. "The woman knows everything that happens here, sometimes even before it does."

"Well, she must not believe Pinky is guilty," I said. "You can release him forthwith. Her instincts are infallible."

"Even if we wanted to, he's made it clear he won't go," Lynn said. "He insists we charge him."

I shook my head in disbelief. During my career as an investigative photojournalist, I'd dealt with numerous criminals, but never had I encountered one who refused to leave custody. Why was this man so insistent about being arrested?

"All right. I'll leave you to it." I turned to Lynn. "Before I go, I wanted to let you know I'm rallying the ladies for a happy hour this afternoon at the Knotty Pine to provide Tonya with some much-needed moral support. Would you be able to join us?"

Lynn considered the invitation and shook her head. "I'd better pass. The girls came back from their father's yesterday, and I'd like to spend time with them. Besides…" she shot a look at Raul, "…it would be inappropriate, considering the circumstances."

She was right, of course. A detective investigating a murder probably shouldn't be socializing with the daughter of the victim's girlfriend. I surmised we wouldn't be hanging out much with Lynn until this crime got solved.

All the more reason to move fast. Hopefully, my friends and I could produce some answers over wine and snacks.

As Lynn headed back to the interrogation room, Raul took me by the elbow and leaned in. "I know what you're planning, but don't. Your little gaggle of girlfriends doesn't need to engage in a crime solving quest. There are professionals for that. I happen to be one of them, and I assure you we're perfectly capable. You all eat, drink, and be merry, but leave the investigating to us."

I ducked my head and sighed. "Oh, Raul. Must we go through this dance every time? You are the main man. Detective extraordinaire. I bow to your wisdom and expertise." To demonstrate, I bent at the waist.

"I mean it, Callie." he said sternly. But I saw him stifling a smile as he turned away.

Chapter Thirteen

usk was falling as the creatures and I arrived at the Knotty Pine Resort, my parents' lodge and home for the past ten years. Strokes of crimson and amber painted the sky, and the air was crisp and cool. I marveled again at how much I loved this place. Why had I ever left it for the hustle and bustle—and smog—of the big city? I guessed absence did make the heart grow fonder.

An image of Sam popped into my mind at the thought. In his case, presence made the heart grow fonder. I remembered my pledge to win over his parents. Wednesday was my chance—possibly my last chance—to make that happen. Perhaps I'd enlist the help of my "gaggle of girlfriends," as Raul referred to them, to help me plan.

But only after we'd dissected the murder of Eugene Murray and deliberated about where Vivian Corwin might have been all these years.

I looped my camera bag over my shoulder and carried Carl across the parking lot, with Woody trotting at my heel. When the glass door of the lodge slid open, a heady mixture of cedar, wine, and food aromas drifted out. My stomach rumbled. I paused at the coat rack and struggled out of my jacket, transferring Carl from one arm to the other in an awkward pirouette. Woody's tail pulsed like a metronome. "Hang in there, big guy," I said.

Once I hung my coat on a wooden peg, I scanned the Great Room. Flames crackled in the oversized fireplace, giving off a soft glow. Through the floor-to-ceiling windows, Mt. O'Connell loomed like a titan. The scene reminded me of a Norman Rockwell painting. Or maybe a Callahan Cassidy photo, like the ones lining the walls of the lodge.

I spotted Jessica and Summer sitting on a loveseat. Since they were the only people in the room, I acquiesced to Woody's desire to join them. "You can go. Just use your manners."

He gave me a lofty look, as if I'd insulted him, and loped across the room, where he planted his head on the loveseat. My two friends cuddled him and caressed his thick fur.

Carl twisted in my arms. "Jealous, are you?" He meowed haughtily, but I knew the truth. The cat loved my friends as much as the dog did—he was simply more reticent to admit it.

I carried him to the couch and plunked him down between Jessica and Summer, then tucked my camera bag under the coffee table. The cat arched his back and allowed the women to take turns stroking fingers down his spine. Satisfied he'd been adequately adored, he curled into a ball.

"How's the food?" I asked.

Jessica snatched up an unidentified delicacy and popped it into her mouth. "Divine."

"Do you ever feel guilty that we eat so much of your parents' food, even though we're not paying guests?" Summer asked.

"And drink so much of their wine?" Jessica added, picking up her mug and gulping the steaming liquid.

I laughed. "Not one bit. They love having us here. We return the favor by imbuing the place with class."

"Still, we should do more to show our gratitude," Summer said. "Isn't their anniversary approaching?"

"Next month," I said. "Forty-nine years."

"Remarkable," Summer said.

Jessica patted her partner's knee. "That'll be us someday."

A tender smile passed between them, and my heart swelled. I was forty-six years old, so it was unlikely I'd ever achieve a golden anniversary. But more and more, I was thinking I wouldn't mind getting to a silver one.

"We should pitch in and get them a gift card," Summer said. "Maybe Pearly's Steak and Chop House."

Jessica gawked. "Pearly's? Surely we can do better than that."

"What's wrong with Pearly's?" Summer said. "You seemed to enjoy it just fine last time we went. Gobbled up an entire ribeye, if I remember correctly."

"There's nothing wrong with Pearly's, as it goes," Jessica said. "I just think we should find a place in Boulder...or even Denver. Something with a three-star rating and an owner who doesn't look as if he's bathed in a deep fryer."

I smiled at her description of Ken Pearly. A short, squatty man in his early fifties, he exuded the image of a guy in a New York City alley trying to sell you a knock-off Rolex. He and Dan, Sam's server at the Snow Plow Chow, could be cousins, based on their similar physical characteristics and unexpected levels of intelligence. Though Pearly and I had never grown to be friends—I still called him Mr. Pearly and he referred to me as Ms.

Cassidy—I had to admit, his restaurant served a better-than-decent steak.

"That's a nice thought," I said, "but I'm sure my parents would tell you it's unnecessary. Our presence ensures the snacks don't go to waste, especially during non-peak season. Speaking of which, I'm going to fill my plate. Keep an eye on the creatures, will you?"

I sauntered over to the buffet, where Mr. Farmington was checking the hot plates. As I greeted him, I appraised the evening's fare with appreciation. Crab-stuffed mushrooms, fried mac-and-cheese balls, and creamy pumpkin hummus with wheat crackers. The only dish that caused me to turn up my nose was the bacon-wrapped Brussels sprouts. Why ruin a perfectly wonderful piece of bacon by folding it around something green?

"You've outdone yourself, Mr. Farmington." I used silver tongs to transfer my choices from serving platters to a plate. "I'm not ashamed to admit I worried the buffet might suffer when Jamal left for the Snow Plow Chow. You haven't missed a beat, though. This looks and smells delicious."

Mr. Farmington smiled with pride. "If I'm being honest, that young man taught me everything I know—about managing the lodge, that is. Though I could teach him a thing or two regarding American history."

I laughed. Mr. Farmington had spent decades teaching history at Rock Creek High School alongside my mother, a former English teacher. Working with teenagers all those years had layered the two of them with thick skins and sharpened senses of humor. When Mr. Farmington retired two years ago, he found himself at loose ends just as Jamal, their former night manager and chef-in-training, left. The fit was perfect. Mr. Farmington exhibited the perfect combination of firmness and patience. He handled guest complaints with charm but didn't cater to over-the-top demands.

Also, he brewed a mean urn of mulled wine.

I ladled some of the steaming red liquid into a mug, added an orange wedge, and stirred it with a cinnamon stick. "I'm sure my parents have updated you on current events."

He nodded. "Butch filled me in on the young man's death. Another dark chapter in our village's history. I said I'd be happy to stay on tonight as long as they need me."

"That's kind of you. They're lucky to have you."

I turned to join my friends as the front door slid open. Renata, the local high school hockey coach and Raul's younger sister, entered, accompanied by the newest member of our gang, Fudge Factory owner Pamela Ashton. The two of them hung up their coats, waved, and made a beeline to the buffet.

I tucked myself into the corner of a couch, smiling as Jessica stuffed her last mac-and-cheese ball in her mouth and washed it down with wine. With her spiky red hair and pale, freckled skin, Jessica would have been well cast as a pixie in a fantasy film. But the scrappy woman proved the idiom about not judging a book by its cover. Her small stature housed a ferociously protective core—especially when someone she cared for was threatened.

The same might be said of her wife. Summer, who made her living teaching courses designed to heal and relax, also harbored an intense protective streak. Despite her claims of pacifism, I didn't doubt she'd throttle anyone who tried to harm one of us—but only if easing them into a serene state of mind didn't do the trick first.

Plates filled, Renata and Pamela seated themselves on adjoining chairs. Jessica pointed at each of us, as if checking roll. "Is Lynn coming?"

"Not tonight," I said. "Professional conflict, she said."

"What about Mrs. Finney? Her superior sleuthing skills would come in handy."

"I invited her, but she declined," I said, ignoring the implication that Mrs. Finney was our primary mystery solver rather than myself. "She and Mr. Purdy are otherwise engaged."

Pamela's cheeks tinged pink. "Oh, dear. I don't want to visualize what that might mean."

Renata grinned. "Good for her. I only hope I'm as active at her age, and as much in love."

Pamela reached over and poked her. "With Ethan," she said, referencing Renata's boyfriend and my business partner.

Renata made a mock angry face, and we giggled like schoolgirls. Woody wagged and trotted from woman to woman, as pleased at the hilarity as if he'd caused it. Carl lifted his head long enough to glower.

When the laughter subsided, Summer took a sip of wine and dabbed her lips with a napkin. "When can we expect Tonya? I've prepared a special meditation."

Jessica shook a finger. "No meditating tonight. We're not here to offer solace. Our job is to unite our superior brains in a quest for answers."

Summer sighed, and Jessica elbowed her in the ribs. "You're right about one thing, though. Our guest of honor is late."

I smiled ruefully. "You know Tonya. The woman enjoys nothing more than making an entrance. She'll arrive soon. And when she does, she'll need every ounce of our crime-solving ability." I raised my mug. "So, let's lubricate those brain cells, my friends."

Chapter Fourteen

As if to prove my point, Tonya swept through the front door with a flourish. Monika, her cub reporter, stepped in behind her. Tonya blew a kiss our direction, while Monika locked eyes with me and shot me a mini glare. I blanched, realizing I'd neglected to return her calls.

The two of them wriggled out of their jackets and ambled toward the buffet, chatting with Mr. Farmington as they filled their plates and mugs. As always, Tonya was a vision. Her hair hung to her shoulders in waves, and her signature red lipstick popped against her dark, glowing skin.

When the two of them finally joined us, Tonya sat beside me and planted a kiss on my cheek. I'd be wearing a lipstick stain for the evening, but that was fine by me. Rarely a day went by that I didn't glance in the mirror to find Tonya's lipstick on my face. I wouldn't have it any other way.

Monika plopped down on the other side of me and

poked me with her elbow. "I can't believe you're trying to freeze me out. I thought we were partners."

I noticed the merriment in her eyes and realized she was teasing me. "Sorry," I said. "This day was nuts."

She grinned. "No worries. We're together now. Let's get this party started."

Jessica rubbed her hands together. "If we're going to continue investigating crimes, we should have an official name. Something like the Estrogen Murder Club."

We all groaned.

"Fact-Finding Females? Ladies of Detection?"

"Enough!" Summer said, placing a hand across Jessica's mouth.

"Let's hope we won't need a name because this will be our last murder in the village," Renata said. "Rock Creek Village is developing a reputation."

We nodded in agreement, and Summer clapped her hands. "First order of business. Tonya, how are you handling the stress? As I mentioned before you arrived, I've prepared a brief meditation that might help—"

"Oh, thank you, Summer, but that's unnecessary," Tonya said, a little too quickly. My best friend possessed a gerbil brain much like my own. Neither of us easily succumbed to the calming effects of Summer's teachings, though we both kept trying. "Honestly, I'm fine. I'm sorry Gene is dead, but it's not as if he and I were bosom buddies."

Summer sighed. "Well, if you change your mind..."

"How's Lydia?" Pamela cut in.

Tonya shrugged. "Lydia's Lydia. What can I say? She fluctuates between fortitude and crying jags—crocodile tears, if you ask me. I'm not sure Lydia experiences genuine emotions. She acts the way society expects her to, but I doubt she feels anything at all."

I raised my eyebrows. Even for Tonya, this seemed harsh.

She closed her eyes. "Sorry. Now I'm coming across as the one without feelings. I'm just so tired of the drama that accompanies my mother every time she waltzes into town. And now she might end up as a suspect in her boyfriend's murder."

I cocked my head. "Why do you say that?"

Tonya cast a glance at Monika. "We made a deal before we got here, right, Mon? Nothing leaves this room?"

Monika gave her a thumbs up. "I'm here as a friend, not a reporter. Though when the time comes..."

Tonya smirked. "Don't worry, you'll get the scoop."

I shifted in my seat. "We're burning daylight, ladies. Let's get on with it. Tonya, why do you say Lydia might be a suspect?"

She twisted a strand of hair around her finger. "Well, when Raul told us Gene was dead, she didn't seem especially surprised. I mean, she covered her face with her hands and acted like she was crying, but it appeared manufactured to me." Tonya stared off into the distance. "I suppose her reaction wasn't uncharacteristic, though. Those of you who know Lydia get it. It's how she is."

"I sense a 'but' coming," I said.

Tonya's gaze dropped to her tapered red fingernails. "It's just that...I'm pretty sure she lied to Raul."

"Go on," I prompted.

"He asked where we'd been that morning—a routine question. I said I'd been reading the newspaper and answering emails before heading to the office at nine. David left for his bookstore before I got up—big delivery. I figured Gene had gone for a run, as he did every morning. Lydia told Raul she slept in and didn't roll out of bed until after nine. But that wasn't true. When I was leaving for work, I noticed the guest room door cracked open, and I peeked in to say goodbye. But the room was empty."

No one spoke for a moment as we digested the implications. "Could she have been in the bathroom?" Pamela asked. "Taking a shower maybe?"

Tonya shook her head. "The door to the bathroom was open, too."

I frowned. The lie didn't look good. "You didn't mention this to Raul?"

Tonya clasped her hands in her lap. "No. I should have, but...ladies, I can't figure out what to do. Lydia and I don't have the best relationship, but ratting on my mother feels wrong. Besides, there might be an innocent explanation..."

"The lie doesn't prove she did anything wrong," I said. "But it's concerning. Why don't you just ask her?"

Tonya cringed. "I can predict how that conversation would go. She'd say her whereabouts were none of my business, and things would deteriorate from there."

"Have David there with you," I suggested. "Lydia is always on her best behavior when he's around."

"She loves David," Tonya agreed. "But he isn't likely to take my side on this. He despised Gene. He was thrilled when Lydia told us she was preparing to dump him."

"Wait, what?" Jessica said. "I didn't know Lydia was planning to end the relationship."

"I'm not sure it's relevant," Tonya said, fidgeting with her ring.

"Come on, Tonya," I responded. "You're smarter than that. This could give your mom a motive. Stack that beside the lie regarding her whereabouts...You should have mentioned this to Raul and Lynn."

"You don't understand what it's like, Callie," Tonya

snapped. "You hit the mother lottery. Stop being so sancti-monious."

I reeled back. My first instinct was to defend myself, but then I glimpsed the agony beneath Tonya's anger. Instead of responding, I wrapped my arms around her. It took only a moment before I felt her squeeze back.

"I'm sorry, sugarplum," she murmured.

"No, I'm the one who's sorry," I said. "You don't need my lectures. You need my support."

She disentangled from my embrace and reached into her purse, pulling out a handkerchief and swiping her eyes. "You support me best by being honest with me." She swept her gaze around the gaggle of girlfriends. "I'm lucky to be surrounded by friends who will tell it like it is. And Callie is right—I'm obliged to tell Raul and Lynn what I know."

We were quiet for a moment. Then Pamela said, "Why did your mother decide to call it off with Gene?"

Tonya sighed, her expression cynical. "Several reasons." She began ticking them off on her fingers. "Gene was only into her for the money. He was preoccupied with family business. He wasn't paying her enough attention. But if you want my opinion, she'd simply grown bored. Lydia's not much into monogamy. She won't admit it, but I suspect she already has boyfriend number...whatever it might be...waiting in the wings."

Monika drummed her fingers on her knee. "I'm not so sure the looming break-up bodes badly for your mother. It could be interpreted as a lack of motive. If Lydia was planning to dump Gene anyway, why bother killing him? Besides, don't take this wrong, but your mother doesn't strike me as the type to exert that much physical effort."

Tonya pondered. "Fair point. Honestly, I don't believe Lydia has the capacity for murder. In my experience, her pattern involves abandoning whatever doesn't please her.

Don't get me wrong, she has a temper. But she's more prone to lashing out with her tongue. Physical assertion might result in a broken nail."

"So, what are you going to do?" Renata asked.

"Would you care to meditate over it?" Summer chimed in. "We could do it here or head over to Yoga Delight. I have the perfect program for unleashing the flow of decisions."

Jessica rolled her eyes. "No one wants to meditate, Summer. We're action people, not overthinkers. Fill us with sugar and wine and give us something to do."

Summer grinned, undeterred. "Yoga? That's active."

We shared a cathartic laugh. Tonya got to her feet and stretched. "I don't need mind-freeing meditation or yoga. I've made my decision. I'm going home to ask Lydia where she was this morning. Then I'll insist we meet with Raul and Lynn first thing tomorrow to clean up the lie."

"What if she refuses?" I asked.

Tonya shrugged. "I'll go without her. One way or the other, I'm not bearing the burden of her secret any longer."

We stood and wrapped Tonya in a group hug. Woody nosed his way into the center of the group. Carl stood on the couch and offered an appreciative meow. Perhaps his sentimental side was evolving.

Then he indulged in some inappropriate personal grooming, and I put that thought to bed.

Once Tonya left, the rest of us cleaned up our plates and mugs. As the the ladies headed toward the coat rack, I put a hand on Monika's shoulder. "Do you mind sticking around?"

Her green eyes lit up. "Are we going to do some sleuthing?"

I smiled. "I have so many thoughts rolling around in my brain. I was hoping to run them by you."

"Absolutely. Maybe we can create one of your famous suspect lists while we're at it." She reached in her pocket and pulled out the pen I'd given her as a gift a few months back.

I rummaged in my bag and pulled out a legal pad. "And this is why we make such a good team."

Chapter Fifteen

We refilled our mugs and situated ourselves across a low coffee table. Fortunately, we had the place to ourselves.

Monika drew columns across the page and labeled them suspect, means, opportunity, motive, and questions. "Where should we start?" she asked, pen poised above the yellow pad.

Before I could respond, the lobby door slid open. My mother and father entered and headed toward us, bypassing the door leading upstairs to their condo.

Woody met them halfway, and Mom's lips curved into a tired smile as she stooped to embrace him. Carl jumped off the couch and rubbed against Dad's ankle.

"How's Vivian?" I asked.

Mom's smile faded. "No serious injuries, thank goodness. But still no memory."

"Not even her name?"

Dad shook his head. "I thought she might be on the verge of recognizing Pinky, but that's the closest she got."

"I noticed that, too," I said. "It could be a good sign. Maybe her memories are lurking just beneath the surface."

"I hope so," Mom said. "In the meantime, the doctor says he'll release her tomorrow afternoon. We've insisted she stay with us. Where else would the poor woman go?"

Monika frowned. "The detectives can't track down any family or other contacts now that they have her full name?"

"Forty years ago, we had her name and still couldn't find anything on her, and that's when the trail was fresh," Dad said. "No driver's license, no bank accounts, no social media in Vivian Corwin's name. It's as if she ceased to exist in 1988. We never stopped searching, though. Even after we believed..."

Even after they believed she was dead, I finished in my mind. "She must have acquired a new identity," I said.

Dad lifted his palms. "But why? What happened that caused her to leave her husband, the village..." He paused and looked at Mom, "...her friends? All without any explanation?"

Mom sighed. "All we can hope is that Vivian recovers her memory and fills in the blanks. Now, I'm going upstairs to prepare the guest room."

"Wouldn't it be easier to put her in one of the lodge rooms?" I asked.

"No!" my parents said in unison.

"We need to keep her close," Dad added.

Dad had been searching for Vivian for forty years and wasn't willing to have her that far from his sight. Still, with cameras strategically placed around the exterior of the property, the Knotty Pine Resort felt safe. When Mr. Farmington left each night at eight o'clock, he locked the lobby doors and guests had to use their key cards to enter. I doubted Vivian would be in any danger here.

Mom turned toward their door. "Coming, Butch?"

His eyes traveled from me to Monika to the legal pad on the coffee table. "Think I'll stay here and keep the girls company for a bit."

Mom smiled. "Don't be too long, sweetheart. You need some sleep."

As soon as she headed upstairs, Dad sat next to me on the couch and glanced at the paper. "Not much progress."

"We were just getting started when you and Mom walked in," I said. "You distracted us. Otherwise, Monika and I would already have the culprit in custody."

Monika picked up her pen. "Shall we start with a list of suspects in Eugene Murray's murder?"

Dad leaned back in his seat. "Before we do that, I'd like to hear Callie describe the crime scene. Visualizing how this might have happened could help us focus on who did it."

"I can do you one better." I retrieved my camera bag from under the table and pulled out my Nikon. Scrolling through the grave rubbing photos, I paused when I got to the crime scene images. I passed the camera to Dad, and Monika rose and moved behind the couch so she could see over his shoulder. Carl settled into Dad's lap and peered at the small screen.

Once we'd studied each photo, Dad handed the camera back to me and sighed. "It never gets easier."

"What doesn't?" I asked.

"The sight of an unnatural death. Gene Murray was a man in his prime. Someone stole decades of his future. No one deserves that."

The three of us remained silent for a moment. I realized for the first time that I'd learned my ritual of respect for victims at my father's knee.

Monika returned to her seat, and I pointed to the legal pad. "Get us started, Dad. Who should be first on the list?"

He rubbed his hand across his chin. "Gotta start with Pinky. The man confessed, after all."

"Did they arrest him?" I asked.

Dad shook his head. "I talked to Frank on the way home. No evidence that warrants holding him."

"Except his confession," Monika said.

"People make false confessions all the time," Dad responded. "Frank said they practically had to handcuff Pinky to get him to leave. Still needs to be on the list, though."

As Monika jotted the name in the suspect column, I thought again how little I knew about Pinky. When had he moved to Rock Creek Village? Where was he from, and what had he done prior to his life here? He was as much of an enigma to me as Mrs. Finney—or Vivian.

"Were Pinky and Vivian friends when she lived in the village?" I asked.

Dad stared into the fireplace, watching the flames crackle as he thought. "You were in second grade when Pinky moved here. He bought the grocery store a few months later. I only remember because you made us stop at the grand opening to buy an apple for your teacher."

Monika snickered. "An apple for your teacher? What a nerd."

"Hush. I got excellent grades that year." I looked at Dad. "Was Vivian living here then?"

"She arrived sometime that year, if memory serves. As for the two of them being friends, I don't recall one way or the other. When Vivian disappeared, we questioned every-one. No connection between them came to light."

Monika tapped the pen against the pad. "All right. Pinky's confession earns him a spot on the list. What should I put in the means, opportunity, and motive columns?"

I chewed my bottom lip. "Means is easy, though not especially helpful. Mr. Fallow said he left the murder weapon—a mattock—lying beside one grave when he went off to tend to another. It would have been easy enough for Pinky to snatch it up on his trek through the cemetery."

"But then, anyone could have," Monika said.

I touched my nose. "Precisely. As for opportunity..."

"No way of knowing at the moment," Dad said. "Last I heard, the cops were still searching for witnesses who might put him somewhere other than the cemetery."

"Okay. Motive?" Monika asked.

The three of us looked at each other blankly. "Only one thing comes to me," I said. "What if Pinky came across Gene attacking Vivian and swung the mattock in her defense?"

"If that were the case, why wouldn't he just say so?" Monika asked.

I pointed at the paper. "Write that in the questions column."

Monika scribbled on the pad, then looked up. "All right. Who's next?"

I hesitated and shot Dad a glance. "We need to add Vivian, right? She was at the scene of the crime and had blood on her hands."

Dad stiffened. "That was her own blood, from her head wound."

"Probably," I said softly. "But we don't know that for certain."

"Not yet," Dad said.

A silence fell over us. I waited, knowing Dad would get where he needed to go. He was still grappling with self-imposed guilt over Vivian's disappearance, but he was a cop at heart. Deep down, he understood the necessity of considering Vivian.

Finally, he gave a reluctant nod. Monika added Vivian's name and quickly filled in the means and opportunity columns. "Motive?" she asked.

Dad drew a hand through his hair. "Self-defense? Like we said with Pinky, it's possible that Gene attacked her, and she swung the mattock to protect herself."

"And fell on George's grave, knocking herself unconscious?" Monika asked.

"Seems coincidental," I agreed. "Also, how would she have gotten hold of the mattock?"

"And why would Gene attack her?" Monika said. "Am I missing something?"

"We're just spitballing tonight," Dad said. "Can't expect to have all the answers. Not yet." He snapped his fingers. "Just realized something. No one has mentioned Gene's phone."

My eyes widened. "Raul gave instructions for crime scene techs to bag it if they found it, but I never heard anything further on the matter."

"Frank didn't mention it," Dad mused. "Then again, I didn't ask."

"Is it important?" Monika asked.

"I doubt he'd have gone for a run without his phone," Dad said. "If it wasn't on the scene, it's only logical to assume the killer took it. And Vivian didn't have it."

His implication was clear: if the killer took the phone, and if Vivian didn't have it, she must not be the killer. His logic was a stretch, though. Vivian might have tossed the phone into the trees, for instance. But I kept my mouth shut. Let Dad deal with this however he needed to.

As Monika wrote a note to ask about the phone, my train of thought took a detour. "How did Vivian get to

Rock Creek Village? She wasn't carrying car keys or ID. Not even a purse."

"All she had in her pockets was cash," Dad affirmed. "Quite a bit, though. Over three hundred dollars."

Monika cocked her head. "She could have left her belongings somewhere in town—a rental, maybe—and walked to the cemetery."

"Then why carry all that cash?" I asked.

We took a minute to ponder the puzzle, but none of us could produce a satisfactory answer. "Add it to the list, and let's move on," I said.

Monika scribbled a few words. Then her pen hovered over the suspect column. "Lydia next? The spouse or partner is always top of the list, right? Tonya said Lydia and Gene's relationship was on the outs. Also, Lydia lied to Raul regarding her whereabouts at the time of Gene's death."

"Yup. Frank told me all about it. Better write her down," Dad said.

"Anyone else?" she asked once she'd added the information.

Dad thought for a moment. "Gene's background isn't...wasn't...squeaky clean. The Murray family isn't the crime syndicate they were in the old days, but they must still have some enemies."

"I'm sure there's plenty of dirt on them," Monika said. "I'll see what I can dig up."

We scanned the list. "Anyone else?" Dad asked.

"This may sound farfetched," I said, "and I can't begin to suggest a motive, but Cedric Fallow had means and opportunity."

Monika's forehead creased. "Who's Cedric Fallow?"

"The caretaker of the cemetery," Dad said. "Ill-tempered old guy, protective of his graveyard. I see your point, Sundance. The murder weapon belonged to him. As you say, though, motive is elusive."

"Gene could have trampled one of his well-tended graves for all we know," I said. "Seriously, Mr. Fallow has lived in the village forever. He recognized Vivian when he saw her. Maybe there was bad blood between them."

"Not that I ever heard," Dad said. "But you might as well add him. No stone unturned, as they say."

Monika wrote his name, and we scanned the list again. "We're weak on motive," Dad said. "Lots of research lies ahead of us. Who wants to tackle what?"

Monika raised a hand. "I'll research the Murrays."

"I'll follow up on Lydia's talk with the detectives," I said. "I'm also going to see what I can find out about Pinky. There's something we're missing there. If he didn't kill Gene, why confess?"

Dad drew a deep breath. "Okay. I'll oversee Vivian. If she's involved in Gene's death, I'll figure it out."

I knew how much it cost him to take that on, and I felt a surge of pride and respect.

We agreed to meet at Rocky Mountain High in the morning to debrief. I tucked the legal pad into my bag, promising to scan the list and forward it to them. Monika pocketed her pen. Dad raised his index finger. "Remember, nothing we do can in any way interfere with the police investigation."

Monika and I looked at each other. "Of course," I said. "Why would you even say such a thing?"

Chapter Sixteen

The next morning, the first thought I had was that I hadn't talked to Sam in nearly a day, and I missed him.

The second thought was that there'd been another murder in Rock Creek Village yesterday.

The third thought was that my mouth felt hairy...

Opening my eyes, I discovered a swath of orange fur resting across my face. From experience, I knew it belonged to Carl. Since the cat often slept curled around my head, this wasn't an unusual occurrence, but I still hadn't grown accustomed to finding the tip of a tail in my mouth first thing in the morning.

I untangled him with care. Experience had also taught me that sudden jostling while he slept resulted in welts along my cheek. He snarled halfheartedly but allowed me to tuck him in beside the golden retriever nestled at the foot of the bed. Woody shifted to accommodate the cat, and the two of them returned to dreamland.

I gazed at the creatures, wondering when I had become

such an aficionado of canine and feline companionship. If someone had told me ten years ago I'd be cuddled up in bed with a dog and a cat, I'd have scoffed. I was too busy and too independent for pets. But when I'd discovered Woody as an abandoned pup on the side of a busy Washington, D.C. road, I'd taken him home, supposedly temporarily. Then, a couple of years ago, Woody decided to adopt a stray cat we named Carl. Now...well, I didn't even consider them pets. They were family.

I glanced at the clock. Seven a.m. Earlier than I normally got up, but a full day awaited me. I shimmied into a sitting position and grabbed my phone, hoping for a text from Tonya. Nothing.

When I called her last night, she'd told me Lydia was already in bed when she got home, so she'd been unable to confront her over lying to Raul. "In bed?" I said, incredulous. "It wasn't even eight when you left the lodge."

"Lying to the police must be exhausting," Tonya had replied.

"Are you sure she didn't sneak out again?"

"She's in there. She said goodnight to David, and he watched her go into her room. When I got home, I stole a peek. After what happened this morning, I don't trust her."

"Like you ever did."

"True. Anyway, I'll speak to her first thing in the morning."

"You'll keep me in the loop?" I asked.

"Of course, sugarplum. You'll be my first call."

That had been over eight hours ago. I considered prodding her with a text but decided to give her a couple more hours. Instead, I messaged Sam, certain he'd be awake on this lovely Tuesday morning. Though he'd relinquished the bulk of Snow Plow Chow's cooking chores to Jamal and Rodger, old habits died hard. I figured he'd always be an early riser.

Good morning, handsome, I typed.

As anticipated, his response came fast. *Hey, beautiful. You're up early.*

Are you at the café? I asked.

Not yet. Waiting for the folks to leave on their adventure. I'll head over about nine.

Want some company for lunch?

Tired of Pop-Tarts and frozen entrees?

I grinned, enjoying our comfortable banter. *Haha. I don't need you to feed me. I just want to wrap my arms around you.*

Three dots danced on the screen, followed by a flame emoji. *It's getting hot in here.*

I responded with a heart emoji and cringed. Emojis? When did I get so goofy? *See you soon*, I wrote.

Can't wait.

AN HOUR LATER, I'd showered and dressed, fed the creatures, and indulged in one of the Pop-Tarts about which Sam teased me. Then we headed off to Sundance Studio. Woody and Carl joined me at the gallery most days. Aside from the fact that I enjoyed having them around, I'd concluded they boosted sales. Customers relished a greeting from my lovable golden retriever and mysterious tabby cat, and the creatures savored their role as studio animals. Plus, they had treats and beds and toys in my office—a home away from home.

As we drove toward the upper village, the sun peeked

over the eastern mountains, sending pink rays across Mt. O'Connell. The aspens shivered in the breeze. I rolled the window down a crack and let the crisp, cool air stream into the car. Autumn was my favorite season in Rock Creek Village—until winter rolled around and became my new favorite. Then spring. Then summer. Turns out, there wasn't a bad season in our mountain town.

The traffic light at the park entrance turned red, and I obediently hit the brakes. As I waited for the light to change, my eyes drifted toward the cluster of buildings on the left. I spotted Renata's SUV among the cars parked at the Ice Zone. As assistant coach for the hockey team, her days started even earlier than Sam's, especially during the season. My gaze wandered to Pinkerton's Place, the village grocery store owned and operated by Pinky. I noticed the proprietor sweeping the stoop and decided to make a quick pit stop. I'd tried researching Pinky's past last night and came up dry. Perhaps a personal conversation would net me insider info.

Pinky eyed me with suspicion as I pulled into a parking space. When I climbed out of the car, he avoided eye contact and kept the broom moving. I didn't get the idea he was thrilled to see me.

"Morning, Pinky!" I said cheerfully.

He looked at me through narrowed eyes. "Here for some produce?"

I wrinkled my nose. "Got any Pop-Tarts?"

"I don't carry that garbage." He started sweeping again. "If you're here to discuss murder and confessions and such, you're wasting your time, missy. I have nothing to say."

I put my hands on my hips. "Pinky, I thought we were friends."

"Not sure what led you to that conclusion."

I gestured toward the Ice Zone. A while back, an incident occurred there that brought us together—if only temporarily. "After everything that happened back then...I thought we'd formed a bond."

"Guess you were mistaken."

I shifted from one foot to the other, trying to devise a plan of attack. Pinky's broom maintained a rhythmic swish. At last, I aimed at what I hoped was a soft spot.

"Vivian's being released from the hospital today. She'll stay with my parents until...well, until she regains her memory. If she does."

He stopped sweeping but didn't raise his eyes. "How's she doing?"

I lifted a shoulder. "Mom says her injuries are superficial, according to the doctor. They can't tell what's causing the amnesia. Shock, maybe. Or psychological trauma."

A moment passed. Without uttering a response, he resumed his task.

"Were the two of you friends back when Vivian lived here?" I asked.

"I knew her."

I bit my lip. It was easier to get Carl to obey a command than it was to pry information out of the man. "Have you been in touch with her since she left the village?"

His jaw tensed. "As your father must have told you, she just disappeared one day. Didn't know if she was dead or alive." He paused and gazed toward Mt. O'Connell. "Glad it was the latter."

The silence stretched out between us. Finally, I took the leap. "Pinky, you didn't kill Gene, did you?"

His fingers tightened around the broom handle. "The man deserved to be clobbered."

"But—"

He leveled his watery blue eyes at me. "I'm done talking, Ms. Cassidy. Either head inside and make a purchase or run along."

I held his gaze. "I don't believe you're guilty of this, Pinky. And I'm determined to find out who is."

"Stay out of it," he said. "For once, just stay out of it."

Chapter Seventeen

A few minutes later, I pulled into the alley behind Sundance Studio, surprised to find Ethan's car already in his reserved spot. My business partner was punctual, but the studio didn't open until ten. Unlocking the back door, I followed the creatures inside as they scampered toward the gallery.

Ethan looked up from his spot behind the sales counter, where he stood with our new employee, Zoe Dean. Ah, that explained his early arrival. I'd forgotten it was training day. He glanced at his watch and grinned. "Wonders never cease." He nudged Zoe with an elbow. "Mark this day on the calendar. Callie Cassidy showed up before nine-thirty. This is an event unlikely to occur again in our lifetime."

"Hardy har har," I said, setting my camera bag on the counter. "Zoe, one skill you'll soon learn is how to fake laughter at what Ethan refers to as his wicked sense of humor. Welcome to our dysfunctional little family. I'm glad you're here."

Zoe had grown up in Rock Creek Village and was friends

with Sam's daughter, as well as the twins, Banner and Braden, who usually worked at the studio. The boys were currently in San Francisco on a so-called sabbatical. Their reprobate father had used some of his controversial life insurance money to fund the trip, saying he wanted to start fresh with his sons. I had my doubts, and so did the boys. They'd agreed to the trip but kept their expectations low, determined to enjoy the experience no matter how the relationship part played out. When they'd approached Ethan and me for the time off, they'd mentioned that Zoe was looking for a part-time job to subsidize her online college courses. Since Ethan had been searching for a new employee for months, the timing had been perfect.

Woody whined and wiggled beside me, barely able to contain himself. Zoe came around the sales counter and crouched to pet the golden retriever's head. She wore skinny jeans and a rainbow wool cardigan over a white V-neck shirt that contrasted with her dark skin. Long braids swung around her shoulders, and silver earrings dangled from her lobes. Her smooth, wrinkle-free face made me sigh over my lost youth.

Carl leapt onto a stool and then the counter, issuing a series of insistent meows. I looked at him in surprise. The cat was not the friendliest of souls, but he appeared smitten with Zoe. She nestled him into her arms, where he purred happily.

Ethan raised his eyebrows. "I've never seen him act like that."

"Looks as if Carl approves of your new hire. Good job, partner. And she came to us at the perfect time."

He smirked. "Absolutely. Her presence will give you more time for your investigation."

Zoe's eyes widened. "Oh, yeah. You found a dead man in the cemetery."

"Finding a dead man in a cemetery," Ethan said. "Quite the detective."

I smirked at him and turned back to Zoe. "Yes, finding Gene there was quite a shock."

"Did you know him well?" she asked.

"He was Lydia Fredericks'...um...boyfriend, I guess. You know Lydia, right? Tonya Stephens' mother?"

Zoe nodded, and Ethan turned serious. "Renata said Pinky confessed, but you don't think he did it."

"Sam's parents don't think so either," Zoe said.

I remembered Zoe had joined them on their excursion to Boulder yesterday. "They don't?"

"Nope. They've known Pinky a long time and said he's no killer." She continued petting Carl, who seemed to be in a state of euphoria. I hoped he wasn't planning to abandon me for life with Zoe.

"I agree, though I haven't yet figured out the motivation behind his confession." I waved a hand to change the subject. "Anyway, how was Boulder? Did Elyse enjoy seeing her grandparents?"

"We had a lot of fun," Zoe said with a mischievous grin. "You were a topic of conversation."

I felt my cheeks warm. "Me?"

She nodded. "Sam mentioned you're planning a picnic for tomorrow."

Ethan chuckled. "Sucking up to the boyfriend's parents, huh?"

Heat surged across my cheeks. I characterized myself as a strong, confident woman, and it embarrassed me to admit that I cared what anyone thought of me.

"Just trying to get some face time with them. I've been so busy I haven't seen them yet." I glanced at my watch. "Speaking of busy, I'm supposed to meet Monika and Dad at Rocky Mountain High. Are you two okay holding down the fort?"

Ethan nodded. "Recruiting Mrs. Finney's help? She got back from vacation in the nick of time."

"You mean her impromptu elopement-slash-honeymoon, don't you?" Mrs. Finney had gotten engaged to Mr. Purdy, her paramour and former CIA colleague, a few months earlier. We'd all been fascinated to see what type of wedding the two quirky septuagenarians would concoct, but they surprised us by eloping in Butte, Montana, following one of their ice dancing competitions. It was a disappointment, but they promised to make it up to us by hosting a monumental reception in the village.

My phone dinged with a text from Tonya telling me she and Lydia were on their way to the police station. She promised to call me later with an update.

I shoved my phone into my pocket. "I'm going to pop into the office and fill the creatures' bowls before I go."

AFTER COMPLETING MY CARETAKING DUTIES, I patted Woody on the head and tried to cuddle Carl the way Zoe had, but he was having none of it. I said goodbye to Ethan and Zoe and headed out the front door. A flurry of fallen leaves whisked across the sidewalk in the autumn breeze. I turned toward Rocky Mountain High, pausing in front of A Likely Story bookstore. Through the bay window, I spotted David Parisi, the handsome Italian who'd swept my best friend off her feet and married her. He saw me and threw me one of those European kisses where the fingers and thumb come together against the lips and then burst open. I grinned at him and waved, unwilling to return the flamboyant gesture.

The blinds at Tabitha's Treasures were still closed, so I couldn't spy on Tabitha, but I pictured her sitting in her office smoking a cigarette and completing today's *New York Times* crossword—using a pen, no doubt. She'd indulged in the same morning routine since I'd worked for her one summer as a teenager. Now, at almost ninety, it was embedded into her psyche.

I peered inside The Fudge Factory and saw Pamela arranging squares of gooey chocolate on a tray. She blew me a normal American kiss, and I responded with another wave.

As I approached Rocky Mountain High, I glanced at the shops across the street. The blinds were drawn across Quicker Liquor's windows. No surprise, since the liquor store didn't open until noon. Pearly's Steak and Chop House, situated next door, only opened for dinner, so I was surprised to see Mr. Pearly chewing on a toothpick as he swept leaves into neat little piles.

I called out a greeting. "You might be fighting a losing battle, Mr. Pearly. Seems those leaves have a mind of their own."

He took the toothpick from his mouth, leaned on his broom, and gave me a weak smile. He looked tired, and I wondered if a bout of insomnia had landed him at the restaurant this early. "Mornin', Ms. Cassidy," he said. "Just trying to get as many of them off the sidewalk as I can. Tromping through wet leaves doesn't do much for my customers' attitudes, or their appetites."

He pointed toward the sky, and my eyes followed his finger to the gathering gray clouds. I'd forgotten rain was in the forecast.

"Uh oh," I said. "I don't have my umbrella. Guess I'll have to send a plea to the rain gods to hold out until I get my coffee."

"Pleading to the gods, huh? Let me know how that works for you. It hasn't proven to be a successful strategy for me."

His tone was light, but I glimpsed a flash of despair in his eyes as he resumed his task.

I continued to the coffee shop, reflecting that even in a small town like Rock Creek Village, people managed to keep a part of their souls sealed off.

Chapter Eighteen

The bell above the door tinkled when I entered the coffee shop. Behind the counter, Mrs. Finney and Mr. Purdy had their heads together, murmuring sweet nothings to one another, if my guess was right. Then again, for all I knew, the two former CIA agents might be plotting a coup.

I plopped onto a stool. "What are you two lovebirds chatting about?"

Mr. Purdy reached across the counter and squeezed my hand. At six-feet tall, he rivaled Mrs. Finney's height, but whereas she was broad and firm, he was thin and sinewy. In my mind, they made the perfect couple. The gold ring encircling his finger glinted in the light, and his face glowed just as brightly. "Happy days, Miss Callie. Just talking of happy days."

A smile of pure joy wreathed my face. Two newly married couples in the village—Tonya and David, and Mrs. Finney and Mr. Purdy. Happy days indeed. "I want to hear all about the wedding."

Mrs. Finney waved, not so subtly flashing her own

purple amethyst wedding ring. "Plenty of time for that, dear. This morning, we have a murder to discuss."

Mr. Purdy kissed Mrs. Finney's leathery cheek, then gave her rear end a pat. "That's my girl."

She giggled. "Sweetie, will you prepare Callie's regular order?"

"One dark roast with a shot of vanilla and a pinch of cinnamon, coming right up."

Mrs. Finney caught me eyeing the glass dome atop the counter. "A slice of orange soufflé coffeecake, too," she said. Her husband nodded obediently and got to work on the order.

Picking up her own cup, Mrs. Finney flipped up the hinged opening on the countertop and came through. "Let's sit near the window, dear. Will Monika be joining us?"

I glanced at my watch as we settled at a bistro table. "Should be here any minute. My father is coming, too."

Her bushy eyebrows rose. "Butch usually advises you to let the police handle such matters."

"He has a deep stake in this case."

"Ah, yes. The missing woman. Her reappearance must trigger a sense of failure, misguided though it may be."

I cocked my head. "Exactly. But how did you—?"

"I've been in his position, dear. In my past life, that is."

She waved her hand again, and the ring glimmered. This time, I knew it wasn't an accident. I snatched her hand and gazed at the enormous gem. "Oh, Mrs. Finney, this is divine. I didn't figure you for a wedding ring type of woman."

"I do love a sparkly bauble, dear." She preened as she admired the ring. "Speaking of sparkly baubles, when might we see a ring on your finger?"

As always when faced with the topic, my gut clenched.

But I was pleased—and a little surprised—to note that the clench carried less intensity than before, and it was free of an accompanying sense of dread. "From what I've heard, someone needs to ask first. Besides, I don't think Sam's parents are on board. They're not convinced I'm good for their son."

She gazed at me wistfully. "My advice, my dear, is to be yourself. Why do we love cats? Because they don't waste their time attempting to impress us." She reached into the pocket of her lavender apron and retrieved a pen and a tiny pad of paper. "Something for next month's cups, perhaps."

The cups to which she referred were the axiom-printed paper coffee cups that had put Rocky Mountain High on the map. Mrs. Finney ordered a new series of them every few weeks. Each set was graced with her original wise—and sometimes cryptic—adages, which enchanted tourists and villagers alike.

She finished scribbling and raised her eyes back to mine. "Now, back to the topic of marriage..."

The jingle of the bell saved me from further interrogation. Monika entered like a tempest, yanking off her hood and shaking out clouds of red curls. She spotted us and made her way over, wriggling out of her jacket and plunking onto a chair. "It's raining." Her accusatory tone implied that the weather had schemed against her.

"At least you have a raincoat," I said. "I didn't even bring an umbrella."

"You two act as if a little rain might melt you," Mrs. Finney said with exasperation. "Toughen up. Why, I remember a time in Burma...Myanmar, they call it now... when a savage storm..."

Monika and I shared a look, realizing we were about to be subjected to another of Mrs. Finney's trips down CIA memory lane. Luckily, the door opened again, and my father entered, closing his umbrella and hanging it on a peg beside the door.

"You hoo. Over here, Butch." Mrs. Finney waved her hand. As I'm sure she'd intended, the ring twinkled, and Monika gasped. "That's the most gorgeous ring I've ever seen. What's that stone?"

"Amethyst," Mr. Purdy interjected as he approached with a tray. "My sweetheart loves purple, so purple it is." He placed coffee and a pastry on the table in front of me and leaned over to plant another kiss on Mrs. Finney's cheek.

"Lucky for you, PDA isn't illegal," Dad said as he joined us at the table. "I'd be forced to make a citizen's arrest."

Mr. Purdy grinned and shook hands with my father. "Luck has been with me since I arrived in Rock Creek Village, Butch. No reason to expect it'll run out today. Now, what can I get you folks?"

He jotted Monika and Dad's orders on a pad and sauntered back to the counter.

"Not trying to take over," Dad said, "but can we skip the small talk? I only have a half hour. Maggie and I want to be at the hospital when they release Vivian."

"Certainly," Mrs. Finney said, as if she'd been the boss all along. "I've already been apprised of the generalities— Eugene Murray, mattock in the jugular, Vivian Corwin and her amnesia. We can go from there."

My mouth gaped. "Where did you get all that information?"

"Never you mind, dear. The point is, we don't need to waste time reiterating the facts."

I shook my head. The woman never ceased to amaze me.

"Well, I'm afraid I have little to add," I said, puckering

my lips. "I drew a blank on Pinky. I'm not a super stealthy hacker type like Monika, and Google wouldn't give up any information on him prior to his arrival in the village. I even stopped by Pinkerton's Place this morning and tried to pump him for information, but he wouldn't bite."

We paused as Mr. Purdy delivered coffee and pastries. He glanced at Mrs. Finney's cheek as if deciding whether another kiss was too over the top. Then he leaned in and went for it. She giggled again as he wandered away. Monika grabbed a slice of coffee cake and tore a chunk out of it. Dad wrapped his hands around his coffee cup.

"I talked to Frank this morning," he said. "They haven't turned up any witnesses who can account for Pinky's whereabouts at the time of Eugene Murray's death. However, they haven't discovered evidence placing him at the murder scene, either. There are no fingerprints on the mattock except Cedric Fallow's, indicating the killer wore gloves. As you know, Vivian wasn't wearing gloves."

I weighed my words, knowing how much Vivian's innocence meant to my father. "That's true, Dad. But there's still so much mystery surrounding her return to the village. Until we can get some answers, I think we need to leave her on the list."

He stared at his cup, then nodded. "She's not at the top, though. Not on my list, anyway."

I turned to Monika. "What about you, Grasshopper?" I asked, using my satirical nickname for the young reporter. "Any illuminating tidbits on the Murray family?"

Monika scarfed down the last bite of coffeecake. "Nothing earth-shattering, but I did gather some background info." She produced her phone and scrolled through her notes. "The Murray family has a long history in Las Vegas, where they were once highly regarded and widely feared. Joe, the original patriarch, had his fingers in several illicit businesses—loan-sharking, bookmaking, protection rackets. He and his first wife had a son, Jack, then divorced when the child was eight. Joe remarried and two years later had a second son, Donovan. Eight years later, he fathered a daughter, Valerie, by his showgirl mistress."

The family tree played like a made-for-TV movie, one I wouldn't have the slightest inclination to watch. "No offense, but could we hear the *Reader's Digest* version? I started losing interest at kid number one."

My father narrowed his eyes at me. "Pay attention, Sundance. The devil is in the details."

I sipped my coffee and suppressed an eye roll. For five interminable minutes, Monika droned on about Murray family dynamics and mob machinations. Joe died. Jack took over. Donovan went along with his brother's bidding. Valerie filled the role of family princess. Blah blah blah. Sociopathic entitlement never did much to maintain my interest.

"It wasn't until the seventies that the trouble began," Monika continued. "Ignoring his younger brother's advice, Jack began dabbling in drug trafficking, leading the family to interactions with characters even more shady—and dangerous—than they were. A couple of high-profile murders occurred, nothing that could be linked directly to the Murrays, but by then they'd landed in the FBI's sights. Long story short..."

I sighed dramatically at the phrase, but everyone ignored me.

"Jack was convicted of murder and sentenced to forty years. He died in prison ten years ago."

"Riveting," I said. "I assume all this somehow leads to Gene."

Undeterred by my sarcasm, Monika consulted her

notes. "Donovan, who goes by Van, thus avoiding the Don cliché, took over the business, promising to make it legitimate. Rumor had it Jack still ran things behind the scenes until his death, but the family has largely managed to stay out of the public eye since the trial. Jack's sons, Amos and Thomas, are nearing their sixties. Donovan has two daughters in their forties and one son: Eugene Murray."

"Ta da," I sang.

"Had," Mrs. Finney interjected. "Donovan *had* a son."

We drew a collective breath, pondering Gene's untimely demise. With a family history like his, how ironic that his death would ultimately take place in a small-town cemetery.

"That's everything I had time to ferret out," Monika said, returning her phone to her purse. "I requested Jack Murray's trial records, but that'll take a while."

I exhaled in frustration. The avalanche of information I'd hoped for hadn't materialized.

Mrs. Finney cleared her throat. "If you're all amenable to it, I'll consult with a couple of my old cronies. I don't want to step on your toes, but perhaps my former colleagues can uncover information unattainable through, shall we say, traditional routes."

"My toes would enjoy that," I said. Dad and Monika nodded in agreement.

Mrs. Finney flicked a glance toward the counter, where a cluster of customers had gathered. "I should get back to work. I think Mr. Purdy and I will be able to contact our sources by tomorrow. I'll be in touch."

She scurried off to help her husband and whispered something in his ear. He rubbed his cheek, nodding as he listened.

Meanwhile, Dad's phone vibrated with a text. He skimmed the message, got to his feet, and put on his jacket.

"That was your mother. The hospital is releasing Vivian in an hour. I need to get going."

I rose and hugged him tight. "I'll stop by this evening to check on everyone."

He planted a kiss on the top of my head, popped open his umbrella, and headed out the door.

Monika said goodbye and skipped out after him after pulling her hood over her hair. I peered out the window, willing the rain to break long enough for me to hustle back to the studio without getting drenched. But the fates chose not to comply with my demand.

I felt a tap on my shoulder, and there stood Mrs. Finney, presenting me with an umbrella. "See that you return it," she said. "It's my favorite."

She pressed a button, and the umbrella popped open. It was a gargantuan violet contraption with purple fringe and puffballs hanging from the tips. Forcing a smile, I thanked her and just managed to wedge the huge thing through the door.

Chapter Nineteen

The tank-sized umbrella kept me dry—except for my shoes, which got soaked as I dodged puddles and piles of wet leaves. I darted beneath the studio's awning, shook out the umbrella, and spent a moment figuring out how to snap it shut. Once inside, I hung the monstrosity on the coat rack beside the door and slipped off my shoes.

Fluffing my hair with my fingers, I turned toward the gallery, where Ethan, Zoe, Woody, and Carl watched me with amusement. "What?" I asked defensively. "Haven't you ever seen someone come in from the rain?"

Ethan pointed at the umbrella. "Not toting a gigantic purple parachute."

Zoe chortled. Woody grinned and wagged, and I swear Carl rolled his eyes.

I shook my finger at the humans. "I was planning to treat you to lunch from Snow Plow Chow, but now I'm reconsidering my generosity."

They tightened their lips in a vain attempt to squelch their chuckles. When they both burst out laughing, I couldn't help myself. I joined them. "I'll be sure to tell Mrs. Finney how hilarious you find her favorite umbrella. Prepare yourselves for her wrath."

After updating me on Zoe's training schedule, Ethan mentioned that we'd sold six canvases online yesterday for a tidy profit, as well as three more from the studio. He pointed to the postcard rack. "Stock is dwindling."

I promised to put in an order for fresh canvases and spend an hour in the darkroom to replenish the postcard supply. One of the gallery's enticements was that each postcard was created by hand, which allowed us to charge a bit more for them. Even so, they practically flew off the rack.

On my way to the darkroom, I stopped in the office, where I rummaged through my notebooks of negative strips. I selected a few for the postcards and walked down the hall, past the computer lab where I taught digital photo classes and the small studio I'd set up for portrait work. When I stepped inside the darkroom's revolving door and rotated it, I experienced the familiar rush of exhilaration as it opened into the pitch-black chamber. I smiled as the pungent chemical odor filled my lungs. Only a photographer would welcome that smell with the same pleasure as a pine-scented forest.

Flipping on the overhead fluorescent lights, I spent a few minutes organizing my negatives and choosing which frames to print. Then I put on my apron—a gift from Sam that read "Darkroom Goddess"—readied the enlarger, and turned out the light. Since I was creating color prints, I had to leave the red safelights off, but I was comfortable enough in the space that the darkness didn't hinder me—as long as I didn't dwell on that time I'd stumbled over a dead body in here...

I used the enlarger to expose the photo paper, then situated it into the light-safe drum. With the drum lid securely fastened, I switched the lights back on to complete the chemical steps. At this stage of my career, the process required so little brainpower that I allowed my mind to wander. Mom and Dad were surely en route to the hospital by now. What would happen to poor Vivian? How long would my parents be able and willing to host her in their home? What if she never regained her memory? Would we ever learn where she'd been all these years? Did she have family or friends searching for her, as my father had done for decades?

It seemed likely that Vivian had returned to Rock Creek Village on a pilgrimage to George's grave. But how had she gotten here? Where was her car? Her suitcase? Her purse, for heaven's sake, with her wallet and ID? It was as if she'd dropped from the sky above into the cemetery.

And how did her arrival connect with Gene's murder? My father said the timing might have been a coincidence, but I didn't believe that, and I seriously doubted he did, either. So how did Gene and Vivian both end up at George's grave? It stood to reason that one of them followed the other to the site. My guess was that Gene had done the stalking. For what purpose, I couldn't conjecture.

And what about Michael Pinkerton? Why did he confess to Gene's murder? I'd wager he was trying to divert suspicion from Vivian—but why? There had to be a link between them that we hadn't yet discovered.

The more my brain chewed on the situation, the further I felt myself drifting from the answer. Maybe Lydia knew what bound Vivian and Gene and Pinky and was even now revealing the answers to Raul and Lynn. They might have the entire mystery solved before lunch. I experienced a twinge of envy. I wanted to be in the room where it happened.

I hummed the song from the musical *Hamilton* and

forced thoughts of murder and mystery from my mind. I selected a negative of a majestic elk whose image I'd captured as he tromped through the pines, his antlers raised arrogantly. I set the enlarger, flipped off the light, and made the exposure.

Just as I'd loaded the photo paper into the drum and turned on the overheads, my phone vibrated. Wiping my hands on my apron, I pulled the cell out of my pocket and checked the screen. Tonya.

I plopped onto a stool and answered, putting her on speaker so I could keep working. "Hey, girlfriend. How'd it go at the police station?"

"It was...interesting. Too much to get into on the phone. Are you and Sam available for dinner tonight? David has offered to prepare an authentic Italian dinner. Sound good?"

My stomach rumbled in response, as did my curiosity. "Better than good. But do I have to wait for dinner to learn what happened? Can't I at least get a preview?"

"Well, Lydia's not in jail. Raul and Lynn instructed her to stay in town, but she persuaded them to let her spend the evening barhopping with girlfriends in Valley Ridge. Though I'm fairly certain it's not girlfriends she'll really be with."

"What do you mean?"

"She finally came clean about where she'd been yesterday morning. As I suspected, her new boy-toy has been waiting in the wings, and the two of them engaged in a little...tête-à-tête."

"Oh, my. And you think she's meeting him tonight? The day after Gene's murder? That seems a little..."

"Inappropriate? Yup. That's Lydia. The woman irritates me beyond belief. And now I'm stuck with her—

until she's either cleared or arrested. At this point, I'm not sure which I'd prefer."

I winced but remained silent. A moment later, Tonya snickered. "Guess I'm more like my mother than I care to admit. No sense of decorum."

"That couldn't be further from the truth," I said, rushing to my friend's defense. "You are the polar opposite of your mother, in all the ways that count. In fact, it wouldn't surprise me to learn you were switched at birth."

"Hmm…With any luck, I might be Maggie and Butch's daughter. Not sure how I'd explain the difference in skin tone, but I can't say I care."

I smiled, happy she was making jokes, even if they were grim. "We might be twins," I said.

"How would that work? Let's see…under the influence of anesthesia, Maggie is unaware she's given birth to two daughters instead of the one she was planning for. Lydia turns up at the hospital, just passing through, probably looking for a rich doctor to wed. She takes one look at me and whisks me away."

"Makes sense to me. I've always loved you like a sister. Always will."

"Same," Tonya said, her voice catching. "Listen, I need to get back to work. The Garden Club story may require a follow up. What about dinner? Can you and Sam make it?"

"Count me in. I'll have to check with Sam. His parents are out with friends for the day, but I'm not sure whether they're returning for dinner. I'm heading to the Chow for lunch. I'll ask him then."

She yelped. "Oh, sugarplum, I've been so swept up in my drama that I forgot about your reunion with the Petrie parents. How did it go?"

"Well, I didn't make it to our brunch date. Something came up. Or dropped dead, to be more accurate."

A beat went by, then I heard a low, ironic laugh. "That's so...so Callie Cassidy."

"What's that supposed to mean?"

"Let's just say things never come easily to you. Not in matters of the heart, that is."

I sighed. I couldn't argue the point.

"Anyway, gotta go," Tonya said. "See you at, say, six-thirty. Let me know if Sam's coming."

When we hung up, I heaved a sigh and rested my head on my arms, considering Tonya's words. I'd struggled against the so-called matters of the heart for so long. Now, when I felt myself ready to surrender to love, it seemed to be struggling against me.

Chapter Twenty

Rain continued pouring as I prepared to head to Snow Plow Chow for lunch. I tried to wheedle a more suitable umbrella from Ethan or Zoe, but they both denied bringing one to work. They were lying, no doubt. I suspected they'd hidden theirs just to see me once again hoist Mrs. Finney's purple behemoth. But since I couldn't frisk them, I reluctantly plucked the umbrella off the coat rack.

"I'll get you back," I cautioned. "Sometime when you least expect it."

Ethan grinned and tugged at his short red beard. "Worth it."

I walked out the front door. As I passed by the shop's bay window, I glimpsed Ethan snapping a picture of me with his phone. I'd likely be trending on Instagram before the day was out.

The umbrella caused another momentary stir when I entered the café. I ignored the giggles rippling among the customers and stowed the umbrella on a hook, confident no one would steal it. When I trudged over to Dan at the host stand, he wore a mirthful expression. "Lemme guess. A loaner from Mrs. Finney?"

I smiled. Dan came across as a wise guy, someone who might be kin to the Murray family, but beneath his rough exterior lay an intelligent, protective, occasionally compassionate fellow to whom I'd grown unexpectedly attached.

"Bingo," I said.

He chuckled as he steered me toward a booth beside a rain-streaked window. "Sam said to give you the best seat in the house and tell you he's already selected your meal. I'll get you a Diet Coke and let him know you're here."

I thanked him, situated myself, and let my eyes wander around the café. Ten or twelve customers sat at scattered tables and booths—a good lunch crowd for this time of year. The place looked better than it ever had. The red vinyl booths gleamed beneath the soft overhead lights. Small vases of blue and white forget-me-nots decorated each polished table, and flames flickered in the fireplace. Even the tile floors appeared freshly scrubbed. Now that Rodger and Jamal were doing most of the cooking, Sam had ample time to devote to the café's upkeep.

Also, he'd likely conducted a deep cleaning of the place before his parents arrived in town.

After Dan deposited my Diet Coke, I gazed at the photos mounted on the café's walls. Top-notch offerings, if I said so myself, since they were original Callahan Cassidy images.

When I'd first moved back to Rock Creek Village, the wall hangings at the Snow Plow Chow were...well, atrocious. Shots of grizzly old cowboys, wagon wheels, and other Old West style illustrations contrasted with the otherwise modern and cozy ambience. Once Sam and I had worked our way back together, I suggested a redo and offered him an array of my local landscape and wildlife shots—with the condition that they'd be available for customers to purchase. The photos sold so well that I was constantly replacing them. Between the displays at Sam's café, Mrs. Finney's Rocky Mountain High, and Mom and Dad's Knotty Pine Resort, Sundance Studio sold at least a dozen canvases a month.

As I basked in self-congratulation, Sam strode through the silver swinging door that led into the kitchen. The sight of him broadened my grin. His blond hair swept back from his forehead and fell just to his ears—shorter than he usually wore it, probably in deference to his mother. He wore a blue plaid flannel shirt, cuffs rolled up to reveal muscular forearms, and a pair of jeans that fit just right. Even from across the room, I saw his blue eyes light up as they landed on me. Warmth rushed through me, followed by a small clench of my gut as I remembered how I'd disappointed him yesterday.

I shook off the momentary negativity and scooted over in the booth. Sam snuggled in next to me, draping an arm around my shoulder and leaning in for a kiss.

"Mmm," I said, leaning my head on his shoulder. "How I've missed you."

"Well, you've been busy. Again."

I studied him for signs of irritation. His lips curved up in a smile. He was teasing me, but beneath the lightheartedness I sensed the tiniest bit of annoyance.

"I'm so sorry for missing brunch, Sam. I—"

He sighed. "Yeah, well, don't worry about it. It's not as if you planned to find Eugene Murray dead in the cemetery."

He reached over and picked up my Diet Coke, taking a

sip through the straw. I marveled that the man could make drinking a soda look sexy.

"True. But I want to make sure you know I'll do whatever I can to make it right. I understand how important it is to you that your parents like me. It's important to me, too."

He looked at me for a long moment. "Now it's my turn to be sorry. I've put way too much emphasis on this reunion. Big picture: it doesn't matter. Yes, it would be nice if my folks fell in love with you again, like I have. But if that doesn't happen, so be it. It won't change anything between us."

I froze, uncertain how to respond. Should I feel relieved Sam wasn't resting our future happiness on his parents' approval? Should I be upset that they harbored negative emotions toward me at all?

"What have they said about me?" I asked.

His cheeks flushed. "Nothing bad. They were just... disappointed that you missed brunch."

"Did you explain the circumstances?"

"Of course." He sighed. "We just need to get the three of you in the same room and everything will be fine. Besides, Elyse and Zoe talked you up last night, so my parents are hearing nothing but good things about you."

I pouted. "Great. I'm reliant on a couple of teenagers' reviews to get back in your parents' good graces."

Before Sam could respond, Jamal headed toward us carrying a tray with two steaming bowls. He appeared so eager that I relinquished my vexed attitude and rubbed my hands together. "What has the talented chef prepared today?"

He grinned. "We're calling it Nacho Usual Chili, though I'm not satisfied with the name." He set a bowl in front of me, handed another to Sam, and placed a bread-laden platter on the table. "It's slow-cooker cream cheese chicken chili. A bit spicy. Comes with a side of bacon cheddar jalapeño cornbread."

I hovered over the bowl, letting the spicy aromas fill my nostrils. "Mmm. Smells delicious."

"You'll be the first to try it—except for Sam and Rodger, of course." Dan stepped forward and cleared his throat. "Oh yeah. Dan sneaked a taste, too."

"Highly recommend," Dan said, lifting two meaty thumbs.

They all stood there watching me, anticipating my feedback. I lifted my spoon, dipped it into the creamy, meaty concoction, and brought it to my lips. It didn't take more than a second to know the new dish was a hit. "This is fantastic," I said as soon as I swallowed. "I predict it will be a tremendous success, especially with the weather turning cooler. Jamal, I've said it before, but it bears repeating. You are a genius. An artist. A master chef."

He humbly lowered his eyes, but I detected his pleasure at the compliment. Dan clapped him on the back. "Taught him everything he knows."

We laughed, and Jamal bowed. "Thank you, Callie. You're too kind."

"I meant every word. Listen, can you pack me a couple of to-go boxes? I told Ethan and Zoe I'd bring them lunch, and this will ensure their never-ending loyalty to me."

"Will do."

He and Dan ambled away, and I turned to Sam. "You got lucky snagging that one."

"Luck had nothing to do with it. I know talent when I see it, and I snap it up. For example, look at the photos on my wall."

I smiled, and he leaned toward me. "Between you and me, though, I doubt I'll be able to hang on to him much longer. He's outgrowing the Chow. I expect he'll be ready for a place of his own any time now."

I made a face. Jamal had been a fixture in Rock Creek Village for several years now, first working for my parents at the Knotty Pine while he attended culinary school, then completing his internship under Sam's tutelage. When he graduated, he chose to stay on and learn the ropes in a place that gave him room to experiment and grow. I'd known he wouldn't play second fiddle forever. When he left, it would create a hole in the village, but we'd all be happy for him.

For a few minutes, Sam and I ate in companionable silence. When I wasn't busy reveling in the sumptuous tastes exploding in my mouth, my thoughts skittered to Sam's parents, Conrad and Lila Petrie. If I put myself in their shoes, I could understand why they might be hesitant to give our relationship their blessing. After all, I'd once broken their son's heart — a long time ago.

Thirty years ago, in fact. In the interim, Sam had married, had a child, and divorced. He'd graduated culinary school, opened a café, and raised his daughter. He'd created a life. Then I showed up in town again, hauling my own emotional baggage. Sam and I rekindled our past relationship. No, that wasn't exactly right. We hadn't picked up where we left off. We'd built something new, better, stronger. Now we were two mature, world-wise people who chose each other, who believed in each other. We'd fallen in a whole different kind of love.

But how could his parents understand that? All they knew was that I'd left him once before, hurt and devastated.

I slid my eyes to Sam and caught him watching me with a heady mixture of tenderness and passion. I dabbed my napkin against my lips and kissed him.

"I love you, Sam," I whispered. "I'll never leave you again. I promise you. I'll convince your parents, too. No matter what I have to do or how long it takes."

He smiled and cupped my cheek. "You're such a sucker for a good meal. Food always makes you mushy."

Chapter Twenty-One

Sam asked if I wanted dessert. I did, always, but I remembered I was in store for an Italian feast tonight and displayed a modicum of restraint. When I passed along Tonya's invitation, Sam said his parents wouldn't be back until late, so he'd love to come.

After one last kiss, I retrieved Ethan and Zoe's to-go bags, stepped outside, and popped open the giant purple monstrosity. Drizzle still leaked from the sky, but the clouds had begun to part above the mountains, revealing streaks of light that boded an end to the deluge. As I sloshed across the cobblestones toward Sundance Studio, I worried about tomorrow's picnic and whether I should devise a backup plan. Even though Sam had tried to reassure me, the weight of the event's importance hung on me like a heavy cloak.

I spent part of my walk back to the gallery pondering the Petries' angst toward me. I understood that the breakup had been hard on Sam, and by extension, his parents. But we'd been teenagers, and I'd gone off to college in Texas. Could the breakup really have come as a total shock to two adults? I wondered if there was something more behind their annoyance.

I supposed what really mattered, though, was how I could go about accepting their feelings, even if they never grew to like me again. After all, it wasn't as if they lived close and I'd see them often. But when Sam and I got married...

The unexpected thought stopped me short. Well, it wasn't totally unexpected, of course. Sam had been hinting at his wish for a permanent commitment for over a year, but he'd been patiently giving me space. I chewed my lip. Did my desire for the Petries' approval mean I was ready to move forward?

I took a slow, deep breath, held it, and exhaled. The psychological undercurrents didn't make any difference right now. It was the practicalities that mattered. And that meant the picnic I was planning needed to go off without a hitch.

I STEPPED beneath the Sundance Studio awning and peeked through the window as I closed the umbrella and shook it off. Inside, Zoe stood near the far wall with a lone customer, smiling and nodding as the woman gestured first to one canvas, then another. From the sales counter, Ethan watched Zoe work, looking as proud as a parent at his kid's first dance recital.

When I opened the door, the little bell above it tinkled. The customer turned, and her face lit up as she recognized me.

I had to admit, being the object of admiration gave me a little rush. In my previous life as an investigative photo-journalist, I was accustomed to being recognized, but the looks I'd gotten were usually dirty ones. After all, I'd often been photographing people at the worst moments of their lives, and very few of them wanted me around. Adoring customers offered an ego boost that could get addictive.

I hung my umbrella and coat on a wooden peg and walked over to Zoe and the customer. The woman beamed as she stuck out her hand. "You're Callahan Cassidy. I'm so excited to meet the famous photographer!"

A blush crept up my neck as she introduced herself. I shifted the bags I was carrying and shook her hand. "I don't know about famous, but I am the photographer. Pleased to meet you."

"Not half as pleased as I am," she gushed. "I learned about you on Creative Entrepreneurs and drove in from Aurora to visit your gallery."

I smiled. She was referencing a podcast hosted by my social influencer friends Bradley and Tim, who had visited the gallery a year ago, talked it up on the air, and put us on the map.

"What a lovely compliment," I said. I turned to Zoe and handed her the lunch bags. "Why don't you and Ethan go eat before this gets cold? I'll keep our visitor company."

Zoe said a polite farewell, and she and Ethan disappeared into the kitchen wearing gluttonous smiles.

Meanwhile, the woman traversed the gallery, oohing and aahing at each canvas. I'd concluded she was a browser, here for a second...or third, or fourth...tier celebrity sighting, so it surprised me when she selected two high-end landscape canvases to purchase.

"These will be perfect in my bedroom," she said, handing over her credit card.

As I rang up her order and wrapped the canvases in butcher paper, I told her the story behind the photos—when I'd shot them, the trek up the mountain, the lighting that day. Customers loved hearing those details, and this woman seemed particularly rapt. I helped her carry the canvases to her car, noting with relief that the drizzle had ceased.

After posing for a selfie with the adoring fan, I turned back to the gallery, only to find Raul standing there with his arms crossed and one hip pressed against the wall. Droplets winked in his dark hair.

He smirked as he pushed away from the wall. "The famous photographer has a fan club."

"What can I say?" I shrugged. "People come from far and wide to meet me. No problem, as long as they make a purchase."

He chuckled and followed me inside, across the polished concrete floor to the sales counter, where he perched on a stool. "I guess it's time I joined the masses. I don't yet own a Callahan Cassidy original."

"You must rectify that at once. I'd recommend the large canvas in the center of the gallery. But don't peek at the price tag. It's my most expensive piece."

When he smiled this time, it didn't reach his eyes. Something was troubling him—and if my instincts were on target, it had nothing to do with the case. He looked surprisingly exposed.

I sat across from him and rested my chin on my hand. "So, why are you visiting a lowly photographer on this overcast morning?"

"I wanted to see if you and your gaggle of girlfriends had solved my case and neglected to inform me."

His cavalier tone spoiled the moment. I felt an injured expression skitter across my face, and Raul grimaced. "Sorry. There's just...a lot going on. Professionally and, um, personally. No reason to take it out on you."

"Things aren't going well with Lynn?" I asked.

He hesitated and looked away. I understood his reticence. Vulnerability didn't come easily to me, either. I waited. After a moment, he met my eyes. "I thought Lynn and I were moving toward something good, but she doesn't seem as sure. She still doesn't want me spending time around her girls."

The pain radiated off him, and I put a hand on his arm. "She's protective of them, Raul. She doesn't want them getting attached until you're both sure the relationship will last. It's one thing to risk your own heart, but with children involved...well, I expect parents will do whatever they can to keep their kids from getting hurt."

"I'd never hurt them," he said, his voice low.

"I'm sure you don't think so now..."

"I know so. I'm not that kind of man, Callie. When I'm in, I'm all in." He shook his head. "I didn't see this coming. I'm thirty-seven years old, and I was content with being single. Didn't think love was in the cards for me. But now that I found it...I'm afraid it might not work out."

My heart swelled. I hadn't expected the stoic detective to offer his feelings up on a platter, and I felt honored he'd chosen to confide in me.

"I know how you feel, except I've got you by ten years. Sam's been ready to propose for months, but I've been resistant."

Raul raised his eyebrows. "Are you saying you're ready now?"

Puffing my cheeks, I blew out a soft breath. "I haven't said it aloud to anyone, but yes. I'm pretty sure I am. But now...his parents...well, let's just say, I'm not high on their list of suitable matches."

Raul sat back and cocked his head. I filled him in on my rocky history with the Petries and the fact that they hadn't forgiven me for dumping their baby boy once upon a time.

He gave me a cockeyed grin. "Listen to us. We've formed our own Lonely Hearts Club. People would be shocked if they overheard us talking to each other this way."

"I hardly believe it myself," I said. "But Raul, Lynn will come around. You just have to be patient and persistent."

"You'll win Sam's parents over, too. You won me over. In fact, that's why I'm here..."

"You mean there's more to this visit than mutual commiseration?"

"Yup. But it may be even harder for me to admit."

My eyebrow shot up. "Do tell."

"Remember at the station when you mentioned the dance we always do? I've been thinking about that, and I've decided you may be right. When the two of us work together, we get things done. What's the point of being at cross purposes?"

"Are you proposing a joint task force?" I asked.

"Let's not get carried away. I'm only suggesting we share information."

I gave him a skeptical look. "You mean I share information while you keep your findings close to the vest?"

His brown eyes glinted. "Would you accept those terms, Ms. Cassidy?"

I folded my arms and glared. "Hardly."

"I figured as much. So, I will commit to sharing what I can, legally and ethically. Does that work?"

"Pinky swear?" I held out my little finger.

Raul smirked. "I'm not a little girl in your third-grade class. I won't pinky swear."

I wiggled my finger and waited. Finally, he wrapped his

little finger around mine. "Don't you dare tell anyone about this."

I laughed. "Be happy I didn't force you to become my blood brother."

"What the heck does that mean?"

"Never mind. Let's focus on our case."

Raul rubbed his eyes. "I can already tell I'm going to regret suggesting this."

I ignored the good-humored jab. "Dad was asking me about Gene's phone. Did you learn anything from it?"

"We don't have his phone," Raul said. "He didn't have it on him at the scene. Lydia said he hadn't left it behind. We didn't find it in Tonya's house or in Gene's car."

I screwed up my face. "That's odd. Where could it be?"

"Our working theory is that the killer took it. No idea why he would, though."

"Or she."

"Or she," he agreed.

I filed the information away for later deliberation and moved to another topic. "Have you uncovered any information on Pinky?"

"Nothing new."

"He's still claiming he killed Gene?"

Raul nodded. "Calls us every few hours insisting we arrest him."

"I just find it hard to believe he's guilty," I said, drumming my fingers on the counter. "In fact, I've been wondering if he confessed in order to protect Vivian. Maybe to keep her out of your crosshairs."

"That would be a logical conclusion, and we've discussed it," Raul said. "But we haven't been able to come up with any connection between them, except that he probably knew her forty years ago when she lived in the village."

"Do you think Vivian could be the killer?" I asked. "I admit I'm a little worried about her staying at Mom and Dad's condo."

"I don't think you have anything to worry about. Between her age and her injury, it seems unlikely that she is responsible for Gene's death. Besides, why would she kill him? We have nothing that remotely ties them together."

That gave me a little peace of mind. I'd expressed my concerns on the subject to my parents, only to be shut down hard and fast. They'd been friends with Vivian in the past, they said, and she was no killer. I knew from experience nothing I could say would sway them. I apparently came by my stubborn gene honestly.

Carl must have deduced that Raul and I were discussing the case, because he scampered out of the office then and wound himself around Raul's ankles. Raul lifted the cat into his lap. "Have you enlisted Mrs. Finney's aid?" Raul asked.

"Saying I enlisted her aid would be a stretch. More like, I caved into her demands for information and her insistence on getting involved. However, she and Mr. Purdy left town this afternoon for another ice dancing competition, so she's not in contact at the moment. I'll call her later and see if her sources have come up with anything."

"And your reporter friends?" he asked. "Anything from them?"

"Now that you mention it, Monika hasn't been in touch. Strange. I'll call her, too. As for Tonya…"

"With her mother as a major player in the case, Tonya can't get too involved," Raul said.

"And just like that, we're finishing each other's sentences," I said. "How'd Lydia's interview go?"

His nostrils flared. "She's…challenging."

I snorted. "That's an understatement. Is she a suspect?"

"She claims she was with a friend at the time of Gene's death."

"A male friend."

He nodded. "She won't give us his name. Says she doesn't want to..." He paused to make air quotes with his fingers. "...*drag him into this mess*. We'll be ratcheting up the pressure on her to tell us, but to be honest, I believe her."

I thought about it and decided I did, too. "So, where does that leave us?"

"We're leaning toward a bad-blood revenge situation between rivaling crime families, but we have no proof. Just speculation."

That would be a best-case scenario since it would mean no one in the village was involved. "Anything else you can tell me?"

He ran a hand across his stubbled chin. "Frank's been behind closed doors with your father trying to figure out where Vivian Corwin has been all these years, but there's nothing new on that front. She vanished like smoke and reappeared the same way."

"Don't tell me you're one of those conspiracy theorists."

"I might be by the time this is over. The whole thing defies logic. We can't make any headway. It's frustrating."

"We'll get there," I said. Carl meowed his agreement. "We always do."

He sighed. "Unfortunately, it often takes a series of catastrophic events to push us across the finish line."

Chapter Twenty-Two

Raul departed as a group of customers entered. These people didn't appear as awed by my presence as my previous buyer, so when Ethan and Zoe returned from their lunch break, I relinquished customer service duties and spent an hour in the office planning the Petrie picnic. Once I'd brooded over the details and finalized a sandwich order with Delilah's Deli in the lower village, I turned my attention back to Gene's murder. Despite Raul's prophecy of catastrophic doom, I was hopeful of a quick solution—probably because Raul's trust made me feel like a valuable part of the team. Now to live up to that trust.

I texted Tonya to tell her Sam would join us for dinner. Then I pressed Mrs. Finney's number. When the call went straight to voicemail, I tapped out a text asking her to call me as soon as her sources got back to her. Pinning down Pinky's role in this mess might help point us in the right direction.

Last, I called Monika. After four rings, just as I was about to give up, she answered. Or at least, I thought it was the young reporter on the other end of the line. All I could make out was incoherent mumbling.

"Monika?" I said. "Are you there?"

She moaned. "Wish I wasn't."

"What's going on?"

"Migraine. Or else a bomb exploded inside my head."

I grimaced. "I'm sorry. Can I bring you anything?"

"Morphine."

"Mmm, no can do," I said. "How about food instead?"

"I'd only throw it up. I took my meds. Need to sleep."

"All right. Call me if I can..."

I heard a thud. When I looked at the screen, I saw that she'd disconnected.

Sympathy and frustration warred within me as I dropped my phone on the desk. I tried to lean toward sympathy, but for goodness sake. Of all times to get a migraine. And as for Mrs. Finney, how many ice dancing competitions did one elderly former CIA agent need to win?

Carl leapt onto the desk and harrumphed. No war of emotions for the cat. The humans in his life perpetually tested his patience.

Meanwhile, Woody made clear a different need. He scampered to the door and whined, then looked at me with urgency. "Bathroom break, Woodster?" When I got up and grabbed his leash, he wagged in gratitude. "I will always empathize with the pain of a full bladder. Let's go."

AFTER OUR OUTING, which consisted of a quick stop on the slope of the ravine followed by five minutes of off-leash gallivanting, I spent the rest of the afternoon tending to studio business. The flow of customers picked up throughout the afternoon, keeping the three of us busy. At four o'clock, students in my digital class filtered into the computer lab. I taught color correction and cropping on Photoshop for an hour, and by then it was five o'clock. When Zoe turned the sign on the door to Closed, Ethan proclaimed the day a financial success. We headed to our cars, tired but satisfied.

As the creatures and I neared the Knotty Pine Resort on our drive home, I glanced at the dashboard clock and impulsively steered the car into the parking lot. I had just enough time for a quick visit before dinner at Tonya's.

Once I put the car in park and switched off the ignition, I swiveled toward the backseat and looked at Woody and Carl. "I'll only be a few minutes. Want to wait in the car?"

From their groans and hisses, I surmised they'd prefer to accompany me inside. I'd expected as much. Woody knew my mother kept an ample supply of treats and was generous with their distribution. As for Carl, he wasn't about to be left out if we humans discussed the investigation.

Creatures in tow, I entered the lobby, waved hello to Mr. Farmington, and trudged up the stairs to my parents' condo, where delicious aromas greeted us. Woody sprinted into the kitchen to explore, and Carl and I followed.

Vivian sat on a high-backed stool at the quartz island, a glass of sparkling water in front of her. Mom turned from the stove and smiled. She ruffled the dog's fur, stroked Carl, and kissed my cheek. "What a lovely surprise. Will you stay for dinner?"

"Can't," I said. "Tonya and David invited Sam and me over for a homemade Italian meal. I only have a few minutes before I have to go home and get ready. I just stopped by to see how everyone is doing." When I raised my eyebrows at Mom in an unspoken question, she responded with a small shake of her head, indicating Vivian still hadn't regained her memory.

"Do you have time for a glass of wine, darling?" she asked.

"I imagine I'll be indulging in a glass or two at Tonya's, so I'd better pass. I'll settle for what Vivian's having." I took the stool next to Vivian's, nestling Carl into my lap. His green eyes surveyed the woman. Woody stayed glued to my mother's calf as she headed to the treat drawer and selected something that looked like beef jerky. He caught her toss midair and loped into the living room to eat his snack in peace.

While Mom poured my sparkling water, I smiled at Vivian. "How are you, Mrs. Corwin?"

"Please, dear, call me Vivian. Though I don't suppose it matters much. No name feels familiar."

She brushed a strand of hair from her face. Though her voice sounded subdued—lost—her gray eyes appeared alert and focused. "But to answer your question, I'm fine. Tired is all. Hospitals are not the most restful places."

Dad made his way into the kitchen and kissed the top of my head before grabbing a beer from the refrigerator. Mom bustled about, chopping vegetables and making frivolous conversation. I sipped my water and joined in the chat. Vivian seemed relaxed as she laughed at Mom's humorous anecdotes about the village, the weather, and local gossip. Fifteen minutes passed, and I stood to leave.

Mom wiped her hands on a dishtowel. "Picnic tomorrow, right?"

"Yup. Pretty exciting." I gave her what I hoped was a convincing smile. "I'm not nervous at all."

She patted my cheek. "Lila Petrie can be a pill. Don't take her personally, darling."

I nodded. As usual, my mother had said exactly the right thing.

I whistled for Woody and tucked Carl into the crook of my arm. Dad walked us to the door. From the slump of his shoulders and the bags beneath his eyes, I could see he was exhausted.

"How are you holding up?" I asked.

"Me? I'm all right. I'm not the one suffering an injury and amnesia."

"This has been an ordeal for you, too, though. You need to take care of yourself. I worry about you."

He gave me a wan smile and hugged me. "You're the best daughter a man could ask for. I appreciate your concern. But I'm okay."

"Still, promise you'll get some sleep."

He gave me a mock salute. "Yes, boss. Between you and your mother, I'll be forced into submission."

I headed to the door. "I need to get going. If something changes, if Vivian remembers anything, call me right away."

I didn't make him pinky swear, but he promised he'd keep in touch. I glanced at my watch and hurried downstairs. The visit had lasted longer than I'd intended, and I'd need to hurry if I wanted to make myself presentable for dinner.

As I hustled toward my car, my eyes swept across the vehicles in the parking lot. When I spotted a black Ford F-150 in the corner, I did a double take. It wasn't the truck that caught my attention so much as the person sitting inside. He turned away and ducked his head, but not before I glimpsed his face. Michael Pinkerton.

Chapter Twenty-Three

Why on earth was Pinky lurking in the parking lot of the Knotty Pine Resort? I considered marching over, knocking on the window, and confronting him, but before I could, he started up his truck and pulled onto Evergreen Way. As soon as I settled the creatures in the car and buckled myself in, I called Dad to tell him about the strange encounter. He sounded surprised and said he'd keep an eye out.

I forced myself to stay under the speed limit as I drove home. Rushing inside the townhouse, I fed Woody and Carl, took a quick shower, and rummaged through my closet for a suitable outfit. My fashion sense would never rival Tonya's, but at the very least I wanted to look like I belonged in the room. Settling on black slacks and a shimmery gold top that reminded me of aspen leaves, I dressed, dried and styled my hair, swiped on a modicum of makeup, and spritzed perfume on my wrists and neck. As I finished, I heard a light knock downstairs, then the sound of the front door opening.

When I popped out of the bedroom, I saw Sam waiting for me at the bottom of the stairs. He wore black Dockers and a long-sleeved maroon button-up shirt with the top button open. Casual, but devastatingly handsome. His expression told me the admiration was mutual.

"Hey, beautiful." As I descended the last step, he swept me into his arms and planted a tantalizing kiss on my lips.

"Now I'm going to need to fix my lipstick," I said. "Most of it's on you."

"Worth it," he said.

Woody nudged Sam's hand with his wet nose. Carl ignored us and paced in front of the door. I grabbed my coat, and the four of us scooted out the door and got in Sam's car.

"So, what interrogative responsibilities am I assigned tonight?" Sam asked.

"None. We're just going to enjoy a nice Italian meal. If we gain any insights, that's gravy."

"I'm a restaurant owner and a chef, and I can assure you Italians don't use gravy. At least, not the kind of gravy we Americans are used to."

"Quite the comedian," I said. "Anyway, Raul filled me in on this morning's interview with Lydia. He said she mentioned an alibi witness but wouldn't give up a name."

Sam raised an eyebrow. "Raul volunteered this information? To you?"

"Surprised me, too. He came by the studio and suggested we work together. As much as possible, legally and ethically." I cast a sidelong glance at my boyfriend. At one point, he'd been threatened by my unconventional working relationship—and later friendship—with the handsome detective, but his expression told me we'd moved past that bump in the road. "Raul mentioned that I was sometimes able to elicit information people wouldn't offer the police."

Sam nodded. "That's true. Did he also mention that you've solved a few cases the professionals couldn't?"

I reached over and squeezed his knee. "I appreciate your support. But sometimes I just get lucky."

He chuckled. "Who are you and what have you done with my girlfriend?"

I swatted his arm. "What do you mean by that?"

"Listen, Callie, you're talented and savvy. Logical and smart. You won numerous awards as a journalist, partly because of how that brain of yours works. All that and gorgeous, too. Let's not talk about getting lucky. Not until we're on our way home from Tonya's, that is."

I laughed, then reached over and kissed his neck as he pulled the car alongside the curb in front of Tonya and David's house. We got out of the car and strolled hand in hand up the sidewalk. Tonya opened the door before we knocked, and Woody sat politely, waiting to be invited inside. Tonya gave him a pat on the head, took Carl from my arms, and stepped aside so our little family could enter. She hugged Sam and kissed my cheek. Sam pointed at the lipstick on my face. "Now we're both marked."

Tonya made a face. "I won't ask for the salacious details. Hang up your coats and join me in the living room for a drink. David is in the kitchen putting the finishing touches on dinner." She shot me a look. "I'm not telling you what we're having. But trust me, you'll love it."

I rolled my eyes. "It's something healthy, isn't it?"

"Don't worry about it, sugarplum. Just eat and enjoy."

She sashayed off, the cat purring in her arms and the dog trotting at her heels. I marveled at how well my creatures behaved in Tonya's presence.

Then again, everyone did. Except perhaps her mother.

Sam and I sat side by side on a plush couch facing a stone fireplace. Tonya plopped Carl into my lap and disappeared into the kitchen. We heard murmuring and a flurry of laughter before she reappeared, drinks in hand and her husband at her side.

"*Cara mia*," David said, bending to brush his lips against my cheek. He squeezed Sam's shoulder. "*Il mio amico*. We're delighted to welcome you to our home."

"We've been here before, David," I said. "Many times."

"And every time you visit is like a brand new gift. Now, if you will excuse me, I must finish the preparations. Dinner will be served in *dieci minuti*."

"Ten minutes," Tonya translated as she handed each of us a glass of red wine. "So, drink up."

"Need any help?" Sam asked David.

"I would never turn down assistance from a renowned chef."

Sam winked at me and followed David into the kitchen. As Tonya sank into an armchair next to the couch, I inspected her over the rim of my wineglass. The woman was exquisitely attired in a black peplum blouse and leather slacks. Silver earrings dangled from her lobes, and the enormous diamond in her wedding ring winked in the light. With her thick brown hair hanging in waves around her shoulders, she might have been a supermodel—except for the hint of red in her eyes and the worry lines etched across her forehead.

"You look like you've been through the wringer," I said.

She lifted a slender shoulder. "Who'd have thought I'd be having mommy issues at this age? But here we are."

"Lydia refused to give up the new lover boy's name, huh? I bet that went over well with the detectives."

"You should have seen the expression on Raul's face. If

he'd had a stun gun in his hand, she'd still be writhing on the station floor."

"Do you believe her?" I asked. "That she was…occupied with another man, I mean?"

"Well, it beats the alternative—that she tiptoed into the cemetery to murder the man she's been sleeping with for the past year." She paused, watching the flames in the fireplace. "As much of a jerk as Lydia can be, I can't see her as a killer. When I try to visualize her swinging that pickaxe—"

"Mattock." Tonya's face squinched in confusion. "Never mind," I said, uncertain why Cedric's lesson on cemetery tools had taken such a hold over me. "Go on."

"She wouldn't want to get her hands dirty that way." She sipped her wine. "Plus, I can't imagine her stepping foot in a cemetery. Too morbid, she says. She didn't even attend her own mother's funeral."

"Yikes. Still, she and Gene were having problems, right? Could she have killed him in a fit of temper?"

She considered the question, then shook her head. "I've rarely seen Lydia swept away by any extreme emotion. She's much more calculating. If she were going to kill someone, there'd have to be something in it for her. I don't see what she gains from Gene's death."

"It gets him out of the picture," I said. "Now she's free to move on to the next Romeo."

"She'd already made it clear Gene's days were numbered. They were done. Why go to the trouble of killing him?"

"Did he have some financial grip on her?" I asked.

"Lydia's much too savvy for that. Besides, you know about Gene's family, right?"

I tilted my head. "Just what you and Monika told me. The Murrays were a crime family, though not major players."

Tonya nodded. "But they retain plenty of assets, from what I'm told. In other words, Gene didn't need Lydia's money."

I pondered. "The fact that Gene is a member of the Murray family suggests there might be plenty of suspects. Even lower-level crime families make enemies."

"That makes sense, though I don't know enough about the inner workings of Vegas mobs to speak intelligently on the subject." She twisted a strand of hair around her finger. "With Lydia so tight-lipped regarding her whereabouts, I imagine she'll remain a suspect until evidence comes to light that suggests otherwise."

"Well, we'll just have to uncover it then," I said.

Tonya wrinkled her nose. "I'm afraid I can't be part of the *we*. I'm too close to the situation. The whole thing is putting a strain on the *Gazette*, too. Between Monika's migraine and my inability to write about the murder, journalism seems to be on hiatus. Poor Phil can't keep up."

I leaned across the space between us and placed a hand on her arm. "This is hitting you from all directions. I'm so sorry. But as far as the investigation part, you don't need to worry. Raul and Lynn have it well in hand."

"And you?" she asked.

I shrugged. "Only if you want me involved."

"I'm afraid you spend as much time clearing my mother of crimes as you do shooting photos."

"That's not true. I've only been involved in Lydia's nefarious deeds one other time." I swirled the last half inch of wine in my glass. "She makes our lives interesting."

David and Sam walked into the adjacent dining room, with David toting a large crystal bowl and Sam carrying a tray of garlic bread. As Tonya and I headed to the table, my stomach emitted an obnoxious growl.

"Enough talk of *tua madre*," David said. "We shall

speak only of joyful topics as we indulge in this evening's repast. That is my decree."

Tonya kissed him on the cheek. "Whatever you say, *mi amor*. When you're feeding me, you're the boss."

Chapter Twenty-Four

The meal began with an antipasto salad consisting of artichoke hearts, pepperoncini, olives, white beans, and cheese. David marinated the ingredients in a mysterious but miraculous dressing that Sam admired. "If you ever decide to sell the bookstore," he said, "I can promise you a spot in the Snow Plow Chow kitchen."

"Ah, but I only cook for people I love," David said, smiling. "I'm afraid I wouldn't provide you with much of a profit margin."

"You cook for Lydia," Tonya said. "Are you saying you love my mother? She's been a thorn in our sides since our wedding. Before that, even."

"She gave birth to the most amazing woman in the world," David said. "Of course I have love in my heart for her. As do you, though you're loath to admit it." He clapped. "But as I commanded, pleasant topics only at this table. Who's ready for the main course?"

Sam and Tonya raised their hands, and after a brief hesitation, I followed suit. Tonya's earlier hint about the meal gave me a twinge of apprehension. People kept trying to convince me that eating healthy was all the rage, but I wasn't entirely on board. True, I'd eaten some delicious healthy foods, particularly during a recent trip to Moonglow Ranch, but I still preferred breaded and fried to baked and gluten-free.

Sam caught my eye. "Keep an open mind, Callie."

Now my apprehension blossomed into full-blown dread. Was David serving raw squid? Or worse, Brussels sprouts? At the sight of me squirming, Tonya snickered. "You're overreacting, sugarplum. You're a grown woman. Suck it up and try the food."

David appeared holding a stone platter. The main dish —whatever it might be—was surrounded by noodles and smothered in melted cheese—mozzarella, if my guess was right. So far, so good. But a glimpse of purple beneath the cheese had me wrinkling my nose.

"Voilà!" David set the platter on the table with a flourish. "My unbreaded eggplant parmesan, secret family recipe, revered worldwide."

Steam rose from the dish. I attempted to plaster an expression of enthusiasm on my face but settled for neutrality. "Yummy," I said unconvincingly.

Sam scooped a serving onto my plate. "Surely a fearless photojournalist like you won't have any trouble eating eggplant."

I took the plate from him and sniffed. "It's so...vegetarian. I thought Italians were all about meatballs."

I waited while the others served themselves. Then all eyes were on me. Might as well get it over with. I used my knife to carve out a bite-sized piece, speared it with my fork, and transferred it to my mouth. I chewed. Tender, spicy, cheesy. I closed my eyes and let the flavors mingle on my tongue. Not bad. Good, in fact. Quite good.

"This is delicious, David," I said. "Who knew something that grows on a tree could taste this good?"

Sam looked amused. "Callie, eggplant doesn't...never mind. Just enjoy it."

Forks and knives clinked against the plates as we dug in. "Be good and finish you meals," David said. "There's pumpkin gingersnap tiramisu for dessert."

"For heaven's sake," I said. "I should have worn stretchy pants."

Throughout the meal, we ate and drank and talked of village gossip. Tonya complained that her reporter shortage meant she'd be covering the local cat festival. "Phil is allergic, so I'm on the docket." Her eyes traveled to Carl, perched on the back of the couch like a king on his throne. "Speaking of the festival, why isn't your little prince entered?"

I guffawed, nearly choking on a noodle. "Seriously? Don't you remember the Fall Festival a couple of years ago? Carl instigated a riot among the beastly contestants. They almost toppled the stage. He'll never be permitted to take part in another pageant."

We all looked at the orange tabby, who indulged in a languorous stretch. Suddenly, his eyes darted to the entry hall. Woody scrambled to his feet, his attention also trained that direction. The front door swung open, and Lydia entered.

If I thought Tonya looked like she'd been through the wringer, her mother appeared to have gone through a woodchipper. Her hair frizzed out of a messy bun, and her cheeks sagged like melted wax. When she got to the living room, her eyes swept around the dining table, taking us in. Her gaze settled on Tonya before she turned away, took off her coat, and tossed it across the back of the couch.

"Lydia," Tonya said, "you forgot to close the—"

Before she could finish the sentence, another figure appeared in the doorway. It was a tall, bony man wearing a heavy peacoat. He shut the door with a soft thud and strolled into the room.

His hair was thick and shiny black—too thick and black for his age, which I estimated at early sixties. Toupee, perhaps. His skin was so pale he looked like a character from an old-time silent movie.

David rose when the man entered, but quickly resumed his seat. Intuition told me he recognized the man, and he didn't appear thrilled at his presence.

I caught Tonya's eye and raised an eyebrow. She responded with an almost imperceptible shake of her head. Like me, she didn't recognize the man.

"Lydia, are you going to introduce us to your...?" Tonya let her voice trail off. Lydia didn't acknowledge the question, except to emit a deep sigh and sink onto the couch.

The man stepped forward. "I'm afraid your mother has had a long and difficult day. Allow me to do the honors. My name is Tommy Murray. Gene is...was, that is...my cousin."

The four of us got to our feet as Tommy approached. He wore a smug expression as he held out a hand to David, who mumbled his name and shook halfheartedly.

Tommy rounded the table and shook hands with Sam, then with me. When he reached Tonya, he lifted her hand and touched his lips to it. David stiffened but said nothing. Tommy took a step back and appraised my best friend with an expression that fell just short of a leer. "The apple doesn't fall far from the tree. Your beauty reflects your mother's."

Woody positioned himself at my side and looked at me, trying to gauge how to respond to this stranger. Friend or foe? Carl bore no such ambivalence. His ears and his tail stood straight up, and his whiskers twitched.

Tonya glanced at Lydia, who'd settled deeper into the couch, as if trying to camouflage herself. Then my friend gave Tommy an insincere smile. "Forgive my confusion, Mr. Murray. My mother didn't mention she'd be bringing you by. In fact, she neglected to mention that you were in the village."

Lydia looked wan. For a moment, I even feared she might faint. The only time I'd seen her looking this green around the gills was the night at Moonglow Ranch when she'd been poisoned.

Tommy took a step back and clasped his hands. "It was a last-minute engagement. I arrived in town this afternoon and asked your mother to join me for dinner. I'm afraid she may have overindulged in the wine. Drowning her sorrows, as I'm sure you can understand. I was tempted to bury my grief in the bottle as well, but since I was driving, I refrained. At any rate, when I returned her to your lovely home, I insisted my almost-cousin-in-law introduce me to you so I could extend my family's thanks for the affection and hospitality you all showed Eugene during the last months of his life. The G-man, as we called him. My beloved cousin."

He bowed his head and remained quiet so long that I wondered if he was observing a moment of silence for poor dead Gene.

The low rumble in Woody's throat indicated that he'd decided the man was a foe. I concurred with his judgment. Jostled from his trance, Tommy slid his eyes to the golden retriever. "And who's this handsome boy?" Woody's rumble mushroomed into a growl. I placed a restraining hand on his collar. Tommy chuckled. "Not so friendly, huh? I get it. I've been known to growl from time to time myself."

He put his hands in his coat pockets and smiled at each of us—a predatory smile, one you might see on a wolf before it pounced on a wounded elk. A shiver skittered up my spine.

"I'd best be going," Tommy said. "Gene's funeral isn't going to arrange itself." He tilted his head at our astonishment. "Sorry. Gallows humor, as they say. That's how the Murray family operates. We can't alter what happened. We can only control how we deal with it. And rest assured, we will deal with my cousin's murder."

He tilted his head and spun on his heel, stopping to brush a kiss on Lydia's cheek. His voice was low, so I couldn't be sure, but I thought he might've said, "Remember what we discussed." Lydia's expression hardened.

As soon as he was out the door, the four of us at the table sank into our chairs as if we'd choreographed the move. Lydia unfolded herself from the couch and headed toward the guest room.

"Just a minute, Lydia," Tonya called out. "What's going on? Why did you go to dinner with your dead boyfriend's cousin? You can't possibly think that's a smart thing to do, especially since his family might view you as a suspect in Gene's death."

Tonya's mother stopped in her tracks but didn't turn around. Her fingers clenched and unclenched at her sides. When she spoke, her voice was low and tense. "I'll thank you not to use that tone with me, Tonya. Like it or not, I'm still your mother. As for my dinner with Tommy Murray, that's none of your concern." She paused, then exhaled. "I'm very tired, and I'm going to bed. Good night."

She plodded into the guest room, slamming the door

behind her. Tonya's mouth hung open in disbelief. She stood up and squared her shoulders. "She'll thank me not to speak to her that way? Wait until she gets a load of this..."

Tonya marched toward the guest room like a bull charging into the ring. Only David was brave enough to intercept her. He stepped into her path and put his hands on her shoulders. "*Mi amor*, I urge you to...what is it Americans say?...look before you leap. Perhaps the situation warrants a cooling-off period."

If I'd said that to Tonya, I'd have gotten an earful—*Don't tell me what to do. I'm a grown woman capable of choosing my own actions.* I braced myself for a raucous lecture on mansplaining. Imagine my shock when my best friend stopped, took a breath, and nodded. "You're right. Emotions are too high. A confrontation would accomplish nothing." She gazed up at her husband, and he kissed her.

Then Tonya turned to Sam and me with a tired smile. "Never a dull moment."

David draped an arm across her shoulders. "How about that tiramisu I promised? I think we could all use something sweet right now."

Chapter Twenty-Five

I woke up way too early the next morning with an unexplained fog of anxiety hanging over me. My mind skittered, trying to pinpoint the root of my dread. Was it Tonya's plight with her mother? Tommy Murray's appearance at our dinner party last night? Poor Vivian and her continuing memory loss? Dad's struggle with guilt?

With a sigh, I pulled myself into a sitting position, picked up my phone and looked at the screen. Calendar reminder: Picnic.

And there it was—the underlying cause of my jitters. Today was my get-together with Sam's parents. My last chance to win them over.

Of course, my therapist would suggest I might be over-dramatizing. It surely wasn't my last chance. There'd be plenty of other opportunities to screw things up.

What would the good doctor advise? I mentally ran through her predictable list of questions.

What's the worst that could happen? she'd ask.

Sam's parents will never forgive me. They'll encourage him to dump me, like I did to him back in college.

Would he do that?

I bit my lip, pondering. Then I smiled. No. He's in this for the long haul. Like me.

Then what do you have to fear?

Nothing, I guess.

Comforting though the thought was, it felt like a simplification. Relationships were difficult enough even with the support of friends and family. The extra challenge of one set of parents balking at the union only increased the strain.

But I'd done hard things before. I could deal with it.

I took a breath to calm my nerves. Now that I'd traversed the worst-case-scenario path, I forced myself to focus on the possibility of a more positive outcome.

They'll forgive me. They'll remember how much they used to like me. Maybe they'll even grow to love me...

Well, let's not skyrocket out of the realm of reality, I told myself. Settle for their acceptance.

I twisted out of bed and walked to the French doors that opened onto a small second-story balcony. Brisk fall air drifted inside. To the east, the sun lingered just below the horizon. Fingers of light reached above the mountains, as if poking the sky to see if it was ready to awaken. I typically wasn't up early enough to greet the dawn, so I took a moment to appreciate the sight.

The day's overture boded well for the picnic. The rain had moved off, leaving the world clean and crisp. Jacket weather, yes, but perfect for being outdoors. I closed my eyes and visualized the scene: aspens rustling, chipmunks scurrying across the path, yummy sandwiches, friendly conversation...I crossed my fingers that the day would play out the way I imagined.

But I had a little time to myself before the social event of the year, and true to form, I used it to contemplate murder. Not the act, but the solution.

I closed the doors and returned to the bed, patting first Woody, then Carl. "I'm going downstairs for coffee on the patio. There'll be treats for anyone who joins me."

Woody bounded off the bed and down the stairs. Carl didn't budge. He'd join us soon enough—he just required control of his own timeline.

Ten minutes later, I was snuggled up on an Adirondack chairs with a blanket tucked across my lap, sipping a cup of coffee as I read through the online edition of the *Rock Creek Gazette*. There wasn't much to it this morning. Tonya's promised blockbuster on the Garden Club, which I didn't even bother skimming through. A few human-interest pieces that proved a bit more intriguing.

The lead story, of course, under Phil and Monika's dual byline, detailed the events surrounding Gene's murder. Detailed might be a stretch, though. The story contained no information villagers hadn't already discerned through word of mouth. It was a simple recap of the basics—the who, what, where, and when, without an explanation of the why.

But the bare-bones article still triggered the synapses of my brain. I rehashed last night's events—Lydia's appearance, followed by Tommy Murray's. I remembered the expression on David's face when he saw Tommy. I felt certain David had recognized the man and that he was less than thrilled to find him in his home.

If I was right, what could have caused the negative reaction? For that matter, how did David know Gene's cousin? Tommy said he'd only arrived in the village yesterday afternoon. A niggle of misgiving tried to take root in my mind, but I thrust it aside. Last time I'd suspected David of something, it hadn't gone well. I'd risked my friendship with Tonya over it, and I wasn't about to tread that path again.

Besides, David was a good man—a loving husband, a loyal friend, a decent human. I truly believed that. If he was hiding something, it must be for good reason. And if Tonya was aware of his secret, she'd tell me in her own time. Or she wouldn't because it would be none of my business.

Still, I filed the seed of doubt in the back of my mind and shifted my focus to Lydia. Her subdued demeanor had been uncharacteristic. Usually, Tonya's mother chattered nonstop. She kept secrets, yes, but never quietly. She'd dodge and deflect when confronted, but I'd never seen her as defeated as she'd appeared last night. Frightened, even. Something was going on with her—and I didn't attribute it to grief.

Finally, I replayed Tommy Murray's appearance. His smug expression. His barely concealed attempts at intimidation. He'd made a show of grieving his cousin, but I questioned his sincerity. No, there was more to Tommy's arrival in Rock Creek Village than simply serving as family representative following the tragedy of Gene's death.

I sighed. What I wanted...needed...was more information about the Murray family's criminal enterprise. Monika's earlier research had only scratched the surface, at least as it related to present times. I wondered if she'd uncovered anything more, especially regarding Cousin Tommy.

I picked up my phone and pressed her number. When the call connected, a groggy voice came across the line. "What time is it?"

"Seven-thirty. Too early?"

She groaned, and I suddenly remembered her migraine. Some great friend I was. "Just calling to check on you."

"Sure you are. I'm lucid enough to know that if you're up this early, you're preoccupied with an investigation."

Though I didn't want to admit it, even to myself, she wasn't wrong. Still, despite my forgetfulness, I did care about the young reporter's well-being. "Whatever. Tell me how you're feeling."

She paused, as if conducting a self-assessment. "Better. Remnants of a headache—pressure behind my eyes and mild throbbing—but I'm on the upswing. What do you need? If it involves staring at screens, I'm afraid I won't be able to help much today."

"Monika, I'm not a monster. I'd never ask you to do something that might cause you pain. Besides, you're the one who's always pestering me to let you get involved. You're the one amassing awards from your stories. But if you're not feeling well enough..."

She chuckled. "So, it is you. I was beginning to wonder if the person on the other end of the line was an imposter. Anyway, now you've penetrated the residual migraine fog and piqued my curiosity. Fill me in. I've been off the grid entirely too long."

I smiled and outlined last night's events. "The Murrays may have lost some of their power, but they're still a crime family. I can't help but think some illicit venture cost Gene his life. If I could get more background on them..."

A few seconds ticked by. I heard rustling and pictured Monika pushing herself up in bed. "I'm happy to help," she said at last, "provided, as always, I get the story in the end. But as I mentioned, screens intensify the pain, so let me take my meds and get some food in me. Hopefully, by this afternoon I'll be able to dig in and conduct more research."

A pang of guilt stabbed at me. "Listen, Monika, don't push yourself. Seriously. There's no hurry. In fact, I won't even be available for a good chunk of the day." I filled her in on my date with Sam and his parents.

"Sounds like you're putting a lot of importance on one picnic," she said. "If you want my advice, just be yourself. We all love you just as you are. If Sam's parents don't, it says more about them than you."

I wondered if that was something she'd read on a motivational calendar, or perhaps a Rocky Mountain High coffee cup. But I knew she was trying to help, so I didn't offer up a snarky response. "I appreciate the vote of confidence. Now, I'm going to hang up so you can take care of yourself. Want me to drop you by something to eat?"

"Thanks, but I have a freezer full of microwavable meals. I'll talk to you soon."

When we disconnected, I sipped my now cold coffee and contemplated my next move. Monika couldn't help—at least not at the moment. Time to turn to my other top resource. I dialed Mrs. Finney and listened as the call again went to voicemail. "You've reached Mrs. Finney, ice dancer extraordinaire. I'm likely on a rink right now, or hoisting my newest trophy…"

"Our newest trophy," said Mr. Purdy in the background.

"Of course, dear. *Our* newest trophy. Leave a message, and I'll get back to you. Toodle-oo."

Despite my frustration at our team's lack of progress, I smiled. Mrs. Finney's extracurricular activity, even in the face of a murder in the village, was a pleasant reminder that life goes on and not everything needs to revolve around crime and investigation—especially for those of us who weren't even cops.

It was a lesson that had always proven difficult for me to learn.

Chapter Twenty-Six

At eight, I went inside, ate my requisite Pop-Tart —brown sugar and cinnamon today—and headed upstairs for personal grooming. Much as I tried to convince myself Monika was right that I didn't need to impress Sam's parents, I couldn't help myself. I showered and even shaved my legs—as if they wouldn't be fully covered—then spent ten minutes in my closet trying to assemble an outfit that sent the right message. Sam's girlfriend should be outdoorsy but feminine. Pretty, but in a low-key way. One shirt seemed too frilly. The next one made me look like a lumberjack. After much waffling, I settled on a pair of jeans that hugged my figure, but not in a wannabe-sexy way, and a long-sleeved, gray and white striped button-up shirt, which I'd wear over a soft gray t-shirt. Hiking shoes, of course, even though the picnic spot lay only a quarter mile from the parking lot.

I dried my hair and spent way too long debating how to wear it. I settled on a ponytail and dabbed on just enough makeup to make myself appear fresh-faced.

Perfume? Nah. No need to compete with the aromas of the great outdoors—or to attract insects.

Since Woody and Carl were joining us, I wrangled them into semi-submission and gave them a thorough brushing. Then I headed downstairs. Woody bounded ahead of me, while Carl sat at the top of the stairs yelling ack, ack, ack because I hadn't deigned to carry his highness down myself. "I have a couple of errands to run before Sam and his parents arrive," I told them. "See if you can manage to stay clean."

A FEW MINUTES LATER, I arrived at my first stop—the police station. Marilyn, the department's administrative assistant, greeted me. "Morning, Callie. Why am I not surprised to see you?"

"Hey, Marilyn. Did Raul and Lynn catch the killer?"

"Not yet. Hope it happens before my last day."

I'd forgotten Marilyn was scheduled to retire at the end of the year. How would the station survive without her? She'd been a fixture since my father's early days as Chief of Police. No one knew more about the inner workings of the department than Marilyn.

"They may have to shut the place down when you leave," I said. "I hope they're offering you a hefty severance to keep their secrets."

She chuckled. "I definitely know where the bodies are buried. So to speak. Frank tells me he'll be hiring my replacement soon so I can train the person. After that, life will go on. One thing age has taught me is that no one in any job is irreplaceable."

I considered her words. I'd been an award-winning photojournalist at the *Washington Sentinel*, once considered a fixture there myself. My ego had tried to convince me how valuable I was to the newspaper. But when I'd chucked it all a few years back, the paper hadn't folded. They hadn't stopped covering crimes or wars or corruption. No, it had been business as usual.

"Life does indeed go on," I said. "Honestly, I find that freeing."

"Then you're wise beyond your years, my dear. For many of us, work is a source of pride, and there's nothing wrong with that. I recognize how much I've meant to this place, to this community. Nothing can erase that. But I'll find other joys, other ways to be productive. And someone else will get the chance to contribute here."

I smiled. "I wish you the happiest of retirements, Marilyn. You deserve it."

"You'll be at my party, right? The Saturday before Christmas."

"Wouldn't miss it."

She straightened in her chair. "In the meantime, there's still work to be done. You're here to see Detective Sanchez, I assume?"

"How'd you guess?"

"Years of practice. Besides, there's been a murder in the village, and you're predictable. He's in his office. You remember the way."

"You don't need to call ahead?" I asked.

She shook her head. "He's predictable, too. Besides, what are they going to do, fire me?"

I grinned as I walked down the hall toward Raul's office. Marilyn was right—I remembered the way, all too well.

When I made it to Raul's open door, I paused at the sound of low voices inside—Raul's first, then Lynn's. It sounded like a tense—and personal—conversation.

Nosy though I was, I wouldn't allow myself to eavesdrop. I cleared my throat loudly enough to be heard and rapped my knuckles against the open door. "Morning, detectives," I said with faux cheer.

Raul sat behind his desk, and Lynn stood with her hands on her hips near the opposite wall of the closet-sized office. They looked surprised and embarrassed, as if I'd caught them in an intimate moment.

A glance passed between them. Lynn dropped her hands to her sides and attempted a weak smile. "Hey, Callie. What are you doing here so early?"

I shuffled from one foot to another, trying to keep my tone light. "I've come across some information, and I'm here to share, as promised."

Lynn glared at Raul. I surmised he hadn't consulted her about our informal arrangement. He stared back defiantly before turning to me. "Come on in, Callie."

"Well, then," Lynn said, her voice tight. "I'll leave the two of you to your investigation. Please let me know when you've made an arrest."

She brushed past me on her way out the door, and I put a hand on her arm. "Lynn, wait, I don't mean to—"

She closed her eyes and took a breath. "I'm not mad, Callie. Not at you, anyway. We'll talk later."

She stalked into her adjacent office. When she slammed the door, I jumped. "I came at a bad time."

"You could say that," Raul muttered.

"Should I come back later? Or text you?"

He leaned back and folded his hands across his stomach. "Sit. Can't let personal problems distract me from the job. What do you have for me?"

I frowned, weighing whether Raul needed the shoulder of a friend or the information of a colleague... well, semi-colleague. If it were me, I'd choose the diversion of a case over the mystifying matters of the heart. Info share it was.

"Remember I told you Sam and I were going to dinner at Tonya and David's last night? Well, something strange happened..."

When I mentioned Tommy Murray, I expected Raul to be surprised, but he didn't seem ruffled by the news. I cocked my head. "Did you already know he was in the village?"

"I'm a detective," he said. "I'm paid to know what's going on in my town."

I crossed my arms. "You didn't tell me. I thought we were keeping each other in the loop."

"Look, Callie, I said we'd share information as appropriate. That doesn't mean I'm going to phone you every time a magpie flutters its wings. I can't spend all day writing reports for you."

"So, as I predicted, this is a one-way street. I come to you with whatever I discover and hope you'll toss me the occasional crumb."

He held up a hand. "Enough. I can't do this with you. Not today."

I bit my lip and studied him. His eyes were hooded. Lines creased his forehead. A wave of sympathy coursed through me. I glanced toward the wall separating his office from Lynn's and spoke in a low voice. "Do you want to talk about it?"

"Not here, and not now." He sighed. "Thanks for asking. But let's stick to business. To answer your question, yes, we were aware Tommy Murray was in the village, though we haven't been able to find out when he actually arrived. He's holed up in an AirBNB outside of town, and the owner hasn't yet returned our request for information. Legally, he doesn't have to, especially since Tommy Murray has broken no laws we are aware of. We're pretty sure he got to town before yesterday afternoon, though. Did Murray say why he came?"

"He played up the grieving cousin role. Said he was here to represent the Murray family."

Raul tapped a pencil on the desk. "Interesting."

"What are you thinking?"

"I told you we suspected Gene might be attempting to recruit local businesses for his money laundering exploits?"

"You did. I was insulted that he never approached me with an offer I couldn't refuse. Is my business unworthy of mob attention?"

Raul didn't crack a grin. He was not in a joking mood.

I threaded my fingers together. My thoughts traveled to David and his peculiar reaction to Tommy Murray. Suddenly, I understood what Raul was getting at.

"You think Tommy might be in town to take over what Gene started?"

"The thought crossed my mind," he said.

That led me to another aha moment. "Could Tommy have killed Gene? Maybe in some sort of power grab?"

"Also crossed my mind. But there's no way to know. Not yet. We have yet to determine a timeline of Tommy's whereabouts. We could ask him, of course, but I'm not sure we want to tip our hand yet."

I mulled over the suggestion that Tommy might have killed his cousin. Part of me hoped that's how it had gone down—the Murray family picking off its own members was a much more palatable thought than Lydia...or Pinky... or Vivian...murdering Gene.

I glanced at my watch. As much as I wanted to continue theorizing with Raul, I needed to get going. Picnic time was fast approaching, and I couldn't afford a repeat of the brunch debacle.

Chapter Twenty-Seven

I left Raul's office, shutting the door behind me at his request. As I turned toward the lobby, I paused in front of Lynn's closed door. I glanced guiltily at my watch, decided I could spare a couple of minutes, and tapped lightly, hoping Raul wouldn't overhear.

"Come in," Lynn called out.

I nudged the door open and wedged my head through the crack. "I come in peace."

Lynn looked up from a stack of papers, smiled, and motioned me inside. I eased the door shut and took a seat. "I wanted to check on you. You seemed...tense earlier."

She flipped her long ponytail over her shoulder. "Yeah, sorry about that."

"Hope I haven't created a problem between you and Raul."

"It's not you. Though I admit I question how appropriate it is that this department involves you so much. And now Raul seems to have deputized you—"

"It's nothing like that, Lynn. We're sharing information. It's expedient. We've always worked well together. When we're not at each other's throats, that is."

She lowered her eyes. "I thought Raul and I worked well together, too. But now he's pushing me away."

I lifted an eyebrow. Was yet another reticent detective opening up to me? First, Raul. Now, Lynn. Maybe I should get my license in relationship counseling.

Physician, heal thyself, I thought.

"It must be tricky navigating a working relationship and a personal one," I said tentatively.

Her head bobbed. "Harder than I expected. I'm wondering whether taking this job was a mistake."

I leaned across the desk and covered her hand with mine. "Trust me, it wasn't. You are a first-rate detective, as well as a cherished friend. We're lucky to have you here."

I hesitated, then decided to speak my mind. "Lynn, we both know the strain between you and Raul has nothing to do with your working relationship. It's the romantic partnership that's in tumult."

She blew out a breath. "We never should have gotten involved..."

"I'm not saying that. The thing is...well, Raul's obviously in love with you."

Her head jerked up. "Did he tell you that?"

"He didn't have to. Every time he looks at you, it's written on his face." I took a breath, wondering how far to take the conversation. I couldn't violate Raul's confidence, but the two of them were clearly struggling.

"Look, Lynn. I get the sense that you're keeping Raul at arm's length. My guess is that it has to do with your daughters. Am I right?"

She nodded. "I don't know what to do. I want to let him into our lives. If it was only me, no problem. But the girls…They've been through a failed marriage. I can't allow them to get attached, only to see them get hurt."

"You want to protect them, Lynn. I get that. And whether or not you admit it, you want to protect yourself, too. Believe me, I know how that feels. I spent months doing the same thing with Sam. But let me ask you this. Are your girls happy?"

Her face lit up. "They are. They're the most upbeat, high-spirited kids in the world."

"So, the divorce didn't steal their happiness. They're resilient. I've never been a mother, so my words may not carry much weight. But it's my opinion that you can't shield children from life. You can only show them how to live it to the fullest. And that means embracing love when it comes and mourning it if it leaves. Which, by the way, won't be the case for you and Raul. You were made for each other."

Lynn chewed her bottom lip, then a spark of mischief flashed in her eyes. "Since you seem to be the guru of relationship wisdom, let me ask you a question of my own. Why aren't you and Sam married by now? Speaking of people who were made for each other…"

"Do as I say, not as I do?" I responded. "Between you and me, we might be getting close. If only I could win over his parents." I looked at my watch and jumped to my feet. "Speaking of, I have to run. If I'm late for this picnic, my fate is sealed."

Lynn smiled. "Take a breath. You'll be fine."

"Hey, will I see you at Summer's wine yoga event tonight? She created it special for our gaggle of girlfriends, as Raul refers to us. It'll do you good, body and soul."

She smiled again. "Wine? You bet. Yoga? I can do that. It may seem unprofessional, but I need it. I'll arrange for a babysitter. Right now, though, I'm going next door to have a word with my partner."

I RACE-WALKED to my car trying to convince myself I had plenty of time to pick up our sandwiches and make it home in time to greet Sam and his parents. But when I entered Delilah's Deli, that hope faded. Four people stood in line ahead of me. I considered my plight. Would it be rude to butt in, since I only had a pickup? Might as well try.

I approached the harried-looking teenager at the counter. "Excuse me, but I have a to-go order. Is there someone else who handles those?"

"I'm the only one here," she grumbled. "Except Delilah, who's in the back making sandwiches. Sorry, but you'll have to wait in line."

I issued a heavy sigh and staked out my spot at the back. As I twisted my phone in my hand, wondering whether I should give Sam a heads-up, the kitchen door swung open. A stocky woman emerged, her face glistening and her hair tucked into a bouffant cap reminiscent of the ones my high school lunch ladies had worn. She toted a large paper bag by its twine handles.

"Delilah," I said, relief coursing through me. "Is that for me?"

She beamed. "Just finished packing it. I added a half dozen chocolate chip cookies and a few treats for the pets. On the house."

I took the bag from her. "That's so nice of you."

"Important event, right? Maggie mentioned a picnic with the potential in-laws." She waggled a finger at me. "Best get moving. Don't want to be late."

My cheeks flushed as I thanked her again and hurried back to my car. I'd need to have a word with my mother about privacy issues. In this case, though, she'd gotten me free dessert and helped me cut the line, so perhaps another time.

I hightailed it home and pulled into the alley behind my townhouse just as Sam's car rounded the corner into the neighborhood. I squealed into the carport, leapt out of the car, sprinted into the house, and moved at warp speed to transfer the food into an oversized picnic basket. As I placed the bag of cookies inside, a tap came on the front door, followed by Sam's key in the lock. I glanced in the mirror, thankful I'd had the foresight to don my picnic attire before visiting the police station.

Retrieving a small cooler filled with drinks, I whirled around as my boyfriend entered the kitchen.

"Hey, beautiful." He took the cooler from my hands and set it on the table. He tucked a strand of loose hair behind my ear and leaned in for a kiss—one that lasted entirely too long for someone whose parents were waiting in the car.

"Shouldn't we get moving?" I asked, smacking my lips.

He twirled me around the kitchen in an impromptu dance move. "That's what we're doing."

A grin curled his lips, and the tension seeped from my body—no doubt just as he'd intended. I cupped his cheek. "Have I mentioned that you're the best?"

"Can't hear it too often." He took a step back and looked me up and down. "You're gorgeous."

"And you're stunning." He wore a long-sleeved denim shirt, jeans, and hiking shoes—and I'd never seen anyone wear them better. "But enough of the mutual lovefest. I'm here to win over your parents, not you."

He placed his hands on my shoulders and stared into my eyes. "I want you to stop thinking that way. This is only a picnic, nothing more. No pressure. My parents will grow to love you, just like they used to."

I thought back to our teenage years, when Conrad and Lila had welcomed me into their home and their lives. I'd liked them so much—they'd been friendly and accepting back then. Would we be able to recapture those good feelings?

"But what if they don't?" I asked, hearing the whine in my voice.

"It doesn't matter. Not to me. I love you, and that's what counts."

After a quick hug, he picked up the picnic basket and the cooler. I tucked Carl into his backpack carrier and snapped Woody's leash to his collar. I wanted to breathe in Sam's confidence, but I couldn't help but feel a pang of dread. "Hope I'm not organizing deck chairs on the Titanic," I said to myself.

SAM'S FATHER occupied the front passenger seat, so I sat in the back beside Sam's mom. "Hi, Lila, hi Conrad," I said brightly. "It's so good to see you again."

Conrad waved at me over his shoulder as Lila studied me through narrowed eyes. "Glad you could make it."

"Mom," Sam said, "I explained what happened. Let it go."

I forced a smile. "I'm so sorry about that. But I'm happy to be here now. Lovely day, isn't it?"

Lila sniffed. Woody's head appeared over the seat. Before I could stop him, his tongue slurped Lila's cheek.

"Woody," I scolded, reaching out to push him away. To my surprise, Lila smiled broadly and stroked the dog's head, cooing at him like he was a baby.

When I glanced at Sam in the rearview mirror, he wore a lopsided grin. I leaned back against the seat, thinking maybe, just maybe, this get-together would work out fine.

Chapter Twenty-Eight

Turned out my optimism was premature.

When we pulled into the parking lot at Moraine Lake, it was as empty as I'd expected. Late autumn usually means a relative scarcity of visitors to the Rocky Mountain National Park, especially on a weekday. Then I spotted two yellow school buses, and I cringed. "Field trip."

"No worries," Sam said. "We all love kids."

The four of us climbed out of the car. Sam opened the hatchback, and I slung Carl's backpack across my shoulders. Lila frowned. "You carry your cat around like a stack of books? That seems unkind."

"Oh, he likes it," I said. Carl chose that moment to yowl piteously. Lila pursed her lips. "I swear he does. The vet told me this type of carrier makes cats happy. They enjoy being included in the action. We do this all the time."

"Humph," Lila said. Conrad glanced at his wife and avoided looking at me.

The picnic spot lay next to the lake, an easy quarter-mile walk. Woody led the way, tugging at his leash in his excitement. Toting the lunch basket, Sam hung back with his mother and whispered something to her. Though I couldn't make out the words, his tone was stern.

A moment later, he caught up to me and smiled apologetically. In the distance, we heard the whoops and hollers of children. Five minutes later, we rounded a bend and found ourselves lakeside.

The water glinted in the sunshine. A musty, earthy aroma drifted on the breeze. The scene was picture perfect —except for hordes of school children screaming and chasing each other around the picnic tables. I felt as if we'd landed smack dab in the middle of *Lord of the Flies*. I closed my eyes, fighting off despair. Sam shifted the picnic basket and laid a hand on my shoulder.

"It's no big deal, Callie. Their horseplay will give us energy."

I nodded morosely, plastered a fake smile on my face, and turned to Lila and Conrad. "Nothing says picnic like an elementary school field trip. If we spy an army of ants, the day will be perfect."

Conrad started to smile, glanced at his wife, and twisted the grin away. Still, it was a promising sight. If my sparkling personality prevailed on Sam's father, perhaps Lila would have no choice but to follow suit.

Hope springs eternal.

We made our way toward the picnic area, dodging nine-year-olds as we searched for a vacant table. Woody barked happily at the children's antics. Carl squirmed in the backpack, but I didn't get the idea he was eager to play.

Just as I began to think we should pack it in and try a different location, a harried looking teacher approached us. "Sorry for the chaos. We'll be out of here in ten minutes. In the meantime, we'll clear off a table for you."

I wanted to kiss the woman. The four of us stood aside as she and two other teachers gathered mounds of trash.

Then a young boy addressed me, his demeanor polite. "Lady, can I pet your dog?"

"Sure," I said. "He's friendly. His name's Woody."

Woody sat, his tail swishing the dirt. The boy dropped to his knees and began petting the golden retriever's back. "Good boy," he murmured. "Good dog."

Several other children crowded around, all wanting a turn. Woody was in the height of his glory, licking faces and soaking up the attention. Lila smiled at the scene. If I was unable to win her over, maybe my dog could.

When the teachers finished clearing the table, Sam placed the picnic basket and cooler on the bench. I handed him Woody's leash and rummaged inside the basket, pulling out a plastic tablecloth to spread across the table. Before I unpacked the sandwiches, a whistle shrilled. The children gathered around the teachers for instructions. Moments later, they lined up and marched down the trail.

Peace and quiet abounded at their departure. Possibly too much of it. Now we'd be obliged to fill the silence.

"Before we eat, I'd love to get a photo of the three of you by the lake," I said.

Lila brightened, and I guided the family to a shady spot near the water. The mountains rose behind them. Lila stood between the two men, curling her arms through theirs. I took several shots from varying angles, studied the camera's screen, and declared the venture a success.

Sam pried the camera from my fingers and handed it to his mother. "Will you take a picture of Callie and me? She's always behind the lens, meaning I don't have many good shots of the two of us."

Lila scrunched up her face. "That gadget looks complicated. I doubt I'd be able to work it."

Sam placed the camera in her hands and pointed at the shutter button. "Nothing to it. Just look through the viewfinder, turn the focus ring until we're not blurry, and press this button."

He guided me to a spot beside a pine tree and wrapped his arm around me. "Ready when you are," he said to his mother.

She fumbled with the camera for a moment as Sam and I smiled for the picture. When she snapped the shutter, it was obvious she hadn't bothered to put much effort into the photo. But I thanked her, took the camera back, and led the way to the picnic table.

Sam's parents sat side by side as I unzipped Carl's carrier. Lila pointed to him. "Won't he run away?"

"That's not his style. He was a stray when my mother brought him in from the cold. Woody loved him right away and adopted him as a brother. Carl is a pampered prince now. I think he's done with the idea of life on his own."

As if to illustrate the point, Carl clambered out of the backpack, jumped onto the bench between Sam and me, and curled up in a furry orange ball. Woody parked himself near the head of the table, awaiting the possibility of leftovers.

"So," I said cheerfully, "I ordered roast beef and provolone from Delilah's Deli. I don't think her place was here when you lived in Rock Creek Village. It's delightful."

"Delilahtful," Sam chipped in. My laughter boomed way out of proportion to his dumb joke.

"Help yourselves," I said. "There's potato salad and chips, too. What can I get you to drink? Iced tea, lemonade, water?"

"Lemonade sounds good," Conrad said.

Lila pulled her jacket tight around her shoulders. "Too cold for lemonade. Just water, I guess."

I tried not to flinch beneath her barely concealed criticism. Instead, I kept a smile on my face as I handed over a plastic water bottle. Lila took a sandwich and lifted the thick sourdough bread, peering at the contents. "Is this gluten-free?"

"Gluten-free?" A flush crept over my cheeks. "I didn't realize...Sam, you didn't say anything about gluten-free."

Sam smacked his palms on the table, startling us all. "That's because there's nothing to say. Neither of my parents has ever before requested gluten-free food."

"You're not around much," Lila said with a whine. "You don't know everything there is to know about us."

"I know that I've had dinner with you three nights this week and the word gluten has never once crossed your lips."

I put a hand on his arm. "Sam, it's all right..."

"No, it's not. I've had enough." He wrapped an arm around me. "Look, Mom. This is the woman I intend to marry—if my parents don't drive her away first."

Conrad's brow furrowed. "Samuel Aaron Petrie, do not speak to your mother that way."

Lila choked back a sob. Carl chose that moment to sit up on his haunches and hack, faking a hairball. I closed my eyes and held my breath, hoping this was all a bad dream. But when I opened them, the tableau remained. Sam scowled, Lila snuffled, Conrad fumed, Carl hacked. Even Woody appeared worried, but I figured he was only envisioning an end to his table scrap fantasy.

I sighed. "I think we should go."

No one spoke as we packed up the uneaten sandwiches and trudged to the car. This time, Conrad sat in the back with his wife, while I slouched into the front seat. Sam gritted his teeth so hard I worried he'd need to make an emergency visit to the dentist. I had to do something, say something, to make things right.

As Sam maneuvered the winding roads, I studied the scenery, hoping it would inspire some profound words. My hand rested on the console, clenched in white-knuckled anxiety. I sucked in a breath and willed myself to relax. These were not white-robed gods sitting atop Mt. Olympus, meting out punishment for my past sins. They were not judges ready to lock me up for my transgressions. They were Sam's parents, and they didn't hate me. They just wanted to protect their son.

I cleared my throat and turned to the backseat.

"I think it's time to clear the air," I began.

Lila huffed. Sam glared at her in the rearview mirror. Conrad looked from his wife to his son before resting his eyes on mine. "I agree with Callie."

When Lila bristled, Conrad put a hand on her knee. "It won't hurt you to listen, dear."

She hesitated, but at last offered a reluctant nod. I shot Conrad a grateful look and took the plunge. "When I left for college almost thirty years ago, Sam and I promised each other distance wouldn't come between us. But we were teenagers. We couldn't know how things would go."

Sam watched the road, expressionless. He hadn't been the one to break it off, after all. It was time for me to take full responsibility. "Sam did his best to keep us together. But life pulled me in a direction I hadn't anticipated. I won't say I regret leaving Rock Creek Village and following the path I did. It made me who I am, for better or for worse." I winced, realizing I'd just quoted traditional marriage vows.

Conrad shifted in his seat. Lila stared out the window. I felt Sam beside me and wondered what he was thinking.

"But what I do regret—the biggest regret of my life, in fact—is hurting Sam. He's by far the best person I've ever met—the kindest, strongest, most loving man in the world. I wasn't ready for him back then. But I'm ready for him now. And you don't have to worry. I will never leave him again. I'll be beside him as long as he'll have me."

Sam looked at me with such tenderness my breath caught. Lila lifted her chin, refusing to speak. Conrad's blue eyes, so much like his son's, softened. He gave me a quick wink.

I turned back in my seat with a smile on my face. I couldn't foresee the future, but I'd done the best I could. As Sam would say, let the chips fall where they may.

Chapter Twenty-Nine

That evening, I was more than ready for some girl time, even if getting it meant contorting my body into impossible poses. Summer's friends-only wine-and-yoga session at Yoga Delight proved just what the doctor ordered.

I sat on my mat, knees akimbo and the soles of my feet pressed together. Summer faced us, her legs twisted in a way that made me grimace in vicarious pain. Eyes closed, she hummed a mantra the rest of us attempted to mimic. Jessica sat beside her, squirming on her mat. It still mystified me that two opposites formed such a loving union. Then again, Sam and I weren't similar in our personalities.

Next to Jessica sat Lynn, her back straight and her expression one of fierce concentration. Beside her, Renata appeared equally determined. The young hockey coach was blessed—or cursed—with the same competitive gene as her brother, Raul. Then there was Pamela, owner of The Fudge Factory, who appeared content and relaxed as she stretched her neck and shook out her arms. Even Monika had turned up, saying a yoga session might be what she needed to eliminate the dregs of her migraine.

On my left, my best friend Tonya sipped from her tumbler of wine. "That's against the rules," I whispered. "Summer says yoga first, wine after."

She winked. "Since when have you known me to abide by the rules, sugarplum?"

"Excellent point."

"Tsk tsk, ladies." Summer opened one eye and shot us a warning look.

A chime rang, and I blew out a breath. "Saved by the bell."

Everyone opened their eyes and shifted on their mats. Summer gave us a pleased smile. "Wonderful program, my friends. I hope you're rested and open to the universe."

Jessica lifted her glass. "Here's to being rested."

The rest of us raised our tumblers in a toast. "Here's to the universe," Renata said.

I struggled to my feet and switched from the mat to a low stool. "The universe is telling me I'm getting too old to spend that much time on the floor."

The friendly laughter and gabbing began then. I regaled the girls with the tale of the picnic. They sympathized and ladled out advice. Summer said, "You need to relax and let them come to you. When you try too hard, the universe rebels."

Jessica nudged her wife. "You're sounding an awful lot like Mrs. Finney. I wonder if she'd pay you to write adages for her cups."

When Lynn began opening up about her own relationship woes, my mouth fell open. Like Raul, Lynn was stingy about getting too personal. Now the sympathy and advice flowed her direction. The group's supportiveness was limitless. I'd spent so many years priding myself on my self-sufficiency and independence that at first, I'd found such intimacy unsettling. Yet here I was, finally able to identify the sentiment that had been growing in me for the past couple of years.

This was what *happy* felt like.

Eventually, as I'd known it would, the discussion turned to mystery and murder. "So," Summer said, her eyes trained on Lynn, "what's new with the investigation?"

Lynn graced Summer with a taciturn smile. "No can tell." She cocked a thumb at me. "But I won't object to whatever Callie shares."

All eyes turned to me. I glanced at Tonya, wondering if her mother's involvement made the topic taboo, but she appeared at ease, even intrigued. I decided to talk, without divulging anything Raul had told me in confidence. The more brilliant minds in the game, the more likely we were to unearth answers. "Which do you want?" I asked. "Mystery or murder?"

Jessica clapped her hands. "Mystery first. I'm fascinated by the Vivian Corwin situation. An enigmatic woman who disappeared from the village forty years ago hits her head on her husband's tombstone and loses her memory...It's like a gothic novel. Has she remembered her past life yet?"

"Nope," I said. "The doctor is hopeful, though he mentioned that long-term memory sometimes fades away forever following a head injury."

"I heard Vivian's bunking with Maggie and Butch," Pamela said. "How long will that arrangement last?"

"As long as it takes, I'd venture to guess. Dad feels responsible for her. He carries a lot of guilt over not finding her all those years ago. And Mom..."

"Maggie is the patron saint of lost causes," Tonya said.

I chuckled. "Should I take that as an insult? Am I one of those lost causes? Seriously, though, Mom's solution driven. She won't let Vivian linger long before she formulates a plan to jog her memory."

There was a pause as everyone sipped their wine. Monika broke the silence. "Here's what I've been wondering. Could Vivian Corwin have killed Gene Murray?"

Lynn's eyebrows rose, but she didn't speak. "Believe me, I've considered that," I said. "Especially since she's staying in my parents' guest room. But I can't make the logistics work. Vivian fell—or was pushed—against George's tombstone. An unconscious woman wouldn't be able to swing a mattock."

"If she really was unconscious," Monika said. "We only have her word for that."

"Her scalp was bleeding," I said. "And the doctor confirmed a head injury."

Monika made a face. "Maybe she stumbled and fell into the tombstone after striking Gene with the mattock."

"Could be, I guess. But the woman is in her seventies. Gene was young and strong. Wouldn't he have seen the attack coming and put a stop to it?"

Monika sighed. "I suppose you're right. But if we're talking logistics, what other explanation makes more sense? For no reason, Gene attacks Vivian? Then an unknown perpetrator enters the cemetery and kills Gene? Who? Why?"

"Dig into it, young reporter," Tonya said. "I realize you've been sidelined with a headache—"

"Migraine," Monika interrupted. "If you'd ever experienced one, you'd know the difference. I get them a few times a year, and they can be debilitating."

Tonya held up a hand. "Sorry. Didn't mean to diminish your suffering. But now that you're better, work your computer magic. Figure out where Vivian has been all these years and how Gene figures into this mystery. Heck, I wouldn't be surprised if you found Amelia Earhart while you were at it."

Monika's eyes narrowed. "I get the impression I'm being mocked."

We laughed. "That's how you know you're part of the group," Pamela said.

"Here's the bottom line," Jessica said. "If Vivian didn't kill Gene, who did?"

Renata folded her arms. "It must be related to Murray family business. They aren't exactly salt of the earth. Someone Gene crossed killed him in revenge."

We considered the notion. Summer said, "Don't forget, though—Pinky confessed."

Lynn shook her head decisively. "Pinky didn't do it."

Last I'd heard, he was still on the detectives' suspect list. What had changed? "How did you come to that conclusion?" I asked.

"Something that came to light just before I came here," she said. "A camera at the Ice Zone faces Pinkerton's Place. Officers were able to access the feed, and they found video of Pinky entering his store just before dawn. He didn't leave again until he headed to the hospital."

"Not the most ironclad evidence," I said. "He could have sneaked out the back door."

"You sound like Pinky," Lynn said. "Even with video evidence to the contrary, he still insists he's guilty. But his car never left the parking lot. He would've had to hoof it seven or eight miles to the cemetery."

"He could've called an Uber," Renata suggested.

"Have you noticed droves of Uber drivers in Rock Creek Village?" Jessica asked.

I tapped my fingers on my knee. "Okay, Pinky's out. So, who's in?"

"My money's still on Vivian," Monika said. "You haven't convinced me otherwise."

I made a face. I wasn't buying Vivian as a killer. Gene's criminal exploits seemed much more likely to create a pool of suspects. Still, I couldn't expound on my suspicions. I'd promised Raul I wouldn't mention his speculation that Gene was trying to recruit villagers into his money-laundering scheme. I kept my lips pressed shut.

I caught Monika eyeing me with curiosity and gave her an innocent smile.

"Anyone considering Mr. Fallow?" Jessica asked. "He was on the scene."

I shrugged. "He had opportunity, as well as means."

"But he's a million years old," Pamela protested.

"He's in great shape, though," Summer said. "Caretaking a cemetery must be a fabulous workout. But what would his motive be?"

"Trying to scrounge up another customer?" Renata said.

We chuckled uncomfortably and fell silent. Tonya cleared her throat. "I realize you're trying to protect my feelings, and I appreciate that. But there's no need. We can't ignore the obvious."

I put my hand on my friend's knee. Despite her cavalier attitude, she had to be suffering. I couldn't imagine having to wonder whether my mother might be a murderer.

Summer was the first to speak. "I can't believe Lydia would be capable of that."

"What has she said about it?" Jessica asked.

"Nothing. She refuses to discuss it. Even David, whom she worships, has had no luck getting her to open up."

Pamela snorted. "She didn't have any trouble opening up last night."

"What are you talking about?" Tonya asked.

"Just that Lydia was quite...forthright at dinner last night," Pamela said.

I shook my head, confused. "You had dinner with Lydia?"

"Of course not." Pamela directed her gaze to Tonya. "No offense."

Tonya lifted her glass. "None taken. I wouldn't have dinner with her either, if I didn't have to."

I rolled my hand. "This dinner you mentioned?"

"Willie took me to dinner at Pearly's last night—"

The girls began tittering and teasing. "Oooh," Renata said. "Fancy dinner date."

"Romance in the air?" Jessica asked.

"Hush, all of you," I said. "Except you, Pamela. Keep talking."

Pamela's cheeks had turned pink at the teasing, but it was obvious it pleased her. Like me, she'd been lonely, craving friendships she didn't even know she was missing. We'd offered her a place to fit in. All well and good, but right now, I wanted information more than I wanted touchy feely.

Pamela twisted a bracelet on her wrist. "Willie and I had finished our steaks and ordered dessert when a ruckus broke out."

"A ruckus?" Lynn asked.

"Lydia started yelling. The man she was with just grinned. The insolence on his face..." Her eyes flicked to the ceiling as she replayed the scene. "I'd have slapped him if I'd been Lydia." She shot a look at Tonya. "Your mother didn't. Remarkable self-restraint. She held her own, though. Stood up and shook a finger at the man. I couldn't make out any specifics, but she was ticked, and he didn't seem to care."

"What happened next?" I asked.

"Ken Pearly came out of the kitchen and told the two of them they were disturbing the customers. I thought sure he'd tell them to leave, but the man said something I couldn't hear, and Ken went back into the kitchen. Everything was peaceful after that."

"Who was the man Lydia was with?" Lynn asked.

Pamela shrugged. "I didn't know him."

"Would you recognize him if you saw him again?" she asked.

Pamela considered her question. "Sure. Probably, that is. Is it important?"

Lynn scrolled through her phone, then turned the screen toward Pamela. Tonya and I both wriggled around to get a look.

"That's him!" Pamela said.

Lynn tucked her phone in her pocket and glanced from me to Tonya. Neither of us was surprised. After all, Lydia had allowed the man into Tonya's home last night.

The man who'd caused a scene at Pearly's was none other than Tommy Murray.

Chapter Thirty

I slept fitfully that night, tossing and turning so much that the creatures abandoned me for their pet beds. Gene's murder loomed in my mind. Every time I drifted off to sleep, the image of his body behind George Corwin's grave startled me awake. Then I'd picture Vivian floating through the fog like a ghost. The two of them must be connected...but how?

I tried to think in practical terms. In my mind, the most obvious suspect in Gene's death was his cousin, Tommy. No one had come up with a specific motive, but did families like his need motive? Destroying each other seemed to be part of their genetic makeup. Maybe Tommy was jealous of Gene's rank in the family. Maybe Gene had figuratively stepped on Tommy's toes during a business dealing. Heck, maybe he'd stepped on his actual toes once and Tommy had carried a grudge and vowed revenge.

I couldn't ignore the money laundering aspect, though. If Gene had ensnared a Rock Creek Village business owner or two into his web, that meant more suspects —local ones.

Ugh. I was running off on a speculative tangent, one that wasn't leading me anywhere. I forced thoughts of murder from my mind and finally fell into a dreamless sleep.

SLUMBER DIDN'T LAST LONG, though. Wide awake at five-thirty, I groaned, kicked off the covers and got in the shower. Might as well make the most of yet another pre-dawn rising.

I'd insisted Ethan and Zoe take the morning off. They'd been working nonstop covering for the twins, as well as my own frequent absences from the gallery. Since I'd be solo from opening until one, I decided to go to the gallery early to work on a special project.

By the time I dressed and dried my hair, Woody was awake and ready for action. Carl was not so solicitous. Like me, he preferred to sleep in, so he grumbled and hissed as I carried him to the car.

In the darkness before daybreak, the town felt abandoned, like I was the lone survivor of an apocalypse. But soon enough, we arrived in the upper village, with its smattering of lights as the early-opening businesses prepared for the day. Within a few minutes, Rocky Mountain High would open to caffeine seekers. Down the street, Rodger and Jamal were probably bustling around the Snow Plow Chow kitchen, prepping for the breakfast crowd. In between lay Quicker Liquor, Pearly's Steak and Chop House, the Fudge Factory, Tabitha's Treasures, and A Likely Story, all shuttered and dark. Had Gene approached any of the owners? Fran? Pearly? Pamela? Tabitha? Surely not David, Lydia's son-in-law—though that might account for his odd reaction when he saw Tommy Murray.

I glanced upstairs to the office above the gallery and considered Willie Wright, Rock Creek Village's realtor. Wouldn't a realty business serve as a perfect cover for a money-laundering scheme? And what about Parker Lyons' Rocky Insurance Company?

I was heading down a rabbit hole. Best to clear my mind with some photography work.

I parked in the alley and herded Woody and Carl inside, arranging their food and water bowls and plumping up their pet beds. Carl resumed his interrupted slumber. Woody happily chewed a rawhide bone. I took my Nikon from the storage cabinet and headed to the computer lab.

My morning project involved printing a photo of Sam and his parents from our brief visit to Moraine Lake yesterday, before irritation and tears led to the picnic's premature demise. I scrolled through the day's pictures, smirking when I came across the one Lila had taken of Sam and me. It was just as I'd guessed—Sam looked great, but my eyes were closed and my mouth drooped open. I wouldn't be placing that one on my mantle.

The photos of Sam with his parents were much better. I settled on one where the sun shone at just the right angle across their faces. All three of them wore genuine smiles— blissfully unaware of the coming debacle.

I connected the camera to my brand new iMac Studio computer and transferred the image. When it appeared on the screen, I cropped it, sized it, and color corrected it. I crossed to the printer in the corner, loaded a sheet of 8x10 glossy photo paper, and printed a copy.

Back in my office, I rummaged through the storage cabinet and selected a rustic gray frame. I situated the photo inside, pressing on the back and twisting the tiny hinges to hold it closed. When I inspected the final product, I nodded in approval. I didn't know whether Sam's parents would ever like or even accept me, but they couldn't argue with this photograph's perfection.

A glance at my watch told me I still had an hour until opening. I used half the time to prepare the gallery—switching on lights, adjusting canvases, and booting up the computer behind the sales counter. Then I exited through the front door, locked it behind me, and hustled down the street to Rocky Mountain High for my morning caffeine fix.

Since Mrs. Finney was still out of town, I took my coffee and pastry to go and headed back to the studio. Promptly at ten, I opened the blinds on the bay window, turned the sign on the door from Closed to Open, and waited for customers.

And waited.

By eleven, only two visitors had entered the gallery—one mistakenly believing Sundance Studio was a Robert Redford movie store, and another who shuffled through the postcards and left without making a purchase.

I'd retreated to the computer, planning to use the slow time to try compiling information on Tommy Murray, when the bell jingled over the door, followed by a cheerful greeting. I smiled at the sight of two of my favorite people.

"Bradley! Tim!" I rushed over and wrapped the esteemed social influencers and podcasters in a hug. A couple of years ago, the two of them had happened into my fledgling studio and made a huge purchase that kept me flush with Pop-Tarts for months. More importantly, they'd promoted Sundance Studio on their booming social media sites. The rest was history. They still plugged the gallery regularly and kept customers flowing to us.

"I'm so happy to see you," I said. "What brings you to the village?"

Bradley handed me his suede coat and smoothed his

hair. "It's you, darling. We're in the market for two more Callahan Cassidy originals for our collection."

"We're adding another room to our little bungalow," Tim said as he draped his leather bomber jacket over my arm.

I hung their coats on the rack by the door, picturing their "little bungalow"—a three-thousand-square-foot mini-mansion in the woods. Then I joined them as they ambled around the gallery scrutinizing my newest offerings.

"What are you looking for?" I asked. "Landscapes? Wildlife? Any specific season?"

Tim rubbed his chin and gazed at the canvases. "Nothing particular in mind."

"We'll know it when we lay eyes on it." Bradley shooed me away. "Leave us be, Callie. We'll call if we need you."

I knew better than to be insulted. This was how the two of them operated. They'd argue and haggle and compromise and summon me when they reached a decision. I returned to my spot behind the sales counter.

Twenty minutes later, they were escorting me around the studio, pointing out four of my largest—and most expensive—canvases. "We couldn't settle on two," Bradley said.

Tim put an arm around me. "We'll simply have to expand the addition."

I beamed. "Gentlemen, you've kept food on my table for another month."

"We live to serve," Tim said.

"Where's that sweet ginger partner of yours?" Bradley looked around, searching for Ethan.

I filed away the description for future teasing. "I told him to take the morning off. You're stuck with me."

Bradley leaned an elbow on the counter. His eyes twinkled. "So, darling, we hear our resident amateur sleuth has stumbled across yet another murder."

Tim crossed his arms. "When can we get you on the podcast?"

I narrowed my eyes. "This visit wasn't about my photography at all, was it? You two heathens are bribing me for a scoop."

Bradley wagged a finger. "Don't be such a cynic."

"We heard it could be mob related." Tim glanced around furtively, as if Al Capone might be lurking in the gallery's wings.

I pasted on my most innocent expression. "I have no idea what you're talking about."

"Mmm hmm," Bradley said. "I suppose you also know nothing about a mysterious woman's reappearance in the village after...what?...a century's absence?"

"Where on earth are you getting—?"

The bell jingled again, and I breathed a sigh of relief—until I saw who it was. My eyebrows flew to my scalp.

"Conrad? Lila?" I plastered on a smile. "Welcome! Come in. I'm...happy you're here."

Bradley cocked his head and studied the couple. "Ahh, you must be the handsome hunk's parents."

Tim nodded. "I can see it." He gestured to Lila. "Sam has your eyes."

Bradley pointed at Conrad. "And your chiseled cheekbones. That boy got the best of you both."

Lila preened, and Conrad puffed out his chest. How did my two benefactors always know just the right thing to say?

"How kind," Lila said. "I don't believe we've met." She shot me an expectant look.

"Oh, of course, sorry," I stuttered. "Conrad and Lila,

meet Bradley and Tim. They're..." I was at a loss for how to label the two multifaceted millennials.

Bradley saved me the trouble. "Tim and I are social influencers and podcasters. We help talented people make money." He launched into an explanation while the Petries listened blank faced. I could identify. I didn't entirely understand what Bradley and Tim did, either.

Tim nudged his partner. "They don't need our resume, Brad. Suffice it to say, we tell people what to buy, and they often do."

Conrad nodded. "You're advertisers."

"In a broad sense." Tim cocked a thumb my direction. "But more importantly, we are this young lady's biggest fans."

Young lady? I mentally rolled my eyes. I was at least fifteen years older than the two of them. "Bradley and Tim's recommendation put Sundance Studio on the map," I said.

"It wasn't hard to do," Bradley said. "Callie is the most brilliant photographer we've run across. Her work is..."

"It's art," Tim finished. "She's also one of the best people we know. She never backs away from returning our favors."

I chuckled. "Subtle, fellows."

When I glanced at Conrad and Lila, I noted the look of approval on their faces. Now I owed Bradley and Tim an even bigger debt. I sighed, envisioning another podcast in my near future.

"Callie, darling, we must dash," Bradley said. "We'll stop back by this afternoon to retrieve our purchases." He lifted Lila's hand to his lips. "It was a pleasure to meet Sam's beautiful mother and distinguished father."

"We think the world of your son. And he hit the jackpot with this one." Tim tilted his head to me.

When they left, I shuffled my feet awkwardly, then snapped my fingers. "I have something for you. Let me go get it."

I hustled into the office, snatched up the photo, and hurried back to the gallery, placing the frame in Lila's hands. "I suspect you don't have many pictures of the two of you with Sam now that he's an adult."

Lila stared at the picture before passing it to Conrad, who looked at it with a smile. "It's wonderful, Callie. Thank you."

"I'd love to get one with Elyse, too. Maybe next time you're in town..."

I trailed off. Lila's gaze had dropped to the floor. Was I trying too hard?

When she lifted her eyes, they were brimming with tears. Oh, no. How had I managed to make things worse?

"Callie, we owe you an apology," she said. "We've treated you poorly, and we're sorry."

I grimaced. "Did Sam tell you to—?"

"No," Conrad said. "We didn't even let him know we were coming here. Lila and I had a heart-to-heart last night."

"We realized how cold and unforgiving we'd been," Lila said. "It's been thirty years since..."

"Since the breakup," Conrad said. "You were only teenagers..."

"We've been so petty. It's just..." She shot a look at her husband, who gave her an encouraging nod. "It was a hard time for Sam when you left. And for us. Even though you were both young, we held on to a dream that you'd be together forever."

Conrad took his wife's hand. "The two of us were teenagers when we met, you know, so the idea didn't seem farfetched."

"And then later, when he married that Kimberly woman..." They both shuddered at the mention of Sam's ex-wife. "At least Elyse came of the union, and she's a blessing for which we are eternally grateful. But my goodness."

"We had to watch our only child grapple with the loss of another relationship," Conrad said.

Lila looked up at him, and a single tear spilled down her cheek. "Not really our only child, though. We...we don't talk about this much, but before Sam was born, we had a daughter. She was just six months old when..."

Conrad put an arm around his wife, pulling her close. "Heart abnormality," he said, his voice husky.

I blinked back tears of my own. "I didn't know. Sam never said anything."

"As I said, we don't talk about it much, even to our son," Lila said. "We never wanted him burdened with our pain."

"We only bring it up now because...well, we've come to the conclusion it may be the root of our overprotectiveness —even now, when our son is an adult."

Lila wiped her eyes and took a breath. "Anyway, the bottom line is that we were wrong to behave as we have. We hope you can forgive us."

The tears I'd been holding back begin to fall, and I didn't try to stop them. I took Lila's hand in mine. "There's nothing to forgive. Let's just start fresh from today."

Lila squeezed my hand, and Conrad patted my shoulder. A weight lifted from me, and in its place lay hope for the future.

That feeling lasted all of fifteen seconds. Then the door thumped open, and chaos returned to my world.

Chapter Thirty-One

Tonya and David entered the studio looking anxious. Tonya gave Sam's parents a strained smile and a quick hug. Sensing something was up, the Petries made a hasty departure.

As soon as they left, I locked the door, turned the sign to Closed, and lowered the blinds. "What's up?" I asked.

Tonya stared up at her husband, who squirmed beneath her gaze. "David has an admission," she said tersely.

I watched and waited. David shifted on his feet. Tonya crossed her arms. "Tell her."

After a deep breath, he told his tale. When he finished, I responded without hesitation. "Raul and Lynn need to hear this right away. Do you want to call them, or should I?"

"Told you," Tonya said to her husband.

David shook his head. "I disagree. Getting them involved increases the danger."

"They're cops," I said. "It's their job to keep people safe. But to do that effectively, they need the facts."

After a moment's silence and a hefty sigh, David nodded. "All right. Call them."

Fifteen minutes later, an insistent knock sounded at the gallery door. I opened it and ushered Raul and Lynn inside. At the same time, Ethan entered through the back door, looking confused. "What's happening? Why are the blinds closed?"

"Good timing, partner," I said. "Something's come up. Do you mind taking over? I'll fill you in later."

Raul cleared his throat. "As much as I'm able," I amended.

Ethan nodded. "Zoe should be here any minute. The two of us can handle the gallery."

I thanked him, grateful I'd had the good sense to make the man my business partner. I led the rest of the group through the gallery and into the cramped office.

Raul leaned against the wall, arms crossed. Tonya and Lynn took the guest chairs, while I sat behind my desk. David stood nervously beside Tonya as Lynn pulled a notebook and pen from her bag and flipped to a blank page.

This time, it didn't take any prompting for David to launch into his story. "It started during one of Lydia and Gene's prior visits..."

He tapped Tonya's shoulder, like a wrestler tag teaming his partner. "It would have been mid-August," Tonya said.

David resumed the narrative. "One afternoon, Gene came into A Likely Story with a proposition. He said his family was recruiting local businesses to partner with them. They'd been doing this for years in other towns, he said, and had the experience to make it work. He told me I could make a *tidy sum*..." He lifted his fingers in air quotes.

"And it would be in my best interests to agree. 'Mutually beneficial,' he said."

Lynn looked up from her notebook. "Did you understand what he meant by *proposition*?"

"Of course. I'm Italian. *Proposizione* is one of the first words Italians learn. The Murrays wanted me to help wash their *denaro sporco*. Dirty money. I refused, told him I ran a legitimate business. He...how do you say?...smirked. Said, 'As I mentioned, it's in your best interests.'" He mimicked Gene's intonation. "I asked if that was a threat. 'Take it however you want,' he said. 'Believe me, you'll come around. They all do.'"

Raul shook his head in frustration. "It would have been helpful to have this information at the time it happened."

David lowered his eyes. "Gene said I shouldn't mention our conversation to anyone. Not Lydia, not Tonya. He hinted that there would be repercussions if I did." His brow furrowed as he looked at Tonya. "I was afraid for my wife's safety, and her mother's, so I kept my mouth shut."

"Secrets," Tonya said, her voice quivering. "We said we'd never keep them from each other."

I mentally kicked myself. I'd had a gut instinct that David was hiding something, but I'd pushed my suspicions aside, unwilling to give them voice. My investigative edge must be eroding.

Now, as I looked at David, forlorn and shamefaced, I realized that was a price I was willing to pay. Sympathy swept through me. "It's understandable, David. You were trying to protect the people you love. It must have been hard keeping this to yourself."

Raul narrowed his eyes at me, and I narrowed mine back. He could look as cop-like as he wanted, but under the same circumstances, I had no doubt he'd have kept quiet, too. Tonya gazed at me in surprise. Then her face transformed from disappointment to tenderness. She took David's hand in hers. "Tell them the rest," she said gently.

He squeezed her hand gratefully. "When Lydia and Gene showed up last week for another of their impromptu visits, Gene took me aside and told me the time had come. His family wanted an answer, and Gene wasn't going home empty-handed. He said if I didn't hook up with them, a price would be paid, and it would be paid by people I cared about. I said he'd have to give me a couple of days to make arrangements. I was on the verge of going to the police, when..." Tonya rose and stood beside him, offering silent moral support. "I'm ashamed to admit it, but when I found out Gene was dead, my first reaction was relief. Then I realized if anyone found out he'd been pressuring me, they might suspect me of killing him. I was torn. Then Tommy showed up..."

Another piece of the puzzle fell into place. "Tommy swooped in to take over where Gene left off."

David nodded. "He stopped by the store the morning after Gene's death, said he just wanted to introduce himself. I was concerned, but he didn't mention anything about a proposition. I thought—hoped—maybe all that ended when Gene died."

He twisted his hands together. "So naive of me. When Tommy walked into our home that night, my heart sank. I knew the battle had begun all over again, had never really ended. Tommy visited me at A Likely Story this morning, and...well, I'll just say that Gene was a pussycat compared to Tommy."

Carl jumped on my desk and meowed. David flicked the cat a glance and continued. "I was terrified. I knew I couldn't go on that way. I didn't want to become part of the Murray family enterprise, but I wasn't about to let anything happen to my wife. There was no right answer. When Tommy left the store, I closed the place and went straight to Tonya's office. I told her everything, and she insisted we come straight here."

"I knew we had to tell you," Tonya said to Raul and Lynn. "David wasn't so sure it was the right thing to do. I figured Callie's input would help tip the balance."

Raul's eyes met Lynn's. She gave him a subtle nod, letting him take the lead.

"I wish you'd come to us sooner," he said. "Lynn and I have been poking around in Gene's activities for weeks now. We knew about the Murray family's money-laundering ventures and speculated they might be trying to expand into Rock Creek Village. It would have aided our investigation if we'd known all this back then."

David started to apologize again, but Raul held up a hand. "Water under the bridge."

He ran a hand across the stubble on his chin. While he thought, I jumped in with a question of my own. "Was Lydia aware of what Gene was up to? And now Tommy?"

Tonya poked her tongue into her cheek. "If she was, she never mentioned it to me. Then again, she hasn't said much of anything since Gene's death. If I had to guess, she didn't know. She adores David. I doubt she'd have let that happen."

"But she must have an inkling by now," I said. "Pamela told us she saw her arguing with Tommy at Pearly's. I'd guess it had to be over that."

Tonya nodded. "Agreed. When I asked her about that dinner, she clammed up tighter than a botoxed smile. For a woman who loves the sound of her own voice as much as my mother, it's been an anomaly."

Raul tapped a foot. "I wonder if Gene attempted to recruit any of the other business owners in the village."

"He didn't approach me," I said. "And I'm sure he didn't talk to Sam. He would have told me."

I winced when I saw David's cheeks flush. I hadn't meant to call him out.

Lynn paused in her note taking. "David, did Gene mention any names to you? Maybe in an attempt to persuade you to join the ranks?"

David shook his head. "He only said the family wanted to branch out into small towns. Less scrutiny, he said. He tried to convince me the plan was legitimate, but I knew better. Why else would he warn me not to tell anyone?"

Raul pushed away from the wall as Lynn rose from her chair. "We need to track down Tommy Murray," Raul said.

"Good luck," I said. "Let us know if we can be of any help."

The side of Raul's mouth curled up. "You're on my speed dial."

Chapter Thirty-Two

Tonya and David left a few minutes after Raul and Lynn. A few customers roamed the gallery, but Ethan and Zoe had everything well in hand. I was in my office debating between doing some darkroom work and ordering canvases when my phone rang. A glance at caller ID put a smile on my face.

"Good afternoon, Mrs. Finney. How's the competition?"

"Proceeding as expected, my dear. We've advanced to the finals. We're up against a short chubby woman in a pink tuxedo and her partner, who looks as if he was stolen from a grave and propped up on skates. I predict our victory is well in hand."

I chuckled. Mrs. Finney wasn't in any position to pass judgment on her competitors' attire. I pictured her lavender ice skates and purple onesie adorned with a taffeta skirt. Mr. Purdy complemented her ensemble with his tight lavender slacks and ruffled silver shirt. "Well, I'm rooting for you," I said. "Can't wait to see another silver cup in your collection."

"We may have to add another display shelf," Mrs. Finney mused. "Anyway, Callahan dear, I'm not calling to brag. Mr. Purdy and I heard back from our sources."

Pinky's background might be a moot point, since detectives had already cleared him of Gene's murder. Still, I was curious. My friend, a former CIA agent, had access to sources who could ferret out information no one else seemed able to obtain. So, I experienced a surge of disappointment when she said, "They couldn't uncover any information on Michael Pinkerton prior to his arrival in Rock Creek Village."

"Nothing? How can that be?"

She tsked. "Honestly, dear, Mr. Purdy and I are stumped."

A loudspeaker crackled in the background. "Must run," Mrs. Finney said. "Or skate, rather. Mr. Purdy and I are up next. We'll discuss the matter later."

I opened my mouth to wish her luck, but she'd already disconnected. Her news—or lack thereof—deflated me. No information at all? It was way too cloak-and-dagger for my taste, especially considering a crime family presence in the village and the mysterious return of a missing woman. There had to be something connecting all the moving parts.

My phone rang again, and my mother's name popped up on the screen. "Hey, Mom," I said.

"Hello, darling. I wanted to ask a favor of you. Are you free this evening?"

"Of course. As long as this favor doesn't involve manual labor."

"I know better," she said. "At any rate, it's actually a favor for Vivian."

That piqued my interest. "What does she need?"

"She's begun recovering a few memories. Gentle tugs

on her psyche. Images of George, mostly. They're hazy at best, but it's a promising sign. She wants to visit the house they shared, thinking it might trigger more recollections. We've discussed it with her doctor, and he's given us the green light."

"That's fantastic!" I said. "Sounds as if Vivian might be on the road to recovery."

"The doctor cautioned her it will be a slow process. Progress followed by regression. Anyway, since George had no heirs, his estate is still in limbo. In the meantime, the court made Willie Wright responsible for maintaining the house. Would you mind going to his office to pick up the key? I've already spoken to him."

"Sure," I said. "Do you want me to drop it by the lodge?"

"Well, darling, I was hoping you'd join us at the Corwin house to shoot some photos. I'm thinking that having a few tangible images to revisit might be beneficial for Viv."

"Happy to do it," I said. More than happy, truth be told. My investigative nerves tingled at the idea of being present if Vivian's memories flooded back.

While I was on the phone with Mom, I'd missed a call from Sam, so as soon as she hung up, I sat down at my desk and called him back.

"Hey, beautiful."

"Hey, yourself. From the tone in your voice, I'm guessing something good is going on."

"It is, as you already know," he said. "Mom and Dad filled me in on their visit to the studio. Sounds like the three of you mended fences. Just as I predicted."

"Humph. Be honest. You were worried we'd never make nice."

"Not true. Callie Cassidy wins over even the most recalcitrant of souls. I think the photo did the trick."

"Doubtful." Woody traipsed over and put his head in my lap, and I scratched behind his ears. "Your parents came to the studio this morning to apologize. They explained their fears over you letting me back into your life. It was... emotional, Sam. Heart wrenching, even. You never told me you had a sister."

He was quiet for a moment. "I wasn't even born when they lost her, and it's not something they discuss much. They're very private about it. It's a surprise to me—and a big deal—that they told you about her."

"I'm honored that they trusted me with their story," I said.

"It's a huge step in the right direction. I couldn't be more relieved."

I smiled at the joy in his voice. I only hoped the reconciliation was a permanent one.

He said he and his parents were about to leave for Boulder to meet Elyse for dinner and a show, and I told him about my mother's request to join them at the Corwin house. When we hung up, I spent an hour taking care of gallery business before heading to Willie Wright's realty office. As I stepped outside, a brisk wind whipped my hair into a frenzy, indicating another cold front making its way through the foothills. I shivered as I jogged up the stairs.

The compact office area—about a fifth of the size of my studio—consisted of a currently unoccupied receptionist's desk, a cubby containing a printer and file cabinets, and a tiny bathroom. The focal point was Willie's oversized oak desk, complete with an enormous leather chair reminiscent of a modern-day throne.

Willie, who fancied himself the king of the realm, looked up from his paperwork. His scowl constituted a knee-jerk reaction. He'd never completely forgiven me for once suggesting he was a murder suspect. Since he'd finally accepted I was in the village to stay, he did his best to conceal his low-level animosity, but the occasional expression of disdain still sneaked through.

"Hi, Willie," I said brightly. "How are things going in the real estate world?"

"Slow for now. Should pick up after the first of the year. That's been my experience." He pasted on a polite smile. "And you?"

"Same. Slow but steady."

He nodded. I smiled. An uncomfortable silence ensued. We'd concluded the small-talk portion of the visit.

"Maggie mentioned you'd be stopping by to pick up a key to the Corwin house," he said. "Let me get it."

Willie rose and buttoned his designer jacket. I restrained an eye roll. All alone in his office at day's end and still donning his jacket and tie. I glanced at my own jeans and flannel shirt and realized he was likely passing judgment on my outfit, too.

He sauntered to the key safe hanging on the far wall and made a show of unlocking it. Once upon a time, he hadn't bothered securing the safe. That bad habit had come back to haunt him when someone had pilfered an extra key to my gallery and used it for nefarious purposes.

Once the safe was open, he selected a key and held it out to me. "See that I get this back. Until the Corwin estate is settled, I'm legally responsible."

"Sure thing. Will you be putting the house on the market?"

He shrugged. "That's what I expected would happen following probate, but with George's wife back in the picture, we'll have to wait and see."

I tucked the key into my pocket. I hadn't considered

the ripple effects of Vivian's reappearance. "Well, thank you for your help, Willie."

He gave me a stern look as he returned to his desk. "Don't forget to lock the house when you leave."

Another mental eye roll, and I headed for the door.

As I put my hand on the knob, I hesitated, remembering that Gene had tried to enlist David in the family's money-laundering scheme. Raul had wondered about other business owners Gene might have approached. Could Willie be one of them?

I turned back to him. "Quick question. Did you ever have any...um, interactions with Eugene Murray?"

Willie frowned. "The man who was murdered? Interactions? What do you mean?"

His tone was guarded. He probably wondered if I was adding him to another suspect list. "Oh, I don't know," I said casually, trying to deflect his concerns. "Did he come in to explore real estate options? Or...any other business dealings?"

Willie shook his head, appearing confused. "Was he looking for a house in the village?"

"Not that I heard...What about his cousin, Tommy?"

"The guy arguing with Tonya's mother at Pearly's last night? Why would he come to my office?"

I sighed. If either of the Murray cousins had tried to suck Willie into their unholy alliance, I felt sure I'd see evidence of it on Willie's face, but it wasn't there.

"Never mind," I said breezily. "I'll return the key tomorrow."

As I left Willie's office, I paused for a moment to look up Evergreen Way. Across the street, Fran from Quicker Liquor stood on the sidewalk chatting with Mr. Pearly. I shifted my gaze to Tabitha's Treasures. I certainly couldn't picture the prickly owner succumbing to the crime syndicate's demands. Then I looked at the Fudge Factory. Now that Pamela was part of our girls' group, she surely would have mentioned it to us if Gene had tried to enlist her services. And then there was Rocky Mountain High. Even Gene knew better than to attempt to recruit Mrs. Finney.

So, who? Which of my neighbors might have caved under the temptation of Murray family money?

I blew out a breath. I was just being paranoid. *Wasn't I?*

Chapter Thirty-Three

George's ranch-style home was situated on the outskirts of Rock Creek Village in an area remote enough that neighbors weren't spitting distance apart. I neared the place just before five o'clock, as the sun hung low on the horizon, casting long shadows through the blue spruce trees. I wound down a long gravel driveway and pulled in beside Mom's green Jeep Grand Cherokee. I didn't feel it was appropriate to take Woody and Carl inside, so I opened the back windows a crack to give them some air.

Mom, Dad, and Vivian waited for me on the front porch. A ramp led from the driveway to the porch, though from what Dad had said, George's wheelchair had rarely traversed it in the years since Vivian left.

After a quick hello, I took the key from my pocket and handed it to my father. Vivian's face was so wan that I wondered if this was a good idea. Mom seemed to harbor the same doubts. She placed a hand on Vivian's arm.

"Are you sure about this, Viv? If you're not ready, we

can come back another time. The house isn't going anywhere."

Vivian squared her shoulders. "The memories are dancing around me like fireflies, just out of reach. I want to catch them, inspect them, hold them close. The only way to do that is to go inside."

Dad unlocked the oversized front door and nudged it open. Tension weighed in the air. I cast a glance at the fragile woman who'd come here to search for her past.

Ever the cop, Dad indicated we should hang back as he entered, flicked on lights, and surveyed the interior of the house. Satisfied all was well, he stood aside so we could enter. Vivian hesitated, took a deep breath, and stepped across the threshold.

Mom followed, and I brought up the rear. Dad closed the door behind us, and we stood in a living room that appeared plucked from the seventies. A well-worn floral couch and a matching chair and ottoman dominated the room, accented by a glass-topped coffee table and end tables. Low pile carpeting stretched across the floor, flattened where the wheelchair regularly crossed it. Wood paneling covered the walls. The pièce de résistance was a front-opening projection television, the height of luxury fifty years ago.

Vivian's hand went to her chest as she inspected the room. When her gaze fell on a tall, narrow curio cabinet, she gasped. Hurrying to it, she placed a tentative finger on the glass. We gathered behind her and peered over her shoulder at dozens of delicate figurines lining the shelves.

"I remember these," she murmured.

She opened the cabinet door, reached inside, and selected a small green and red glass parrot. She cupped the bird in her hand and gazed at it. A solitary tear trickled down her cheek. "Georgie gave me this on our wedding day. I'd pestered him for a Costa Rica honeymoon, but it was tax season, and he said he couldn't take the time off. He felt awful. This little guy served as his promise to take me there someday."

Her voice trembled. "We never did go. At least, not that I can remember..."

She closed the cabinet door but kept the glass parrot clenched in her hand.

When she turned away from the cabinet, her eyes were as determined as I'd seen them. She pointed toward the back of the house. "The kitchen is that way."

Mom and Dad followed her through an arched doorway. I hung back and, as my mother had requested, took photos of the living room and especially the cabinet containing Vivian's treasures. Afterwards, I joined the three of them in a kitchen that reinforced the home's seventies theme. Embossed linoleum floor. Avocado colored Formica countertops, lowered in deference to George's wheelchair. Harvest gold appliances, including a state-of-the-art KitchenAid mixer. It was as if we'd entered a time capsule.

"Georgie didn't change a thing," Vivian whispered.

She stumbled as she made her way out of the kitchen, and Dad caught her by the elbow. This trip down memory lane might be taking a toll. "We shouldn't stay much longer," Mom said.

"A few more minutes," Vivian insisted. She led my parents down a narrow hallway as I shot a few pictures in the kitchen. Then I tagged along after them, glancing into a cringe-worthy bathroom with a fluffy green toilet seat cover, followed by a guest bedroom with a pink quilt spread across the double bed.

A moment later, I stood with them in the main bedroom. The space was basic: a queen-sized bed covered with a blue chenille bedspread. Dresser, end tables, lamps. The focal point was the wall behind the bed, which was adorned with a geometric arrangement of stick-on mirrors.

Vivian smiled at the sight. "Georgie argued against those mirrors. Called them ostentatious. But he indulged my wishes." Her eyes filled with tears again. "That man would have given me the moon."

She lifted a framed photo from the nightstand and stared at it. "Our wedding day," she murmured.

When she turned the photo so we could see it, my eyes welled up, too. The couple in the photo looked so young, so full of love and hope. What tremor in the universe had disrupted their promising future?

Suddenly, Vivian's eyes widened. She drew a quick breath, and the glass parrot dropped to the carpeted floor. She turned to my father and gripped his arm tight enough that he winced. Her voice quaked.

"Butch, did Georgie...did he die in this room?"

Dad reeled back. He shot a quick glance at my mother, who also appeared distressed.

"Please," Vivian begged. "I need to know."

After a moment's pause, Dad said, "Yes, Vivian, he did. He passed peacefully in his sleep. The doctor said his heart just stopped beating. He wouldn't have been in any pain."

Vivian crumpled onto the bed, buried her face in a pillow, and sobbed.

Mom started to sit beside her but stopped herself. I understood. The spot seemed almost sacred. To touch it would feel intrusive. She stooped to pick up the little parrot, then stood a few feet from the bed, far enough to give Vivian space but close enough to bear witness to her pain.

Vivian cried for several minutes. When her tears finally subsided, she sat up against the headboard and clutched the pillow to her body. She looked up at my mother. "I remember Georgie now, and how much I loved him. I remember our life together. I sense his presence, almost as if he was still here." She took a tissue from the box beside the bed and swiped her eyes. "But what won't come back to me is this—why did I leave him? Oh, Maggie, why can't I remember that?"

My mother drew a breath. "I believe your mind is protecting you, Viv. It won't allow you to remember more than you can handle. You just need to be patient."

Vivian's demeanor changed abruptly. She rose from the bed, her eyes steely. "No. I'm done being patient. I want answers." She pursed her lips. "Take me to the cemetery. I need to stand beside Georgie's grave. It's where I lost my memory and where I'm destined to retrieve it."

"Viv, that's not a good idea," Mom said. "Going back there—it's too much, too soon."

Vivian folded her arms. "I was asking for a ride, not permission. If you won't take me, I'll find someone who will. I'll walk if I have to."

My mother flinched. Vivian saw it, and her face fell. She took Mom's hand in hers. "Forgive me, Maggie. You've been nothing but kind to me." Her eyes passed over Dad and me and returned to my mother. "You all have. But I must insist on this. My instinct tells me going to the cemetery might unlock whatever door has closed in my mind. You have to trust that I know what's best for me."

Mom and Dad exchanged a glance, a wordless communication honed by years of marriage. They both nodded. "All right, Vivian," Dad said. "We'll take you. But not today. It's nearly dark, too late to go now. We'll make the trip tomorrow afternoon when it's warmed up a bit. When you're rested."

She frowned but relented. Then she turned to me.

"Will you go, too, Callie? I'd feel better if you were there. You were the first person I saw after..."

She trailed off, and I smiled at her. "Of course. Whatever I can do to help."

Vivian took a moment to let her eyes drift across the room. "I was happy here," she murmured.

Tears sprang into my eyes for the umpteenth time. I wanted to go to Sam, wrap my arms around him, and never let him go.

Vivian led the way down the hall to the front door. She opened it, turned back for one last look, then stepped outside. She looped her arm through Mom's, and the two of them went to the car. I hung back with Dad as he locked the door.

"That was rough," I said quietly.

He wore a worried look as he glanced Vivian's direction. "I hope the trip to the cemetery isn't too much for her."

"She seems unshakable on the subject," I said. "I doubt you'd be able to talk her out of it."

He nodded and glanced at the key in his hand. "I'm going to hang on to this for a few days in case Vivian wants to come back. I'll let Willie know."

Dad and I walked across the gravel and got in our cars. They left first. I took a moment to settle the creatures and buckle myself in, then pulled out. As I neared the end of the long driveway, a black truck rolled by on the road, just a minute behind Mom's Jeep. An alarm bell rang in my head. The Corwin place was the last house on this remote stretch of road. Where would that truck have been coming from?

I puffed my cheeks and exhaled, chiding myself for my paranoia. Sometimes a truck is just a truck.

Chapter Thirty-Four

The next morning, I arrived at Sundance Studio just as Ethan and Zoe did. Zoe looked surprised to see me, which produced a twinge of guilt, especially since I'd be gone part of today, too.

"I promise you, Zoe, I do work full days," I said.

Ethan tugged at his beard. "Yes, I recall that special day a few months back..."

I smacked his arm. "I pull my weight around here."

"That you do." He chuckled. "People come from far and wide to buy Callahan Cassidy originals, so I can't complain—as long as you keep us in inventory. Are you working in the darkroom today, or will you be on the sales floor?"

"Well..." I winced as I delivered the news that I'd be leaving at noon for a lunch date with Sam and his parents.

"Planning the wedding?" Ethan teased.

I shot a look at Zoe, one of Elyse's best friends. I didn't want that rumor traveling back to Boulder and reaching Sam's daughter. "Don't be silly. It's just that the Petries are flying back to Florida tomorrow, and it will be the last chance I get to see them for a while."

"One more opportunity to make a good impression," Ethan added.

Zoe smirked. "From what I heard, you don't need to worry about that. Elyse said you're all besties now."

My cheeks warmed. "I wouldn't go that far, but we've made progress."

I changed the subject by saying we needed to get to work. Zoe and I walked around prepping the gallery while Ethan made a list of stock I needed to replenish. Then it was time to open. For two hours, we hosted a steady stream of customers, unusual for this time of year. But then I recalled that Bradley and Tim had once again promoted the gallery on yesterday's podcast. I owed those two a debt of gratitude—and perhaps even a discount on their next purchase.

Mid-morning, Mom texted they were planning to be at the cemetery at three o'clock. Vivian had asked if I'd bring Woody and Carl, since they provided her with comfort.

I grunted. I could see Woody providing comfort, but Carl? He was less a nurturer and more a get-things-done and let's-solve-a-murder guy. I told Mom I'd left them at home today, but I could swing by the townhouse after lunch to pick them up.

At eleven forty-five, I said my goodbyes to Ethan and Zoe and drove to Sam's house. Though he'd lobbied for lunch at Snow Plow Chow, Lila insisted on preparing the meal herself. When she laid out the chicken and dumplings, buttermilk cornbread, and green pea salad, I nearly salivated. After a few bites, I remarked that it was easy to see where Sam had gotten his talent in the kitchen.

Lila's face lit up. "I always knew my son would be a chef. From the time he was itty bitty, he'd climb on a stool to help me cook. As he got older, he started creating the most amazing meals. He's a natural."

I grinned. "Agreed. I've traveled the world, and he's the best chef I've ever come across." I speared a dumpling with my fork and lifted it. "Well, maybe second best."

Too late, I considered the ramifications of mentioning my world travel. Would it remind Sam's parents that years ago I'd left him to pursue my career? The remark didn't alter the cheerful mood, though. Conversation flowed, friendly and light, so that by the end of lunch I was almost convinced we might have permanently bridged the gap that had stretched between us.

Sam and Conrad insisted on cleaning up. While they took the dishes into the kitchen, Lila leaned toward me, wearing a conspiratorial smile. "Callie," she said in a whisper, "after all that's happened, I want to tell you that you and Sam have our blessing. If there's to be a wedding, Conrad and I will be thrilled to attend."

My jaw dropped, and I snapped it shut. "I... um...well..."

Lila put a hand on my arm. "No one is pressuring you, dear. But when you're ready, I know Sam will be. A mother knows these things."

The men returned to the dining room, and Sam cast a suspicious glance from his mother to me. I smiled nervously, said I needed to get back to work, wished the Petries safe travels, and hightailed it out of there. As I drove home to pick up the creatures, I tried to figure out how I felt about Lila's declaration. It's what I'd wanted, right? To win over Sam's parents so my relationship with him could move forward unimpeded?

Still, her suggestion of an imminent proposal caught me short. I'd assumed it was coming, but soon? Was I ready for that?

In my mind, I pictured Sam—his lopsided grin, his bright blue eyes, always filled with love when he looked at me. Any trepidation vanished, replaced by warmth, love, and the desire for commitment.

It had taken time—thirty years, in fact—but I believed I was ready.

BACK AT SUNDANCE STUDIO, I got in an hour of work before herding the creatures back into the car. I drove to the cemetery, arriving right after Mom, Dad, and Vivian. The afternoon sun made it warm enough to forgo coats. Vivian wore an outfit I recognized from Mom's closet— black slacks and a red wool sweater. Despite yesterday's bravado, her face looked troubled. Understandable. The memories lurking just beyond her reach might come tumbling back today. Though it's what one part of her surely hoped for, another part must recognize that at least some of those memories were likely to be traumatic, or at least unsettling.

Standing beside Vivian, Mom held a small bouquet of wildflowers, no doubt meant for George's grave. Dad hovered near the women, the lines on his forehead deep.

I climbed out of my car and opened the back door. Woody jumped out and bounded toward Vivian. The dog had a psychic sense for who needed him. Vivian's face relaxed as she crouched and buried her fingers in his fur. His tail wagged fast enough to create a breeze, and he swiped her cheek with his tongue, eliciting a laugh. *Well done, Woodster.*

I plopped Carl into his carrier and slung it across my shoulder. Then I walked over to the group and clipped

Woody's leash onto his collar as he cuddled with Vivian. No way was I running afoul of Cedric Fallow again.

Speaking of the devil, Mr. Fallow appeared, returning from the interior part of the cemetery. With a spade resting on his shoulder, he could have been the Grim Reaper's twin brother. As he approached, I braced myself for a snappish comment about animals in his cemetery. But when he spotted Vivian with her arms wrapped around the golden retriever, his expression...was I seeing this right?...softened. He almost appeared compassionate.

Vivian glanced up and did a double take. She rose slowly, studied his face, and drew a breath. "Cedric," she whispered. "I...I remember you. You were George's friend. And then mine."

Mr. Fallow's eyes clouded, and his lips tightened. "You left, Vivian. Not a word for forty years. George was never the same after. The man was devastated. Why would you do that to him?"

I heard the unspoken part of the question, too—*why would you do that to me, your friend?*

Vivian's gaze fell. After a long moment, she looked back to Mr. Fallow. "I wish I could tell you that, Cedric. It's the reason I'm here. I want answers, too."

Mr. Fallow stared off into the distance. Then he turned on his heel and strode toward his cottage. I expected him to go inside, slam the door, and be done with her.

Instead, he rested the spade against the front porch and came back to us. Without a word, he offered Vivian his arm. She gave him a sad smile and curled her arm through his. He patted her hand. "Let's go get you those answers."

I'm not sure I've ever been so stunned in my life. One glance at Mom and Dad assured me they felt the same.

Mr. Fallow escorted Vivian down the path as the rest of us trailed behind. No one spoke. The only sounds were the chattering of the magpies and the breeze rustling the few leaves remaining on the aspens.

When we reached George's grave, my parents and I hung back. No visible trace of blood remained on the gravestone—Mr. Fallow's caretaking, no doubt. Vivian released his arm and reached out for the flowers. Mom handed them to her, and Vivian propped the bouquet against the marker. She extended a finger and traced George's name.

Suddenly, she stiffened. She lifted her face to the sky and closed her eyes. Her hands stretched outward, palms up. Her breathing slowed, as if she were in a trance. The rest of us stood still, hardly breathing ourselves. Even Woody and Carl didn't move.

A cracking sound, like that of a twig snapping, broke the silence. Vivian's eyes flew open, and she turned toward the trees. "George? Are you here?"

My eyes widened as my gaze followed hers. Was part of me awaiting the ghostly visage of Vivian's dead husband? Of course not.

I scanned the horizon but couldn't detect any signs of life, ghostly or corporeal. Nor did the sound repeat itself. I told myself it must have been a wandering deer or a squirrel searching for nuts for his winter trove.

Vivian's breathing quickened so much I feared she might hyperventilate. Mom went to her side and took her arm. Vivian's eyes skittered to George's grave.

"Please, Georgie." Her voice quavered. "Help me remember."

Her eyes darted around the cemetery, as if she expected a response. After a moment's stillness, she wrenched out of my mother's grasp and dropped hard to her knees, burying her face in her hands. "He's not here. I sensed his presence for a moment, but no longer. And the memories have flittered out of reach."

Tears streaked Mom's cheeks, and Dad put an arm around her. Woody whined. Carl issued a mournful yowl. The humans remained silent, our hands clasped in front of us. All we could do was be with Vivian in her grief.

Then Cedric knelt beside her and rested a gnarled hand on her shoulder.

That's when my own tears began to fall.

Chapter Thirty-Five

Once we all composed ourselves, we walked back to the parking lot in silence. Cedric looked on as Dad opened car doors for Vivian and Mom. Then Dad got behind the wheel and drove off, tires crunching on the gravel.

I turned to thank Cedric for his kindness to Vivian, but he was already trudging toward his cottage. He climbed the porch steps, crossed his arms, and scowled at me.

So much for the salve of human spirit. I'd gotten a glimpse of the good heart hiding beneath Mr. Fallow's gruff veneer, but it might be the only time I'd ever see it.

By the time I arrived at my parents' condo, Mom had taken Vivian upstairs. Dad poured me a Diet Coke. "She's wrung out," he said. "Vivian, that is. Though I imagine your mother is, too."

"And you. You don't talk about it, but I know this must be hard on you, Dad."

He grabbed a bottle of water from the refrigerator and unscrewed the top. His expression was inscrutable as he gazed out the window. Finally, his eyes met mine.

"That poor woman, everything she's going through...I just wish I could help her. If only I knew what had happened. If only I had memories to offer her..." I didn't think I'd ever seen my father so distraught.

Mom came downstairs, took one look at my father, and walked straight into his arms. "Butch, you must stop beating yourself up. You did everything possible."

"My head knows you're right," he said. "But my heart..."

"Well, your heart, good one though it is, needs to butt out right now. Let your head take the lead on this."

Dad kissed her on the cheek and looked at me. "What would we do without this woman?"

I lifted my glass. "May we never have to find out."

Mom told us Vivian was asleep, courtesy of an Ambien the doctor had prescribed. Then she began flitting around the kitchen, whipping up dinner while Dad and I deliberated over the noise we'd heard at the cemetery—the one Vivian had attributed to George's ghost.

"Must have been a deer," I said.

"Could have been, I suppose." He didn't look convinced.

"You're not suggesting you believe in ghosts?"

He chuckled. "Well, Sundance, just because you can't see something..." Then he turned serious. "A ghost wouldn't be highest on my list. It occurred to me someone might have been watching. I was thinking about you seeing Pinky in the Knotty Pine lot the other night, and —"

The jangle of my phone interrupted him. A glance at

the screen showed it was Monika. I raised a "hold that thought" finger and answered.

"What's up?" I asked.

"I have something," she said breathlessly. "A photo you need to see."

"Text it to me."

She huffed. "No way. I want to be there when you see it. Callie, this shouldn't wait."

The urgency of her tone grabbed my attention. I told her I was at my parents' house, and she agreed to come to us. When we hung up, I repeated the conversation to my parents.

"Huh." Dad responded coolly, but his expression betrayed his curiosity.

Mom's eyes sparked, too. "I hope she'll stay for dinner. I have plenty."

A few minutes later, I met Monika in the lobby. She wouldn't give me any hints, but her eyes danced, and her cheeks flushed with adrenaline. She was a reporter through and through. How I remembered that feeling. In fact, I was reliving it now.

Upstairs, Woody greeted Monika with enthusiasm, and Carl stared at her with intensity. Dad took her coat, while Mom poured her a glass of sparkling water. All the while, my impatience swelled. "This isn't a social call," I muttered.

"Now, Callie, Monika's information won't self-destruct because we take the time to be gracious," Mom said.

I blew out a breath, relieved when we finally settled around the dining table. Woody positioned himself next to my mother's knee, hoping for another treat. Carl leapt into her lap and planted his front paws on the table, eager for the big reveal.

Monika wrenched her laptop from her satchel and booted it up. "I finally got my hands on Jack Murray's trial records. Nothing new jumped out at me. The name of the principal witness was redacted. Much as I'd like to know who it was, that level of hacking is above my skill set."

Hmm. Perhaps it was information at Mrs. Finney's disposal, though I doubted the findings would hold much importance.

"Anyway," Monika continued, "I've spent the last couple of hours trying to organize everything I've learned about the Murray family. Did you know they ran with the Rat Pack back in the fifties?" She turned to me. "That's Frank Sinatra, Sammy Davis, Jr., Dean Martin, and...a couple of other old guys whose names escape me."

"I know the Rat Pack," I said. "Surely this isn't the ground-breaking news you've come here to share."

She tapped away at the keyboard, ignoring my agitation. The young reporter had been starstruck when she first met me. She said I'd been one of her heroes through her high school and college years. But after the case we'd investigated together last year, that hero worship had segued into collegiality. Now, the two of us interacted as peers rather than the seasoned veteran training the young pup. I appreciated the growth in our relationship—mostly. Sometimes, though, I wished she' just obey me without question.

After a few more taps, she lifted her eyes. A devilish smile played on her lips. Her pleasure in the dramatic pause reminded me of Tonya, who had mastered the technique.

"Can we get on with it?" I urged.

"Patience," Monika said. "We've talked about these people before, but this photo clarifies everything."

She turned the screen to us and watched expectantly. I leaned in to view what appeared to be a family photo—one that would have been well-placed in the Corwins' seventies-themed home. Men clad in gray, single-breasted sharkskin suits with oversized collars and wide ties. Boys wearing knit polos with thick, colorful vertical stripes. Women sporting knee-high white leather boots and pastel dresses with plunging necklines. Girls in pantsuits covered in bright, concentric circles. They looked like a cross between the Sopranos and the Brady Bunch.

Monika began pointing, using a professorial tone as she spoke. "These are the offspring of Joseph Murray, the family's original patriarch, who died long before this photo was taken. Joseph started out as street muscle for Benny Binion, then climbed the ranks to become Benny's top aide. When Benny went to jail for tax evasion, Joseph branched off, with Benny's blessing, and carved out his own side hustle. It didn't compare in size and scope to the major crime families, but he did okay. More than okay."

She leaned over the computer and pointed to a man sitting in a wing-back chair. A gorgeous woman stood at his shoulder and two young adults sat at his feet. "This is Jack Murray. When Joseph died in 1964, Jack became the family's leader. He's pictured here with his wife and two sons, Amos, who was born in 1964 and died of a drug overdose in 1990, and Thomas, four years younger."

My eyebrows lifted. "Tommy Murray."

Monika looked pleased, like a teacher whose student had just grasped a difficult concept. Then she put her finger on the man in an adjacent chair. "Here's Jack's brother, Donovan. He's ten years younger than Jack, a brother from another mother. When Jack went to prison in 1984, Donovan took over the family business—at least, ostensibly. People speculated that Jack continued to pull the strings from behind bars until he died in 2015. Donovan is eighty now and reportedly in poor health."

She paused for a sip of water, then pointed to the two girls sitting on stools at Donovan's feet. "Donovan's daughters, Paloma and Trish. Both married wealthy men and have no interest in the family business. They have a half-brother, Don's son with a much younger wife, neither of whom are pictured in this photo. But..." She turned the laptop around, clicked a couple of keys, then swiveled it back to us.

She'd minimized the family photo and overlaid a shot of an older Donovan, circa 2000, with his arm draped across the shoulders of a teenage boy. "Here you go. Eugene Murray."

It wasn't much of a surprise. I'd already deduced where Monika's story was taking us. "And unlike his half-sisters," I said, "Gene had an interest in the family business. In fact, he aspired to run it when dear old daddy passed."

"Exactly," Monika said. "But there was a fly in the ointment." She pointed back to Tommy. "As Jack's son, Cousin Tommy believed the mantle should rightfully be his."

Thoughts began pinballing in my brain. A family feud. Rivalry for power. I whistled. "This information points to Tommy as the prime suspect in Gene's murder."

Dad clucked his tongue. "Now, Sundance, let's not get ahead of ourselves." But I thought he believed it, too. After all, the theory made total sense. Family in-fighting, eliminating the competitor for the top job—all the elements of a cheesy made-for-TV movie.

Carl squirmed in my mother's lap, meowed, and reached a paw out to swipe at the computer screen.

"Carl," I scolded, reaching for him.

Mom held up her hand. "Just a minute, darling. I think he's trying to tell us something."

She pulled the laptop closer and enlarged the family

photo. After studying it for a moment, she pointed at the young woman seated near Donovan but slightly apart, as if she were part of the family but not quite. The woman's face was angled away from the camera, like someone out of view had distracted her. "You haven't mentioned her," Mom said.

Monika shrugged. "Valerie Murray, Joseph Murray's illegitimate daughter from a fling with a Vegas showgirl. Eighteen years younger than her half-brother Jack and eight years younger than half-brother Donovan. I haven't been able to uncover much info about her. She's managed to stay out of the public eye."

"Well, she's reappeared," Mom said.

Mom watched as Dad bent toward the screen. Recognition flickered across his face. "It can't be."

"It is," Mom said. "I'd bet my last dollar on it."

Monika rounded the table and peered over Mom's shoulder, scrunching up her face. "I don't get it. Who are we talking about?"

I squinted and studied Valerie Murray's face. She seemed familiar somehow, but...Then it came to me. My heart beat furiously. "Oh, my," I muttered.

Monika put her hands on her hips. "What are you all seeing that I'm not?"

"Valerie Murray is upstairs in my parents' guest room," I said. "But we all know her as Vivian Corwin."

Chapter Thirty-Six

We were quiet as we processed the news. Vivian Corwin was Valerie Murray, half-sister to Jack and Donovan? Eugene and Tommy's aunt?

The ramifications exploded like fireworks, and all at once we were talking at lightning speed.

"How did I miss that?" Monika muttered.

"I missed it, too," I said. "But Vivian's dual identity raises so many new questions. Like, has Vivian been holed up with her crime family in Vegas all these years?"

"I can't believe that," Dad said. "She loved George. That much was obvious when we visited his house and his grave. She wouldn't have left him for the Murrays."

"All right, then, what made her come to Rock Creek Village in the first place?" I mused. "Forty years ago, I mean. Under an assumed name..."

Monika tapped a finger on her chin. "Callie, you say Tommy should be the prime suspect in Gene's murder now. But doesn't this revelation move Vivian—Valerie—to the top of the list? She might've—"

Mom slapped her hand on the table, startling us into silence. "Hush, all of you," she said in a stern whisper. "I don't understand everything that's going on here, but one thing I do know. That woman sleeping upstairs has been through a trauma these past few days, both physical and emotional. I do not want her disturbed. If you can't keep your voices down, I'll thank you to take this conversation elsewhere."

Monika clamped her mouth shut, chastised, as did Dad and I. Silently, I ran my thoughts across the events of the past few days. An unwelcome idea tugged at the corners of my mind. Could Vivian's amnesia be an act? Could her supposed trauma be the machinations of a gifted actress? I'd briefly entertained that idea at one point and abandoned it. My parents knew her from the past and trusted her. But considering what we now knew, was that trust misplaced?

I stared at Vivian/Valerie on the screen and flashed to an image of her clutching her treasured glass parrot. The expression of grief as she looked at the wedding photo on the nightstand. The heart wrenching sobs as she lay on the bed she'd shared with her husband. I shook my head. No, I just didn't believe it was all an act. I considered myself a good judge of character, a trait I'd inherited from my parents. Vivian couldn't have duped all three of us. Right?

I sighed. One thing was certain—we needed to let the police in on this news.

My father had already reached the same conclusion. He picked up his cell phone. "I'm calling Frank."

CHIEF LARAMIE ARRIVED fifteen minutes later, accompanied by Raul and Lynn. We gathered in the living room as Mom laid out coffee and a plate of snickerdoodles. Frank gave Mom a mock salute. "Maggie, you always manage to make unpleasant business more palatable."

She smiled as he bit into a cookie. A moment later, we were all nibbling and sipping—except Raul. "Didn't realize we were here for a tea party," he grumbled.

"Coffee," I said.

"What?"

I lifted my cup. "You said tea party, but this is coffee. As a detective, I'm sure you want to keep your facts straight."

He glowered at me, then turned to Monika. "Let's see this picture that has everyone all worked up."

Mom held up her hand. "Before we get started, I want to caution you all to keep your voices down. I checked on Vivian a few minutes ago, and she's still sleeping soundly. But I'm warning you, I don't want that sleep disturbed. Does everyone understand?"

We all nodded obediently, as if we were a classroom full of Mom's students. Monika passed her laptop to Raul, who sat on the couch between Lynn and Frank. The three of them studied the image on the screen. Raul was skeptical. "You're sure that's her? It's not the best angle."

"It's her," Mom said. "Remember, I knew her forty years ago, back when she looked like this younger version. I'm sure. Valerie Murray and Vivian Corwin are one and the same."

Frank reached into his pocket, pulled out a creased piece of paper, and smoothed it out on the coffee table. We leaned in to see a yellowed flyer displaying a smiling thirty-something Vivian Corwin. Above her photo screamed the word MISSING in bold capital letters, followed by a number to call with information.

If there'd been any doubt, the flyer put it to rest. The

woman in the family photo on Monika's screen, the one on the piece of paper, and the one sleeping upstairs in my parents' guest room were the same person.

"All right, that's settled." Raul looked at Monika and lifted his chin to her laptop. "Can you forward us copies of those photos?"

She pulled her computer across the coffee table and clicked a few keys. "Done."

Raul checked his phone for the documents. "Thank you for bringing this to our attention, Ms. Schiff. We'll be in touch when we have information to release to the press."

It was a thinly veiled attempt to dismiss her, and I couldn't wait to see how she handled it.

She pursed her lips and locked eyes with Raul. "I'd prefer to stay. As you said, I uncovered the information. I'd like to see how this plays out."

Mom glanced at me and sighed. I knew what was going through her head. *Just like Callie.* She'd mentioned more than once that Monika's attitude was a carbon copy of mine at that stage of my career.

"How about a compromise?" Frank said. "Monika can stay if she agrees that everything she hears is off the record until she's told otherwise."

Raul hesitated, his mouth set in resistance. When Frank crossed his arms, Raul acquiesced, but he leveled a stern look Monika's direction. "Nothing in the paper. Nothing online. Not a word to anyone. Not until we give you the go ahead."

She nodded her acceptance of his terms. With that matter settled, I leaned back and watched Raul as the wheels spun in his head. "Do you all believe Vivian's claim that she doesn't recall the events at the cemetery?" he asked.

"I do," Dad said. Mom said she also believed Vivian.

For the most part, I did, too, but a flicker of doubt must have crossed my face. From the corner of his eye, Raul caught the expression. He let it go—for the moment.

"And she still has no memory of her past life?" he asked.

"The trip to George's house triggered memories of their life together," Mom said. "But when we went to the cemetery yesterday hoping to retrieve even more, it turned out to be a lost cause."

Frank leaned his elbows on his knees. "Here's what I'm wondering. When Vivian left Rock Creek Village, did she return to Las Vegas? Has she been there with the Murray family this entire time?" He'd echoed another of my earlier questions, one that Dad had quickly shot down.

My father shifted in his seat as we all considered Frank's question. "It's a possibility," Raul said. "Something we need to follow up on. When she heard the news of Corwin's death, she might have experienced a rush of nostalgia and felt the need to visit his grave. If that's the case, and Gene was already in town with Lydia, the family might've sent word to him to trail her."

Lynn tapped her pen against her notebook. "There's no way around it—we need to interview Vivian."

Mom bristled at the suggestion. "I don't think that's a good idea. Dumping this information on her might undermine her recovery—and to what end? She can't remember anything anyway."

"According to her," Lynn said. "All we have is her word for that."

"And the doctor's word," Mom said, trying to keep her temper in check. "In his expert medical opinion, Vivian is suffering from amnesia."

Lynn didn't respond to that. None of us did. Everyone's gaze lingered on Frank. The decision rested with him as Chief of Police. He took a moment to weigh both arguments, then turned to my parents. "This is a murder investigation. Like it or not, Vivian is deeply involved. We have to talk to her. You'd say the same in my position, Butch."

Mom opened her mouth to object, but Dad turned to her and looked her in the eye. "He's right, Maggie. Much as we want to protect Vivian, we can't let our personal feelings interfere with a police investigation."

For a moment, I thought Mom was going to argue. Then I thought she might cry. But she did neither. She merely responded with a terse nod.

Frank watched her sympathetically. "We don't have to do it tonight. We can wait a day. Give you time to consult her doctor and get some guidance on the safest way to handle the interview."

"That'll work," Dad said.

"Let me stress this again," Frank said. "Do not allow Vivian to leave the premises. And keep an eye out for Tommy."

My eyebrows shot up. I hadn't even entertained the thought that Tommy might pose an imminent threat to Vivian, and by extension, my parents. It made sense, though. If Vivian/Valerie's currently inaccessible memory contained damaging information on the family's dealings, past or present, they'd want her dealt with before she could recall any details.

It was another worry to add to my growing list. I was beginning to think we should arrange for alternate accommodations for Vivian. Mom and Dad wouldn't react well to the suggestion, but—

Dad's phone rang. He looked at the screen and answered. "Hey, Sid, we're right in the middle—"

My father stopped talking and frowned as he listened. "All right. Keep him in the lobby. We'll be right down."

He hung up. We sat on the edges of our seats. "That was Sid Farmington at the front desk. Michael Pinkerton is in the lobby. Says he needs to talk to us. All of us. And he emphasized that it's urgent."

Chapter Thirty-Seven

Although we'd be just downstairs, Mom didn't want Vivian alone in the condo in case she woke up, so she stayed behind, with the caveat that we'd keep her posted.

The rest of us trekked to the lobby, where we found Pinky pacing near the floor-to-ceiling windows overlooking Mt. O'Connell.

Mr. Farmington came from behind the registration desk to meet us. "Sorry to interrupt your meeting, Butch, but this seemed important."

"Thanks, Sid. You did the right thing." He scanned the Great Room, void of guests, and gestured to a seating arrangement near the spot where Pinky stood facing us. "We'll be over there. If any guests come to the lobby..."

"I'll use my charming powers of persuasion to direct them to a different part of the room," Mr. Farmington said.

The six of us headed Pinky's direction. I'd never seen him looking so haggard. He was an older man, but always so robust. Now, his face was drawn, and his eyes carried a weighty sadness. And something else...another emotion I couldn't immediately pinpoint. When Pinky swiveled to meet my gaze, I deciphered it. Fear.

We all took seats near the fireplace. Dad said, "All right, Michael. You have our attention. What's the emergency?"

Pinky pointed a finger at Monika. "What's the press doing here?"

Raul sighed, probably asking himself the same question. "She's agreed to keep everything off the record," he said.

Lynn pursed her lips and stared at Pinky. "If you're here to confess again, you're wasting your time and ours," she said. "We already confirmed you were nowhere near the cemetery."

"I'm not here to confess," Pinky said. "I'm here to find out what you think you know."

A crimson hue edged up Raul's neck. I braced myself. I'd seen that happen before—it meant his temper teetered on the verge of eruption. Then he closed his eyes. His lips moved as he counted to ten.

Seconds later, his eyes were clear and his voice calm but firm. "Mr. Pinkerton, we're in the business of gathering information, not sharing it. I'd advise you to stop playing games and tell us why you're here."

Pinky wrung his hands. Then he turned his attention to Dad and Frank.

"The two of you spent a long time looking for Vivian Corwin. I'm guessing you just learned this, but in case I'm wrong..." He took a deep breath. "I'm telling you now that Vivian Corwin was once Valerie Murray, half-sister to Jack and Donovan Murray."

Dad's jaw tightened. Frank frowned. "How did you...?"

"I've been watching," Pinky said gruffly.

My eyes widened as I remembered seeing Pinky parked in the resort lot the other day. Then the black truck following Mom's Jeep as we left George's house. Pinky had been conducting surveillance.

He glanced at Monika. "I knew it wouldn't remain a secret much longer. When the reporter showed up here tonight, I figured she'd put it all together. If she hadn't, Mrs. Finney's sources would've. Or Vivian would recover her memory and spill it all. It was time to come clean."

Everyone remained silent. I squirmed in my seat. I had so many questions, but surrounded as I was by professionals, I thought it wise to defer to them.

Luckily for me, Raul took over. "Mr. Pinkerton, my partner and I have tried to look into your background—"

"Me, too," Monika interrupted. "And Mrs. Finney. Even she couldn't find—"

Raul glared at her, and she snapped her mouth shut. The detective turned back to Pinky. "For you to know about Vivian Corwin's true identity, you must have had access to insider information. Combine that with your non-existent history, and I'm led to believe you have a past that somehow figures into everything that's happened here. I suggest you tell us about it."

A few seconds ticked by. Raul leaned forward and clasped his hands, his eyes never leaving the man's face. Pinky exhaled. "Vivian isn't the only person in Rock Creek Village who has lived under an alias. Before I became Michael Pinkerton, I was Robert Placke. U.S. Marshal Robert Placke."

By this time, his revelation didn't come as a total shock. But it did help the pieces start falling into place. One of the Marshals Service's primary responsibilities involved helping people disappear. I was developing a hazy image of what must have happened and of the link between Pinky and Vivian, but I had yet to grasp the details.

Frank fixed his gaze on Pinky. "We know Valerie Murray was the daughter of one crime boss and the sister of another," he said. "She showed up in Rock Creek Village forty years ago under an assumed identity. I'm guessing you had something to do with that?"

After a brief pause, Pinky nodded. "Remember back in the eighties when the government indicted Jack Murray on racketeering and extortion charges?"

"Vaguely," Frank said. "I read about it in the newspaper, but I didn't pay much attention. Seemed like one crime family or another faced indictment on a weekly basis back then."

"This one ended up being a long trial with dozens of witnesses," Pinky said. "Ultimately, the jury sentenced Jack Murray to forty years. He was fifty at the time, so it essentially meant life in prison. You may have heard he died ten years ago. Thing is, one of the state's key witnesses in his trial, the one most people say secured his conviction, was..."

At that moment, it all clicked together in my mind. I leaned forward, waiting for Pinky to confirm my conclusion.

"...his half-sister, Valerie."

FOR THE NEXT HALF HOUR, Pinky wove a tale of greed, corruption, and family dysfunction. The Feds had been building a case against the Murray family for at least a decade when they finally persuaded Valerie to turn state's evidence against her oldest brother. Valerie, who hadn't yet turned thirty, worked in the family business as a low-level bookkeeper, apparently nursing no ambition to rise in the ranks. Still, she understood enough of the inner workings to serve as an essential cog in the government's case against Jack. The Feds used the stick-and-carrot strategy on her, threatening significant jail time if she didn't cooperate, while promising a new identity if she testified. Still, she'd demurred—until the state's attorney threw in immunity for her beloved half-brother Donovan. That had sealed the deal.

Enter Pinky, aka Robert Placke. As Valerie's handler, he kept her secure throughout the trial and oversaw her relocation after Jack's sentencing. Robert had offered Valerie three choices of location, and she'd picked Rock Creek Village, Colorado. She packed the few things the service permitted her to take and disappeared into the night, unable to reveal her destination to anyone, even her mother.

"I was only supposed to be in the village a few months," Pinky said. "Just long enough to make sure Valerie was settled and safe. As a front, I took a job at The Village Grocery." His eyes clouded as he focused on the past, on a life forgotten and repurposed.

"Three months passed. Donovan took the reins of the family business, vowing to give up all illegal activities and go clean."

Lynn sniffed. "A vow he didn't keep."

"To be honest, I believe he intended to. He adored Valerie and was deeply touched by the sacrifice she made on his behalf. But once you're in, it's hard to get out, especially when the money dries up."

"I'm sure it's a terrible burden," Monika said with sarcasm.

Pinky ignored the comment. "Eventually, the U.S. Marshals wanted me back in the rotation. Always someone new requiring relocation. But being here in the village made me realize how burned out I'd become. I no longer wanted a Marshal's life. I enjoyed life as Michael Pinkerton more than I ever liked being Robert Placke. So I quit. I used the new identity the service had given me and bought the grocery store. Put down roots."

I quirked an eyebrow. I suspected his motivation went deeper than burnout.

"Long story short," he continued, "Valerie became Vivian. She took a job as an administrative assistant in George Corwin's accounting business. Six months later, they were married."

And there it was. The quake in his voice revealed his longing. Pinky had fallen in love with Valerie, and if I was right, he'd carried that torch for forty years.

"Was George aware of Vivian's past?" Dad asked.

"He never was," Pinky replied. "Not during the marriage, not after Vivian left. The hardest thing I ever had to do was keep mum. Watching him suffer that way..."

He shuddered, then locked eyes with my father. A wave of emotion—and mutual understanding—passed between them.

But the story remained unfinished, and Raul wasn't the patient type. "I get the witness protection angle and the relocation. But why did Vivian later disappear from Rock Creek Village? Did the Murrays catch up to her?"

Pinky sighed. "She messed up. You see, Valerie and her mother were very close. Entering WITSEC meant Valerie could never see her mother again, or even speak to her. A year after Valerie's wedding, she began fixating on the idea that her mother would never know about her life in Rock Creek Village, her marriage to George. It ate away at her."

I thought of my own mother and imagined the enormity of never again being able to contact the woman I loved most in the world. "Poor Vivian," I said. "She ended up reaching out to her mom, didn't she?"

Pinky nodded. "She was smart enough not to call from Rock Creek Village. She drove to Denver and spoke to her mother on the phone for less than fifteen minutes. Then she had an attack of conscience and told me about the call. Much as I hated to do it, I had to inform the Marshals Service. If the Murrays had tapped her mother's phone—which was a distinct possibility—the call might have divulged the parameters of Valerie's location and compromised her safety. Though the call was short enough that the Murrays couldn't have pinpointed the exact town, it was too much of a risk."

I puffed my cheeks. "It's hard to believe Donovan would allow the family to take those measures after what Valerie had done for him."

Pinky shrugged. "Donovan likely served as the family's leader in name only. We always believed Jack continued running the business from his prison cell, though he was too wily to get caught. At any rate, Valerie needed to be moved, but she refused to go. Even though I no longer worked for them, the Marshals Service contracted with me to persuade her, which I did. I convinced her it wasn't only about her—George would be in danger, too. That did the trick. She loved him. She wouldn't risk his safety."

"Why didn't George go, too?" Monika asked. "WITSEC relocates families, right?"

"Valerie wouldn't even consider that option. With George's disability, she feared a move could compromise his health. Besides, all his doctors were nearby. His home was set up to accommodate his wheelchair and all his other needs. His business was here. And she worried that his disability might make it harder to change his identity. She refused to risk his safety."

I thought of the house we'd visited yesterday, stuck in the vortex of the seventies. When Vivian left, George never changed a thing.

Pinky brushed a hand across his scalp. "I've never seen anyone in such pain. But she believed it would be easiest for George if she just left. She wrote him a simple note." He pried his wallet from his back pocket, opened it, and retrieved a well-worn piece of paper. Unfolding it, he read aloud. "*I'm sorry, but I have to go. Someday, I hope you can forgive me.*"

"You have her note?" Lynn asked.

"I was with her when she packed up and left," Pinky said. "As a Marshal, I knew the protocol. She shouldn't— couldn't—leave a note. I slipped it into my wallet without telling her. George never saw it."

And Pinky had carried it with him ever since, a testimony to his love and guilt. What a tragic story, from all angles.

"Where did Valerie—Vivian—go?" Raul asked.

"The service wouldn't divulge that information to me," Pinky said. "Once I convinced her to leave Rock Creek Village, they terminated my role and engaged in no further communication."

"Did she ever contact you?" Lynn asked. "Or George?"

"Never. The fiasco with her mother convinced her it wouldn't be wise. She was determined to follow the rules this time, without exception. But when George died..."

"The rules no longer mattered," I finished.

We sat quietly for a moment, contemplating Pinky's story, until Raul broke the silence. "When did you realize Vivian had returned to the village?"

Pinky rolled his shoulders as his mind returned to the present. "Cedric Fallow came to the store soon after the... incident at the cemetery. The old gossip asked me if I'd heard Vivian Corwin was back. He said she'd been injured and taken to the hospital, and that Eugene Murray was dead. I shooed him out the door, told my assistant manager to take over, and drove to Pine Haven like a bat out of hell."

"Why did you confess to Gene's murder?" Lynn asked. "At that point, you didn't even know it was a homicide."

Pinky snorted. "Well, it wasn't exactly logical to think the man stumbled into the cemetery and died of a heart attack. I knew you'd eventually figure out who Vivian had once been. Then you'd jump to the inevitable conclusion —that she killed Gene. After all, she was the only person in the cemetery at the time of his death—"

"Not necessarily," I cut in. Everyone looked at me. "Who says Tommy didn't arrive in town earlier than we knew? Or any of Vivian's other nieces or nephews? Or her brother Donovan, for that matter? And what about Murray family enemies who might have been trailing Gene? Just because we didn't see anyone else doesn't necessarily mean no one was there."

Pinky narrowed his eyes. "That may be. But the most logical explanation points to Vivian. George dies. Viv appears at his grave, sustaining an injury that supposedly results in amnesia, a diagnosis I'm sure has elicited a measure of skepticism. Her nephew lies dead beside the grave. If I were still on the job, I'd jump to the same conclusion."

His gaze swept across each of us. "But I can tell you unequivocally that Vivian did not kill Gene. It isn't possible."

Raul crossed his arms, unimpressed. "How can you be so sure? And don't tell us again that you did it."

Pinky got to his feet, eyes blazing. "Young man, I was a trained U.S. Marshal before you were a glimmer in your mother's eye. I'm smart, skilled, and intuitive. But more than that, I know Valerie—what she's capable of, and what she's not."

I wanted to point out that Pinky hadn't known Valerie/Vivian for forty years. That people could, and did, change. That time might not have healed her wounds. That, in fact, those wounds may have festered. That seeing Gene in the cemetery may have ripped open her scars.

Maybe George's death triggered a latent rage that had been simmering inside her since she testified against her brother.

But one glance at Pinky assured me this wasn't the time to wax philosophical. Right now, the man appeared capable of inflicting serious damage, and I didn't seek any scars of my own.

I searched the group for the warrior willing to break the impasse. But just then, my phone rang, allaying the tension.

"Sorry," I muttered. I silenced the phone and took a quick peek at the screen. Tonya. I let the call go to voicemail.

A few seconds later, she sent a text. *9-1-1*.

My heart rate notched up. Though my friend possessed a dramatic streak, she rarely veered into the territory of melodrama. She would not send such a distress signal lightly.

"Sorry. I have to take this."

I stood up and stepped away from the group, touching Tonya's number on speed dial. She picked up at once and didn't even give me a chance to speak.

"Callie," she said, her voice distraught. "Lydia's missing."

Chapter Thirty-Eight

I'd rarely heard that level of alarm in my best friend's voice. Not that Tonya was unemotional, not by any means. She displayed frustration, sure. Anger, occasionally. Love, frequently. But my friend was not typically prey to fear. I didn't hesitate in my response.

"I'm on my way."

I summarized the call for the group, then ran upstairs to grab my bag. After informing Mom of Lydia's disappearance, I hurried back to the lobby. Raul and Frank said they'd be right behind me as soon as they settled things here. Lynn would take Pinky to the police station for a formal statement, despite his ardent objections that he needed to stay near Vivian/Valerie. "Tommy Murray is in town," he said, panic edging into his voice.

"I'm staying put," Dad said. "No one will get past me, Michael, I assure you. We'll lock the lobby doors, and I'll instruct Sid not to let anyone but guests inside—we don't have but a few of those right now anyway. The condo door will stay bolted. Sid and I will monitor the security cameras."

Lynn nodded. "I'll assign duty officers to drive by on a regular basis."

Frank put a hand on Pinky's shoulder. "She's well protected. There's nothing you could do here that isn't being done."

Pinky hesitated, his fingers curling and uncurling at his sides. Then he looked at Dad. "You'll keep me in the loop?"

"Absolutely."

Monika caught my eye and lifted her palms in a *what-should-I-do* motion. "I don't think you should go to Tonya's," I said. "This is hard enough for her without having to navigate the dual role of daughter and boss."

I braced myself for her objection, but she nodded. "Call me later?"

"As soon as I can."

IN UNDER TEN MINUTES, I parked at the curb of Tonya's house and charged up the sidewalk, carrying Carl while Woody scampered at my heels. The door swung open, and David stood before me, his face pinched. He escorted me inside and spoke in a low voice.

"Thank you for coming, *amica mia*. I've never seen her this way. She's...how do you say?...beside herself."

"Where is she?"

He gestured to the guest room, and I hurried down the hall, where I found Tonya sitting on the bed, looking dazed. Rivulets of mascara lined her cheeks like tattoos, and strands of hair escaped her low bun. Even her signature red lipstick was smeared. Worry oozed off her like an oil slick.

Woody laid his head beside her knee. Carl paced the

perimeter of the room, sniffing Lydia's belongings. I sat next to Tonya and put an arm around her. She rested her head on my shoulder.

"You know I've always had a rocky relationship with my mother," she said, her voice husky. "But I love her. And I'm scared she's..."

I gave her a squeeze. "Breathe, girlfriend. Pretend I'm Summer, guiding you in a meditation session. Just close your eyes and breathe."

She did as instructed. A minute later, she'd calmed visibly. Footsteps came down the hallway. Tonya sat up straight and swiped her palms across her cheeks as Raul and Frank hustled into the room, with David right behind them.

"Callie tells us Lydia's gone AWOL," Frank said, his eyes sweeping the room.

Tonya swallowed her anxiety and replaced it with stoicism. "I last saw her early this morning. When I got home from work this afternoon, she was nowhere to be found. I tried calling her and discovered her phone ringing in here." She pointed to a cell on the nightstand. "Her purse is gone, but not much else. She didn't pack a suitcase. Didn't take any toiletries or clothes—not even her favorite stilettos. Worse, she left her makeup bag in the bathroom."

No makeup? No zebra-patterned red high heels? This might truly be serious.

"What about her car?" Raul asked.

Tonya shook her head. "They came to the village in Gene's Lincoln, which is in the driveway behind the house. The keys are hanging on the hook by the front door." She clasped her hands in her lap. "My fear is that Tommy Murray kidnapped her. Or worse..."

I pulled her close. "Don't let yourself go there, Tonya."

"Why would he take her?" Raul asked. I shot him a look. Couldn't he see she needed a minute? He caught my annoyance and responded with a clenched jaw. I tilted my head in acquiescence. He was right, of course. If Lydia was in danger, time was of the essence.

I locked eyes with my best friend. "Is there something specific causing you to think that?"

"It's the only explanation I can come up with. Remember the expression on Lydia's face the other night when Tommy followed her into the house? At the time, I assumed she was irritated, but now I'm convinced she was scared. Maybe Tommy believes she killed Gene. Or the family might have dispatched him to bring her in for a...I don't know...a reckoning."

Raul pursed his lips, thinking. "Do you have security cameras that might have captured your mother leaving?"

David hung his head. "I've been meaning to install a system. Never got around to it."

Tonya looked up at him. "Neither of us considered it a priority. Our neighborhood is safe. At least, it used to be..."

Frank rubbed his chin as he devised a plan of action. "Detective Sanchez and I will head back to the station to get a search in motion, starting with a county-wide BOLO for Tommy Murray's car. We've been keeping an eye out for him locally, but it's time to expand the hunt. And we'll send officers door to door around your block. Hopefully, one of your neighbors has a camera that recorded something useful."

We walked Frank and Raul to the front door. When they'd left, David poured wine, and we settled onto the living room couches. A fire crackled in the fireplace, cocooning us in warmth. Woody stretched full length along the hearth, and Carl curled up in my lap. It was such a cozy tableau—almost as if we'd gathered for a friendly chat rather than another crisis.

Tonya began to rant. "Leave it to Lydia to cause all this turmoil. She's probably not in danger at all. You know how she likes to traipse off on escape trips when anything goes wrong in her life. She'll turn up on a cruise ship in the Caribbean, sipping mai tais and courting her next boyfriend."

I wasn't a psychologist, but even I understood what was happening here. My friend was forcing herself into emotional self-protection mode. I'd made that same journey a hundred times. Fear and worry felt too vulnerable, too weak. Anger made us feel powerful and strong. Tonya didn't believe what she was saying, not deep down inside. But I wouldn't call her on it. This coping mechanism wasn't a bad thing, not if it helped her get through the night.

The ring of Tonya's cell startled her, and she nearly spilled her wine. She snatched up her phone and stared at the screen. "Unknown caller." She answered, pressing speaker so David and I could hear.

Lydia's voice trilled across the line. "You must be concerned, darling, but never fear. Mommy is safe and sound. We bought *burner* phones. Can you believe it? Turns out I'm quite adept at this cloak-and-dagger business. It's like I'm the star of a gangster movie."

"We?" Tonya's voice hit a high pitch. "Who are you with, Lydia?"

"You don't know him, darling, but rest assured, he'll keep me safe."

Traffic whooshed by in the background. Tonya's lips were tight. "Lydia, if you left willingly, why didn't you pack a bag? Take your things?"

"Well, I left my phone behind for obvious reasons.

Wouldn't want anyone tracing my whereabouts, now, would I? As for the clothing and the rest, I just figured a girl should have a whole new wardrobe when she goes on the lam."

Lydia tittered, and Tonya squeezed her eyes shut. Was she taking a lesson from Raul and counting to ten? "We've been worried, Lydia. You need to come back. Everyone is looking for you."

"That's why I left, sweetheart. I don't want anyone to find me." Her tone said, *duh*.

"The police will keep you safe," Tonya said.

"The only way to ensure my safety—and yours, too, sweetheart—is for me to stay a step ahead of Gene's family." Her voice turned serious. "The Murrays are not to be trifled with, Tonya. Some of them think I killed Gene."

"Did you?" Tonya asked.

Her blunt question took me by surprise. "Of course not," Lydia responded, sounding insulted. "How can you ask such a question? I don't have a violent bone in my body."

Tonya looked at me helplessly, and I responded with a shrug. I figured there was nothing Tonya could say to persuade her mother to return. Lydia had always done whatever she pleased. And to be honest, her plan didn't seem like such a bad idea. If the Murrays were after her, she'd be leading them away from the village. Taking one for the team, so to speak.

Over the phone, we heard a car horn blast. "I'm going to hang up now," Lydia said. "From what I've learned watching *Law and Order*, even burner phones can be traced if a person stays on too long. Don't try to find me, and don't worry. As I said, I'm with a friend. And I have plenty of money with which to subsidize my travels. I'll be in touch, sweetheart. Mommy loves you."

"But Lydia—"

Lydia disconnected, and the three of us stared at each other in astonishment. Woody's ears perked, and he trotted across the entry hall just before the doorbell rang. David stood up and glanced at Tonya. "I imagine that's the officers Frank said he'd be sending. Are you up to talking with them?"

Tonya issued a sarcastic snort. "Sure, why not? In fact, let's invite the neighbors. Everyone should know what a lunatic my mother is. Perhaps I'll publish a story in the *Gazette*. 'Editor's mother on the lam to escape dead boyfriend's crime family.' Geez." She gave me a look. "Back in high school, you used to complain that your parents were boring. Count your blessings, sugarplum. What I wouldn't give for a little boredom right now."

David appeared shell-shocked. "Okay, but about the police at the door..."

Tonya graced him with a wry smile. "See them in, my sweet. I'll behave."

When the two police officers appeared, Tonya gave them the gist of Lydia's phone call and said they might as well call off the search. "She left of her own volition. No need to waste resources tracking her down."

The cops retreated outside to call for guidance. When they returned, one said, "Detective Sanchez instructed us to proceed. He says locating Ms. Fredericks is in the best interests of the case."

Tonya waved a hand. "Well, if you find her, you have to keep her."

The officers appeared flummoxed at the statement, and David shot them a sympathetic look. They finally elected to pretend the comment hadn't occurred at all. "We're going to canvass your neighbors and hopefully retrieve video footage of your mother's departure," the first one said. "If we're lucky, it will help us determine what vehicle she used. We'll also run her credit cards. Do you have access to her account numbers?"

"As if. My mother considered it crass to discuss the details of her finances. She did mention that she's carrying a large sum of cash and that she's been watching *Law and Order*. I'm guessing she won't use her credit cards, for the time being, anyway."

"That presents a challenge," the officer mused. "But let me reassure you, we'll do our best to find her."

Tonya faked a yawn. "I'm going to bed soon. If you find my mother tonight, you'll have to arrange for her lodging. Preferably on a stiff cot at the police station. Behind bars, please."

Chapter Thirty-Nine

Once again bewildered by Tonya's comment, the officers scrambled to leave. The creatures and I weren't far behind. Lydia's phone call had dissolved Tonya's worry, leaving percolating anger in its place. That would be David's cross to bear.

Besides, I was tired. It was only seven-thirty, but it had been a stressful and angst-ridden day. I looked forward to microwaving a frozen dinner and a curling up with a good book. As I headed home with that goal in mind, my phone rang. I glanced at the screen and smiled as I answered.

"Hi, handsome."

Sam didn't respond with his usual warm greeting. Instead, his tone was tense. "Callie, I'm sure you heard about the fire..."

"What?" My voice hit a pitch that caused Woody to whine. Carl jumped onto the console and into the passenger seat, curiosity dancing in his eyes. "I don't know anything about a fire. What's going on?"

"I'm the one with the scoop? I'm not sure that's ever happened. Too bad I don't have time to gloat."

"Sam, get to the point. What happened? Are you okay?"

"I'm fine. A fire broke out in Pearly's kitchen. Jamal put it out before it spread, but he was injured in the process. They say it's not serious, but they've taken him to the hospital to treat him for smoke inhalation and burns. I'm on my way there now."

My head spun. "Oh, Sam! That's awful. But wait...why was Jamal in Pearly's kitchen?"

"I'm not sure. I haven't spoken to him yet. All I know is when we closed the Chow at four, Jamal said he was staying late to work on a few new recipes."

My mind churned as I processed the newest village calamity. "I'm on my way home from Tonya's. Let me drop off Woody and Carl, and I'll meet you at the hospital."

"I appreciate that, Callie, but it's unnecessary. As I said, it doesn't sound serious. It's just that Jamal has no family here, and I don't want him to be alone."

My heart swelled. Sam's compassion was a quality that had attracted me to him back in high school, and it had only matured over the years.

"It's just rough having to leave my parents on their last night here," he continued. "We didn't have anything special planned, but I feel bad about not being with them."

The little angel I carried with me perched on one shoulder, urging me to offer my services as a companion to Sam's parents. From the other shoulder, her devilish sibling whispered a reminder of how tired I was and how much I'd looked forward to that book on my coffee table.

How many times has Sam forsaken his own plans to take care of you? the angel scolded. *But you never asked for that,* the devil argued. I sighed, reaching up to flick the devil aside.

"Listen, why don't Woody and Carl and I head over to your house? We can keep your parents company."

A long pause ensued. "Are you sure?"

His disbelieving tone delivered a pang of guilt. Or was it annoyance? It wasn't as if I never did anything nice.

"Of course I'm sure. I wouldn't have offered otherwise. It'll be good to spend time with them before they leave."

"Well, then, I'll call and tell them you're coming. And Callie...thank you. This means a lot to me."

The guilt-slash-annoyance melted away. "It's my pleasure, Sam. Besides, your parents adore Woody and Carl."

"They love you, too."

Hmm. *Love* didn't seem likely. Not this soon after we'd made mutual amends. Besides, I didn't need them to love me. I had parents of my own for that. All I wanted was a cordial, friendly relationship with them, for Sam's sake and Elyse's.

But I didn't need to say any of that out loud. Let him believe his parents and I would be, as Zoe put it, besties.

After extracting Sam's promise to keep me updated on Jamal, I hung up. As I turned the car toward Sam's house, I dialed my mother's number.

"How is Tonya?" she asked without a greeting.

I summarized the evening's events, then shifted to the real purpose of my call. "Have you heard about Jamal?"

"Your father just got off the phone with Frank. It sounds as though the poor boy's injuries are superficial. I'm told Sam is on his way to the hospital."

My parents had clearly cultivated a better network of sources than I had. "Does Frank know what—or who—started the fire?"

"Not yet. The restaurant wasn't open tonight, so Ken wasn't on site, nor were any of his employees."

"Pearly's was closed on a Friday night?" I asked. "That's unusual."

"An issue with the ovens, I'm told. It's lucky Jamal passed by when he did and saw the smoke. If he hadn't intervened, the entire place might have been a loss, as well as neighboring businesses if the fire had spread."

"A little good news on this stressful day," I said.

I asked about Vivian and was told that she'd eaten a light dinner in her room and gone right back to sleep. "She's shaken by the visit to the cemetery, I'm afraid," Mom said. "I spoke to her doctor, who advised us to allow a day for recuperation before we hit her with news of her identity as a Murray. The doctor is hoping she'll recover the memory on her own. Frank agreed to hold off talking to her until Sunday unless something happens to force his hand."

Once we said our goodbyes, my mind flitted from one village disaster to the next, finally settling on Vivian. Or was it Valerie? It seemed to me that, except for the fire, every recent traumatic event in the village somehow spawned from her arrival. If only she could regain her missing memories, perhaps we could solve all the mysteries in one fell swoop.

MINUTES LATER, I pulled up to Sam's house: a three-bedroom navy-blue bungalow with white shutters and porch railings. It was the home in which he'd raised Elyse, and I wondered, not for the first time, whether he'd try to persuade me to live there with him. I was starting to believe I'd be ready to say yes if he proposed. And when two people were married, social convention implied they were expected to live together. But I loved my townhouse as much as Sam loved his bungalow. Would moving into his space feel like giving up a piece of myself?

I pushed the thought out of my mind. My mother would tell me worrying about future events was like mortgaging the present moment. Sam and I would cross that bridge if we got to it.

As soon as I released the creatures from the confines of the back seat, the front door of the bungalow opened. Carl darted straight inside, and Woody ran wagging and grinning to sit politely between Conrad and Lila.

When I made my way inside, my stomach rumbled loudly, and Lila put her hands on her hips. "When's the last time you ate?"

I scrunched up my face as I tried to recall. "A snickerdoodle and coffee a few hours ago. Before that, breakfast."

She took me by the arm and led me toward the kitchen. "We have so many leftovers. Let me just warm up a plate for you."

She cocked her head to Woody and Carl, who sat so close together that it was a challenge to discern where one golden-haired creature ended and the other began. They turned plaintive eyes to Lila, looking for all the world as if they'd gone unfed for days. "What about these two guys?" Lila asked. "They look hungry, too."

I chuckled. "Believe me, they're not hurting for food. They won't be wasting away anytime soon."

Lila ignored my sarcasm and turned to Conrad. "Honey, there's a cooked chicken breast and rice in the refrigerator. I'm sure Woody would enjoy that." She tapped her finger against her cheek as she eyed Carl. "And I think we have a can of tuna with this kitty's name on it."

After the creatures and I ate, we settled in for Scrabble—girls vs. boys. Woody sat beside Conrad with his chin on the card table, while Carl curled up in

Conrad's lap and studied the board as if reading the tiles. Conrad and Lila bickered amiably over word choices. We joked and laughed and chatted. These were the Petries I remembered from the old days—and I was starting to believe we might have left our friction behind.

After a few games, the clock in the living room bonged nine, and I stifled a yawn. Lila noticed it and started packing up the game board. "Callie, if you don't mind, Conrad and I should call it a night. We're early-to-bed types, and we still need to pack."

"Oh, of course," I said, grateful for her generosity.

Conrad handed Carl to me. "We appreciate you coming by, Callie."

"Yes, that was very thoughtful of you," Lila said. "I'm glad we were able to put our differences behind us."

"Me, too," I said. "It's a huge relief to me."

"It's been a long time since we've seen our son this happy," Lila said. "Thank you for that."

I blinked back a tear. "I should be thanking you. Sam is a good man because of how you raised him. I'm lucky to have him."

Lila's eyes drifted to a spot behind me. I swiveled to see Sam standing in the doorway, his eyes twinkling. "Don't mind me," he said, slipping an arm around my shoulders and kissing me on the cheek. "Keep talking. My ego could use a boost."

I gave him a light swat. "How's Jamal?"

"He'll be fine. A few burns on his hands and arms—first-degree, mostly, with a couple of second-degree. They dressed the wounds and gave him a cream for them. They also treated him for minor smoke inhalation. He'll stay overnight so they can monitor his lungs, but the doctor doesn't seem concerned."

Conrad crossed his arms. "How did this all happen, son?"

Sam sighed. "When Jamal left Snow Plow Chow, he walked over to Quicker Liquor to get a bottle of wine for a dinner party he was supposed to attend. As he passed Pearly's, he smelled the smoke. The sign on the door said the restaurant was closed for repairs, so he went around back to the alley. Smoke was pouring beneath the door. Jamal looked in the window and saw flames, so he called 9-1-1. Then he broke the glass and climbed inside. He found a fire extinguisher and managed to keep the flames contained until firefighters arrived."

"He's a hero," I said.

Lila tsked. "Hero or not, he's fortunate he wasn't badly injured. Or worse. Salvaging property isn't worth risking a life. If he were my son..."

"I get it, Mom," Sam interrupted. "You care for Jamal like he's family. But I bet Ken Pearly's grateful, as are the neighboring businesses that were saved from damage. Anyway, all's well that ends well."

"Are you picking him up from the hospital tomorrow?" I asked.

Sam shook his head. "He has a friend coming to get him. Young woman, if my guess is correct, though he was tight-lipped about it. Good thing, too. With Dan out of town and Jamal unavailable, Rodger and I will be running the Chow on our own."

Lila's eyes brightened. "Dad and I would be happy to pitch in. Our flight doesn't leave until dinnertime."

She glanced at Conrad, who nodded eagerly. "Your mother can help with the cooking, and I'll wait tables. It'll take me back to my teenage days."

Lila clapped her hands. "It'll be so much fun."

Sam cocked his head and grinned. "Well...I was planning on closing a little early anyway to get you to the airport. Is this how you really want to spend your last morning in Rock Creek Village?"

"Can't think of anything better," Conrad said.

I promised to stop by the Chow for lunch, and Sam walked me to my car. I situated the creatures in the back seat, then Sam pulled me close and placed a lingering kiss on my lips. "Careful, Romeo," I said. "Your parents are probably peeking through the curtains like they used to when we were in high school. Making sure things stay PG-rated."

"I didn't care then, and I sure as heck don't care now."

He brushed a strand of hair from my cheek and kissed me again. His lips were warm and soft, and I closed my eyes and wrapped my arms around his neck. When we pulled apart, I fanned myself. "Oh, my."

His lips curved in a sexy smile. "Hold that thought until tomorrow night when I get back from the airport."

I raised an eyebrow. "Pretty presumptuous of you, mister. I'm not always at your beck and call, you know."

He cupped my chin in his fingers. "Far be it for me to presume. May I call on you tomorrow night, Ms. Cassidy?"

I tilted my head. "You may, sir. I have agreed to have dinner at my parents' house, but after that, I'm all yours."

"I like the sound of that."

One more kiss. Before it could lead to another, I wrenched away and forced myself into the car. I wriggled my fingers at him and headed toward home, smiling and humming to myself. Life was good.

If I could keep from thinking about fires and murders and missing mothers, that was. Just for tonight, I was going to try.

Chapter Forty

Alas, my desire for a peaceful night did not come to pass. When I got home, I made a call to Mrs. Finney, who'd returned from her competition, silver cup in hand, and wanted me to assure her I'd be at the coffee shop in the morning to get her up to speed on local events.

After that, Monika called and further enmeshed my brain in village drama. With a green light from Tonya, the young reporter was preparing a story for the online edition of the morning *Gazette*, and she wanted to rehash the events of the past few days.

"Remember," I cautioned, my tone more like my mother's teacher voice than I was entirely comfortable with, "you promised Frank and the detectives you'd keep everything that happened at the Knotty Pine today off the record."

"I know that, Callie," she said, sounding every bit the petulant teenager in Mom's class. "I spoke to Detective Clarke, who gave me a few on-the-record quotes I can use. Besides, the information I dug up on my own is fair game. I didn't get any of that from the cops, so there's no off-the-record limitation."

"Hmm," I said. "Be careful."

She huffed. "Callie, I live and work in this village. I'm not going to burn my sources. Sometimes I think you forget I'm a professional."

I sighed. Maybe I was turning into an old fogey. "You're right. Sorry. How can I help?"

She started by asking questions to help clarify the information she'd gathered. After reminding her I was not to be used as a source, I answered what I could without stepping over the line Raul had drawn for me.

We ended up talking for almost an hour. By the time we hung up, I was impressed yet again by Monika's intelligence and talent. We had a top-notch reporter in our midst.

The downside of the conversation was that it got me too wired up to sleep. I lay in bed, letting my mind skitter through the facts of the case but getting no answers.

Finally, I managed a few hours of shuteye. When my alarm beeped at seven, I was tempted to smack it and drift off again. But I had a date with Mrs. Finney. If I fell back asleep, I'd only be visited by nightmares about missing it. After a quick shower, I drove into town and dropped the creatures off at the studio.

As I headed down the sidewalk, I glanced across the street to Pearly's Steak and Chop House. From this vantage point, it looked none the worse for wear. The actual damage would be visible only from the back. I pictured shards of glass from the broken window littering the alleyway. The charred walls of the kitchen. The smell of smoke hanging heavy throughout the restaurant. I thought of my gallery. How would I feel if fire had damaged the place I loved?

After a brisk walk, I entered the coffee shop. The place teemed with customers. Mr. Purdy looked like an Olympic sprinter as he ran orders to tables. Behind the counter, Mrs. Finney flitted about in a loose-fitting violet tunic and periwinkle leggings. When she spotted me, she pointed to an empty table and indicated she'd join me as soon as she could.

Heading across the shop, I noticed Mr. Pearly hunched over a coffee cup at a table near the window, with a clear view of his damaged restaurant. Pity coursed through me.

His hands wrapped loosely around his cup. A huge cinnamon roll lay on a plate near one hand—a gift from Mrs. Finney, I surmised. The roll remained untouched. I doubted Mr. Pearly had much of an appetite this morning.

I debated whether to stop and offer my sympathies, wondering whether my presence would be an intrusion. But the man looked so forlorn that I couldn't help myself.

I cleared my throat as I approached. He took a toothpick from the corner of his mouth and gave me a half-hearted smile. "Morning, Ms. Cassidy."

"Hi, Mr. Pearly. Do you mind if I join you? Just for a minute."

When he pointed to a vacant chair, I sat. He looked at his coffee as if he'd forgotten it was there and took a gulp.

"I heard about the fire," I said. "I'm so sorry."

"Thank you," he said simply.

"It's fortunate Jamal happened by. Sounds like he was able to minimize the damage."

Mr. Pearly's eyes clouded, as if a storm was imminent. "The boy was injured. I feel horrible about that."

His voice cracked. Poor Mr. Pearly. He was taking this hard.

Impulsively, I put a hand on his arm. "Only minor injuries, Mr. Pearly. Sam tells me Jamal will be back at work in no time. Besides, he only did what you would have in similar circumstances. Imagine if you'd walked by and discovered Snow Plow Chow on fire. You would have done whatever you could to save the place. Any of us would have. That's what I love best about Rock Creek Village—we look out for each other. We're family."

Mr. Pearly studied me for a few seconds, then nodded. "Family. That's a good way to put it. A nice sentiment." He exhaled. "So many villagers have reached out to me since last night to offer their sympathies—and more. Food. Money. Help with repairs. I'm a lucky man to live in such a place. I'm sorry to say I've taken that for granted."

I smiled. "That's human nature. I took this place for granted so much that I abandoned it for twenty-five years. Sometimes it takes adversity to make us appreciate what we have."

He squeezed my hand. "Thank you for your kindness, Ms. Cassidy. You're a good person, and I'm glad you came back here. Rock Creek Village is a better place with you in it." He drained his cup and stood. "Now, if you'll excuse me, I need to get going. There's work to be done."

As he headed toward the door, I called after him. "You forgot your cinnamon roll."

"Not hungry," he said. "It's all yours."

I WAS EYEING the cinnamon roll when Mrs. Finney approached, bearing a tray with two coffees and the roll's identical twin. She distributed the plates and cups on the table and tsked when she saw Mr. Pearly's untouched pastry. "That poor man. I don't even want to think about how'd I'd feel if Rocky Mountain High went up in flames.

The damage doesn't seem too catastrophic, though. He should be able to rebuild quickly."

She took a sip of her coffee. "Unfortunately, though, I haven't the time to dwell on Ken's misfortune. As I'm sure you see, this place is a madhouse this morning. I mustn't leave Mr. Purdy to handle it alone for long. I'd appreciate an expedited version of current events."

"You probably already know everything I do anyway," I said with a chuckle.

"Quite possibly, dear. But it never hurts to hear from a friend's lips that which one has gleaned from disinterested sources."

I wrinkled my nose. "If that's supposed to be one of your aphorisms, I'm afraid it needs work."

"Yes, well, I'm off my game. All that time on the ice seems to have frozen the flow of wise thoughts." She clapped her hands. "Let's have your recap, Callahan. Time is short."

It took me ten minutes to fill her in on Vivian's connection to the Murray family and Lydia's disappearance. As predicted, little of it seemed to surprise her. The only news that caused her bushy eyebrows to raise was the revelation that Pinky had once been a U.S. Marshal, information her sources had been unable to uncover. She pursed her lips and muttered something about the useless junior agents populating The Company these days.

A throng of customers in ski clothes entered the shop then, and we could see Mr. Purdy start to sweat. "Sorry to cut this short, dear," Mrs. Finney said, "but a girl has to make a living. We'll talk soon."

She scurried back behind the counter. I slurped my coffee and scarfed down one of the cinnamon rolls. Then I wrapped the other in a napkin for later consumption and departed for the gallery. Mrs. Finney was right. Regardless of village chaos, a girl had to make a living.

A STEADY FLOW of customers kept Ethan, Zoe, and me busy all morning. Before I knew it, lunchtime had arrived. I'd promised to stop by Snow Plow Chow to see Conrad and Lila at work, but I hadn't counted on the gallery being so packed. A to-go order would have to suffice. I phoned in an order and left Ethan and Zoe to wrangle customers as I hurried to the café to pick up our food.

The Chow was as busy as Sundance Studio. Conrad darted from table to booth, pencil and order pad in hand and a grin on his face. He was clearly enjoying his server gig. I waved at him and headed toward the kitchen to pick up my order.

When I pushed open the swinging metal door, the aroma of frying bacon hit my nostrils first, followed by the scent of chocolate. No better smells in the world, I reflected. From his workstation, Rodger lifted a chin in greeting as he whisked an egg concoction in a large glass bowl. At the large commercial range, Lila wielded a set of tongs, which she used to turn thick slices of bacon. She gave me a quick smile, then issued a series of stern instructions to her son. Sam turned his back to her and mouthed, "Help!" But I could see he enjoyed having his parents working alongside him.

Lila used the tongs to point to a takeout bag, which I snatched up. I gave her a one-armed goodbye hug, kissed Sam on the cheek, and went back into the restaurant. I promised Conrad we'd talk soon, then dashed back to the gallery, treasures in hand.

The three of us rotated shifts in the office to shovel in

our BLTs and fries as if we were teachers with a fifteen-minute lunch break. Then it was back to customers—ringing up orders, wrapping canvases, carrying purchases to cars. By the time things slowed down at two, the gallery looked like Woodstock after the music had stopped.

"Whew," Zoe said, wiping the back of her hand across her forehead. "I should get combat pay."

"You did great," I said. "It rarely gets this busy. The way you kept up today tells me you'll be able to handle anything."

Ethan reached one hand over his shoulder and patted himself on the back. "I deserve all the credit. I know how to pick 'em."

I pointed at him and smiled. "As do I, partner. I picked you, after all. No time for basking in self-congratulation, though. Those bare walls need replenishing. Let's raid the inventory closet."

We spent the next hour hanging fresh photos on the walls and tending to the now-occasional customer who meandered in. As I returned from the storage closet with the last canvas to hang, the tinkling bell announced a new arrival—Detective Raul Sanchez.

The lone female customer in the store did a double take at the sight of him. I got it. Though there was nothing romantic between us, even I couldn't ignore Raul's smoldering good looks. His black hair, olive-toned skin, chiseled jaw, and broad shoulders resulted in many a swooning female—and a few swooning men, too. Especially on those rare occasions, as now, when he was actually smiling.

He sauntered over, took the canvas from my hands, and positioned it on the wall. I grinned at him. "Thank you, kind sir. To what do we owe the honor of your presence?"

"Got a minute to talk?"

I glanced at Ethan, who cocked his head toward the office. "Go do your Scoop Cassidy routine. We'll come get you if more crowds swarm in."

Raul followed me into the office, where Woody greeted him with a slurp of tongue. Carl pretended to ignore him, but I could see interest gleaming in his green eyes. The cat figured, rightly so, that the detective wasn't here on a social call. As Raul and I settled into chairs, Carl leapt onto the desk and curled his tail around his torso.

"Have you located Lydia or Tommy?" I asked. Neither of us required small talk as a warm-up.

Raul shook his head. "We have law enforcement scouring the county. No sign of either of them."

"Well, you needn't scour my gallery, or my home, for that matter. I guarantee I'm not harboring a fugitive."

"Comforting. We've issued a wide alert for Tommy's car, but of course, we can't do that with Lydia because we still don't know what her...friend...drives. Or even who he is."

"The neighborhood canvass didn't turn up any video footage?" I asked.

"Nope. In that respect, we're at a standstill."

I drummed my fingers on the desk. "I assume you've contacted the Murray family."

He nodded. "I talked to Amos, Tommy's older brother. Though when I say, 'talked to,' it's hyperbole. As soon as I introduced myself, he treated me to a stream of foul language that curled my toes. Then he hung up on me."

"Did you mention Vivian? Or Valerie? Whatever she's called..."

He shook his head. "No. We've decided to keep Vivian's true identity quiet for the time being. Don't want to risk further endangering her."

"Makes sense."

"I also tried multiple times to get in touch with Eugene's father, Donovan, but he's not taking my calls."

"Sounds like there could be a trip to Vegas in your future," I teased.

I knew how much Raul detested Sin City, so when he shuddered theatrically, I laughed. His lips curved into an easy smile. I narrowed my eyes. Given his lack of progress in the case, I'd expect frustration—a clenched jaw, fists opening and closing. Yet Raul seemed almost low-key. There could be only one reason for that.

I leaned back in my chair. "You and Lynn have worked things out."

He gave me a quizzical look. "What makes you say that?"

"You're the image of calm and collected. Not the Raul Sanchez I'm accustomed to. Either you've started taking Prozac, or your love life has improved."

"Prozac makes me dizzy," he said.

"Must be the love life then. Details, please."

"Nothing much to tell."

"Stop it, Raul. We're friends, remember? No need to be shy with me. Besides, I have some salacious info of my own. I'll spill mine if you spill yours."

His eyebrows quirked up. "Bribing an officer of the law? Seriously, though, it's not a big deal. Lynn invited me for a game of mini-golf this weekend."

I felt a little deflated. "Oh. Well, that's great."

"With her daughters."

I clapped my hands. "Fantastic! That's a big step. I predict we'll be hearing wedding bells soon."

"Only if they're yours. Is that you so-called salacious info? Did Sam propose? Or maybe you did..."

"Psssh." I waved a hand. "No engagement here. I've

only just negotiated a cease-fire with his parents. I'm hoping it's a permanent truce, but only time will tell."

"Then what's your big news?"

"I don't have any. I was just trying to get you to spill your guts. A proven interrogation technique. You're welcome to use it sometime."

"Bush league," he said.

"Worked on you."

He chuckled and got to his feet. "All right, Ms....what was it Ethan called you?...Scoop Cassidy. I'm off to conduct some actual police work. Stay out of trouble. And call me when you've solved the case. Or located Tommy or Lydia. Or cured cancer. Whichever comes first."

Chapter Forty-One

When five o'clock rolled around, we closed the studio and ran through a quick clean-up. Then the creatures and I headed over to the Knotty Pine for dinner with my parents and Vivian. I was momentarily surprised to find the lobby door locked—until I recalled the extra precautions for the sake of the WITSEC guest.

Mr. Farmington spotted me through the glass, pushed a button to unlock the door, and gestured us inside. As Woody ambled over to greet him, Carl squirmed out of my arms and bounded into the lobby. My eyes followed him to a seating area occupied by three people, all dressed to the nines. My mother wore a sparkly silver ensemble and heels. Dad donned his best suit and tie. And then there was Vivian, clad in a dress I recognized as one of Mom's, a lovely navy-blue velvet frock. Her hair had been neatly styled, and she wore eye makeup and lipstick. On the coffee table in front of the trio rested three mugs—filled with mulled wine, no doubt—and small plates of hors d'oeuvres.

I glanced at Mr. Farmington. "What is this, prom night or something?"

He grinned. "Your father said Ms. Corwin needed cheering, as well as a little time out of the condo, so they dressed up and came down for wine and appetizers. We sent a notice to our few guests that the lobby was temporarily closed for a private party. It'll only be for an hour, but so far, it's been worth it. Just look at her."

I turned back to the threesome. My father gesticulated as he immersed himself in whatever story he was telling, while Mom listened with rapt attention. Best of all, Vivian threw her head back and laughed with unreserved joy.

I looked at my own attire—jeans, plaid shirt, and sneakers—and frowned. "I'm hardly dressed for such a formal occasion."

Before Mr. Farmington could respond, my mother's voice carried across the room. "Callie, darling, grab some snacks and join us."

At the word *snacks*, Woody trotted toward the couch, tail wagging in anticipation. My mother, always prepared, pulled a treat from a pouch on the table and tossed it to the golden retriever, who caught it with a snap. Carl rejected Mom's offer and climbed onto the arm of the couch, settling in beside my father.

I went to the buffet, selected a few human treats, and filled a mug with steaming wine. Then I joined the three of them. Setting my plate and cup on the table, I took Vivian's outstretched hand as she bestowed a genuine smile on me.

"Callie, it's so nice to see you again."

"Same to you, Vivian. You look lovely." I turned to my parents. "You all do. Unfortunately, I didn't receive the memo requesting formal attire. I'm lowering the fashion level a few notches."

"No worries," Dad said. "We take all kinds here, even riffraff such as yourself."

His eyes danced, and I realized just how tense he'd been for the past few days. It was good to see him relaxed, as if Vivian's laughter lifted a burden from his shoulders. I wished this scene could last, but I knew it was the calm before the storm. Frank planned to question Vivian tomorrow, and I doubted she'd be laughing when he revealed her former identity. I wondered what name she'd taken when WITSEC moved her out of Rock Creek Village and into the third version of her life. The Marshals Service hadn't divulged that information to Pinky so he wouldn't be tempted to search for her once she'd moved on.

I told myself to quit fretting over details and enjoy the moment. Good food, hearty laughter, scintillating conversation. Though Vivian had no significant memory of her life before or after George, she was a charming, funny woman. I listened, talked, ate, and drank. Before I knew it, an hour had passed.

For a moment, we slid into companionable silence. When Vivian spoke, her tone was contemplative. "I can't remember who I was last week. But, you know, maybe that's okay. Perhaps I'm even better off not knowing. I think I could be happy here in Rock Creek Village, with new-old friends and my memories of my life with George."

Mom reached out and patted Vivian's knee. "It may seem that way right now, Viv, but I imagine you'll soon be yearning for more. And no matter how painful you might find the rest of your memories, you have the strength to face them."

Vivian clasped Mom's hand. "I'm sure you're right, Maggie. Better the monster on the table than the one lurking in your head."

I pointed at my mother. "She says that all the time!"

"Great minds think alike," Mom said with a smile. Then she got to her feet. "The roast should be done by now. Let's head up for dinner."

Dad and I collected empty plates and mugs and deposited them on a designated tray. Mom and Vivian started toward the condo door, pausing near the lobby entrance. I saw Mom pointing out one of my landscape canvases hanging on the wall, and I blushed, realizing my mother was bragging about her daughter the photographer.

I was on my way to rescue Vivian from the unsolicited public relations stunt when Mr. Farmington called out urgently, "Maggie, watch out!"

A cracking sound pierced the room as the entry door shattered. Shards of glass rained across the wood floor. I gasped. My eyes darted around, trying to make sense of what had happened.

A stunned silence followed, broken by Woody barking and growling. The dog edged toward the door, but I seized him by the collar before the tiny pieces of glass could prick his paws. Carl yowled but thankfully stayed behind me.

My father, the former Chief of Police, didn't even hesitate—and he wore no collar I could grab. He pushed past me and raced toward Mom and Vivian.

A figure appeared—a man silhouetted in the demolished entrance. He stepped in and flung aside the tire iron he'd used on the door.

It took only a moment to recognize him. The fugitive who had eluded the police was missing no more. We'd found Tommy Murray—or rather, he'd found us.

Chapter Forty-Two

When Vivian saw Tommy, the blood drained from her face. "Jack?" she cried.

Tommy's brow furrowed in confusion, but I understood immediately. Though it was Tommy standing before her, Vivian was seeing the image of her oldest brother, the one she'd testified against forty years ago.

A second later, realization dawned in Tommy's eyes as well, and he smirked. "Everyone says I resemble dear old dad. But he's been dead ten years, you old loony bin. Died in prison—where you put him."

He reached out with his left hand and grabbed Vivian by the arm, pulling her toward him. His right hand went into his jacket pocket and came out with a gun. Dad stiffened, and Mom and I gasped simultaneously. Vivian didn't make a sound.

Tommy yanked her closer. "We've been looking for you most of my life, dear Aunt Valerie. You've gotten away with what you did for a long time, but now it's time to face the music. And it's a tune you're not gonna enjoy."

Vivian squawked in pain as he squeezed her upper arm. Then her eyes turned hard. If my guess was right, the memories were flooding back—and they weren't happy ones.

Dad took a step toward the two of them, but Vivian held up a hand to stop him. She drew a breath and faced her nephew. "I remember you, Tommy Boy. Never the brightest bulb on the tree, as I recall. You overcompensated by turning into a first-class bully. The family has tasked you with apprehending an old lady, have they? Not the most challenging of assignments. You must not be especially high in the pecking order."

Tommy blanched and tightened his grip. "When my father died, Uncle Van became top dog. With Gene gone, that makes me his number two. I'd say that's a pretty decent spot in the chain of command."

"Gene..." Vivian's eyes closed as her mind latched onto a fresh memory. She turned pleading eyes to my father. "Was it Eugene?" Her voice broke. "In the cemetery...the body...was that my nephew? Am I responsible? Did I...?"

"Of course you did, you old biddy," Tommy said. "My cousin came here to tend to some family business. That girlfriend of his turned him on to the place. I can't say exactly what happened because, thanks to you, he's not around to tell us. Best I can guess, he spotted you when he was out for his run. Funny how the fates conspire, putting the two of you in the same place at the same time. You must not have been thrilled about the family reunion, because you swung a pickaxe into his neck."

Mattock, I thought but refrained from saying.

When my father took a step forward, Tommy lifted the gun. Dad ignored him and addressed Vivian. "I don't think that's how it happened, Viv. Remember, you were injured yourself. A more likely scenario is that Tommy here came to Rock Creek Village to get a piece of that 'family business' he mentioned. He came across you and Gene talking in the cemetery and saw it as an opportunity to execute a power grab. The key word being execute. I believe Tommy killed Gene, then shoved you head first into George's tombstone and left you for dead."

I stole a look at my father and realized he was winging it, trying to stall Tommy until...what? None of us had been able to call the police. I sneaked a peek at the registration desk and noticed Mr. Farmington was gone. Hopefully, he'd stolen into the office to dial 9-1-1.

Meanwhile, Tommy's face had turned crimson. "First off, her name is Valerie. Vivian doesn't exist. Second, I did not kill Gene. He was family. We take care of our own."

"Depends on how you define 'take care,'" Dad said. "Your aunt's family, too. Are you here to take care of her? Admit it, Tommy. Eugene had bested you in the brains and talent departments. You were envious. You'd been waiting in the wings way too long. The time was ripe, and you seized it."

Tommy dug his fingers into Vivian's arm. His lips curled into a mirthless smile. "Think whatever you want. I'm done talking. This ends now."

He yanked Vivian toward the smashed door. Woody tugged against my grip on his collar, but I held tight. As Tommy dragged Vivian over the jagged glass of the doorframe, Dad sprang forward. Tommy saw him coming and pointed the gun at him. Mom cried out and took hold Dad's arm, jerking him back.

Tommy grinned. "Good call, lady. No reason for any of you to pay the price for dear old auntie's sins." He used the pistol to deliver a salute. "Folks, it's been real."

He backed away toward the parking lot, his grasp still tight on Vivian's arm. Though she was trembling, she graced us with a resigned smile. "Tommy's right. You all need to stay back. Don't need to worry about me. I'll be fine." *Tough old bird,* I thought.

Tommy snorted. "Fine? If you say so. Whatever gets you through the night."

He kept moving backward, pulling Vivian with him and not taking his eyes off my father. Dad bounced on the balls of his feet, ready to charge. "You can't win against a gun," Mom said to him. "We'll have to find another way."

Suddenly, a voice boomed from outside, just out of our line of vision. "Let her go."

Pinky strode into view and crouched like a wrestler preparing to slam his opponent to the mat. Beneath the wrinkles lining his face, I could visualize the U.S. Marshal he'd been decades earlier. Muscles rippled in his arms. Though the man was in his eighties, he'd maintained a powerful physique. One look at him satisfied me he'd hold his own in a fair fight with the younger man.

But Tommy's gun meant the fight wasn't fair.

"I won't ask you again," Pinky said, his voice fierce. "Let her go."

Tommy scoffed. "Make me, old man."

Pinky didn't bother to respond. Not with words, anyway. He pounced toward Tommy like a leopard. Tommy's eyes widened. His finger tightened on the gun's trigger.

The bullet hit Pinky in the abdomen, slamming him to the pavement. Tommy gaped at the gun as if it had fired on its own. It seemed he hadn't really meant to shoot.

Everything seemed to happen at once. I heard a squeal and realized it was me. Carl emitted a screech that might've broken glass, if it hadn't already been shattered. Woody bucked at my grip on his collar. Dad wrenched his arm from Mom's grasp and started toward Tommy and Vivian.

Mom shouted, "Butch, no!" Tommy recovered his wits and aimed the gun at Dad.

Before Tommy could fire again, Vivian slammed her fist into his forearm, sending the weapon clattering to the pavement. When he bent to retrieve it, she thrust a knee into his nose.

My mouth dropped open. What was it with these old people and their superhuman strength?

Tommy fell to his knees. His hands flew to his bloody nose. He looked up and snarled at Vivian. Then he saw Dad advancing toward the gun and scrambled toward it himself.

I caught my breath. It was a race to the gun, one Tommy appeared poised to win. Mom shouted, "Butch, watch out!"

But before Tommy's hand could wrap around the weapon, Mr. Farmington appeared at the broken door, brandishing a rifle. "I wouldn't do that, son," Mr. Farmington said. "It's always best to know when the jig is up."

Chapter Forty-Three

Dad skidded to a halt and stepped aside to allow Mr. Farmington a direct line of sight. Tommy froze. His outstretched hand hovered an inch from the gun. He looked up at Mr. Farmington, whose grip remained steady on the rifle. Mr. Farmington's normally jovial expression now said he meant business. No doubt in my mind he intended to follow through if Tommy forced his hand. Sirens wailed nearby. Tommy rocked back on his heels and raised his hands in surrender.

"What is it with all you old people?" he muttered, parroting my earlier thought. "It's like a senior citizens' Marvel movie."

Carl chose that moment to enter the fray. He pranced around the broken glass and sidled up to Tommy, reaching out a paw and slashing his claws across the man's arm. "Ow!" Tommy squealed. "I'll wring your neck, you mangy animal!"

Woody leapt to the cat's defense, barking furiously as he dodged the glass. Carl made a chattering noise and skittered just out of the man's reach. Mr. Farmington cleared his throat, drawing Tommy's attention back to the barrel of the rifle. "Butch," Mr. Farmington said, "zip ties are in my coat pocket."

Dad retrieved them and squatted beside Tommy, pulling his arms behind his back and fastening the zip ties around his wrists a bit more tightly than necessary. I nodded in approval.

The second Tommy was secure, Vivian ran to Pinky and dropped to her knees beside him. "Oh, Robert," she cried. "Hold on. Please hold on. Help is coming."

I noted she'd used Pinky's original name. The final spate of memories must have come crashing back.

An ambulance screeched into the parking lot. I hurried out to wave them to us. Dad and Mr. Farmington stayed on the stoop, guarding Tommy, while Mom knelt beside Vivian and Pinky.

As the EMTs grabbed their gear, I rolled my hand to hurry them up. "Pinky's been shot!" They unfolded the gurney and jogged toward the injured man.

Pinky opened his eyes and focused on Vivian. He lifted a shaky hand to her cheek. "Valerie. Thank God you're all right."

Tears spilled down Vivian's cheeks. "Oh, Robert. You swore you'd protect me forty years ago, and you have. You saved my life! And see what it's gotten you? You should have kept away from me."

Pinky's face spasmed in pain. When it subsided, he smiled. "Couldn't do that, now, could I? I love you, Valerie. I never told you, but I've loved you since the day I met you." His eyelids drooped closed again, and his breathing turned shallow.

"Robert!" Vivian sobbed. One of the paramedics gently pulled her away so they could work on Pinky.

Mom tried to steer Vivian into the lobby. "Let's get you inside," she said.

Vivian wrenched away, her expression stubborn. "I'm not leaving him."

"We at least need to move back and let the EMTs work," Mom said. "For Pinky's...for Robert's...sake."

Vivian bit her lip and took a few steps back. Her eyes never strayed from Pinky. Half a dozen cars screeched into the parking lot, as the rest of the cavalry arrived. First came Raul, then Lynn. Two more officers jumped out of another vehicle. Frank pulled up in his truck. A few other uniformed cops joined the excitement.

"Looks like the entire department turned up for this one," I said.

Raul marched toward us. His eyes swept the scene and paused on me. He huffed. I lifted a shoulder. *Wrong place, wrong time.*

Lynn walked over, her hand hovering near her gun. Frank sauntered in behind her. They watched as Raul yanked Tommy to his feet, removed the zip ties, and hand-cuffed him. Tommy spotted Lynn and leered. "Hey there, gorgeous. I got an idea how you and me might put these handcuffs to better use."

Lynn rolled her eyes. Raul jerked hard on the cuffs, and Tommy grimaced. The cops fanned out, roping off the scene with yellow tape and scanning the ground for evidence.

Frank headed toward Mr. Farmington and removed the rifle from his hands as Dad clapped his manager on the shoulder. "Well done, Sid."

"Yes, quite well done," Mom chimed in. "I worked with you for years and had no clue you were such a tough guy."

"Well, I *am* a former teacher," Mr. Farmington said.

"There's a reason my students used to call me The Enforcer."

Lynn went to Vivian and began questioning her. The paramedics transferred Pinky to a gurney and raised it to prepare for transport. Pinky looked rough, his skin so thin and pale that blue veins were visible at his temples. I saw the blood pulsing there—a good sign—but his breathing was labored. *Please let him make it.*

Vivian made a move toward the gurney. "I'm going with him."

Gently but firmly, Lynn restrained her. "I'm afraid we can't permit that. Only relatives are permitted to accompany a patient in the ambulance."

"But he needs me." Vivian's voice bordered on hysteria.

"You need to arrest that woman!" Tommy shouted. "She should be the one in handcuffs, not me! She killed my cousin. Not to mention perjuring herself when she testified against my father."

His remarks did more to mitigate Vivian's agitation than any comforting words could have. Before our eyes, her determination returned. She stared daggers at her nephew. "Neither of those statements is true, Tommy Boy. Your father was guilty, and you know it. You've always known it. As for Eugene, it's obvious to all of us that you killed him. Then you shot poor Robert..."

She stared after the departing ambulance. Raul caught my eye, and I lifted my brow. Neither of us was a hundred percent convinced Tommy had murdered his cousin. Still, he had shot Pinky, so maybe we were wrong.

Tommy snarled again. Carl took a step toward him, and Tommy flinched. Keeping the cat in his sights, he said, "For the last time, I did not kill Gene. I'm a Murray. We take care of our own."

"That line is getting tiresome," I said. "Particularly considering how you've treated your aunt."

He scowled at me. "Valerie's not family, not since she betrayed us. For all I care, she can rot in—"

Raul cut him off. "That's enough. We'll sort this out at the station." He summoned one of the officers. "Take this man into custody and process him. Aggravated assault with a deadly weapon and attempted kidnapping, for starters. We'll amend the charges as necessary. Be sure to read him his rights."

Tommy cocked his head toward Lynn. "I promise to go peacefully if that one takes me in. She can read me my rights all day long."

Raul pulled himself to full height and leaned in, his voice low. "Whether you go peacefully or not doesn't much matter to me. In fact, I might prefer it if you resisted."

Tommy shrank away from Raul. When the uniformed officer began leading him away, he looked almost relieved. But when he passed Lynn, he managed a wink. "You know where to find me, sweetheart."

Lynn didn't bother to respond. Instead, she turned back to Vivian. "Mrs. Corwin, we're going to need you at the station. Come with me, please."

"Am I under arrest?" Vivian asked.

Lynn didn't offer a direct answer. "There are a few things we need to clear up."

Vivian frowned. Mom placed a hand on her arm. "Butch and I will be right behind you, Viv. We'll wait for you at the station and take you to the hospital as soon as the detectives finish with you." She gave Lynn a pointed look. "It won't take long, will it?"

Lynn started to respond, but Frank intervened. "We'll do our best, Maggie, but we have to do our job." He shot a look at Dad, who nodded reluctantly. Once the emotion of the situation dissipated, I knew Mom would see it their way, too.

Lynn led Vivian to her car, and Mom and Dad hurried toward theirs. "Keep me posted," I called after them. Dad responded with a thumbs-up, but I saw the worry lines around his eyes.

As Frank headed over to instruct the troops, Raul pulled me aside. "We'll be needing a statement from you, too."

"I know. This isn't my first rodeo."

He smiled wryly. "If only you could promise it would be your last."

I lifted a hand and crossed my fingers. We stood in silence for a moment, watching the activity. "Looks like the case is wrapped up," Raul ventured.

"Looks that way."

He narrowed his eyes. "You don't seem convinced."

"Nor do you. I mean, it's obvious Tommy is a criminal. But you heard how emphatically he denied killing Gene."

"His word doesn't carry a lot of weight." Raul shrugged. "Besides, most killers deny culpability when they're caught. As they say, jails are full of supposedly innocent men and women."

"True, but..." I mentally replayed the confrontation between Vivian and Tommy. "You should have seen her, Raul. When Tommy shot Pinky, Vivian turned into the Hulk. The way she disarmed Tommy and kneed him in the face...it was powerful. It's not beyond belief that she could have swung a mattock into Gene's neck."

"Do you think that's how it happened?"

I shuffled my feet. Beside me, Carl yowled. I picked him up and peered into his eyes. He seemed poised to convey an important insight, but I was unable to access it. *If only you could talk.*

"No," I finally admitted. "But still...pinning everything on Tommy? It feels too easy."

Raul ran a hand through his dark hair. "Sometimes the simplest answer is still the right one. We'll follow the trail wherever it leads. The truth will come out."

He started toward his car, and I watched him, considering his statement. *The truth will come out.*

He was right—probably. The question was, at what cost?

Chapter Forty-Four

Two days had passed since Tommy had attempted to kidnap Vivian and then shot Pinky. I'd spent most of that time buried beneath the fallout from the investigation—along with an in-depth cross-examination by Mrs. Finney. I also spent hours being interviewed by Monika, who ultimately produced a trio of potentially award-winning stories at least as riveting as the ones that won her the Feldman Award last year.

Today, on a bright autumn afternoon, the creatures and I were headed to the lodge at a summons from my mother. She hadn't revealed the reason, but I wasn't especially curious. Knowing Mom, I was going to be treated to a presentation of another new hobby, or better yet, a taste test of the latest delicacy she'd whipped up in the kitchen. At any rate, the gallery was closed on Mondays, so I was free to be at her beck and call.

As I drove through the village, my mind flipped through the events of the past few days. Following Tommy's arrest, Vivian...Valerie...had given her statement at the police station. The detectives must have found her credible because afterward they allowed my parents to take her to the hospital to be with Pinky. Robert. Whatever. All these aliases were making me dizzy.

Raul said they hadn't entirely eliminated Vivian from the suspect list in Gene's murder, but they had no evidence to implicate her. Besides, none of them believed she'd done it. They also felt confident she wouldn't follow Lydia's example and flee—not with Pinky fighting for his life.

Thankfully, it looked as if it was a fight he'd win. Surgeons had repaired the gunshot wound and patched him up. He still faced the risk of infection, but barring that, doctors said he'd eventually be back to normal, except for a scar serving as a permanent reminder of his heroism. They expected to release him later in the week, though he'd require at-home care for at least a month.

No trouble finding someone to take on that duty. Vivian had volunteered, or rather, insisted. Pinky's declaration of his forty-year love had opened a floodgate of emotion. Mom predicted Vivian and Pinky would be together "until death do they part."

I hoped that day lay far into the future. I was still concerned over the prospect of Murray family retribution, though. Frank had contacted the U.S. Marshals, who assured him they'd keep the Murrays on their radar. They'd even offered Vivian renewed WITSEC protection, a proposal she refused. "I'm seventy-two years old," she said. "Whatever the consequences, I'm through running."

As I'd assumed, Tommy's appearance at the Knotty Pine had sparked the full resurgence of her memories, from childhood through her recent return to the village. Only the hours before and after her head injury remained out of reach. Doctors warned her that time was likely gone for good—a bitter prediction, since it meant Vivian wouldn't be able to identify Gene's killer or her own attacker.

Everyone was convinced of Tommy's guilt anyway. But the case wouldn't be an easy one to win. The cops lacked solid evidence against him for Gene's murder. As far as the other charges, word had it Tommy planned to plead not guilty to the multiple counts of racketeering, money laundering, attempted kidnapping, and the biggie: aggravated assault with a deadly weapon.

As I pulled into the Knotty Pine parking lot, I sighed. The investigation seemed to be drawing to a conclusion, yet we still had no definitive answers to the most important question—who killed Eugene Murray?

MOM MET us in the lobby and hurried us to the condo door.

"What's going on?" I asked. "This feels like more than a few new sweaters you've knitted for the creatures."

"Vivian's brother Donovan reached out to her," she said breathlessly. "They've scheduled a Zoom call, and Viv requested that you attend."

"Me? Why?"

"She says you've been kind and helpful since the day you found her in the cemetery. She also referenced your keen investigative mind."

I blushed. "Are Raul and Lynn also attending this sibling reunion?"

Mom shook her head. "Vivian refused to get law enforcement involved. Your father will be there, of course, but Viv doesn't think Donovan would speak openly with detectives present. We persuaded her to record the conversation on my phone, though."

I clucked my tongue. "An unauthorized recording won't be admissible in court."

"Dad mentioned that, but Viv doesn't care. She said she'd never testify against Donovan anyway. Not for any reason." Mom glanced at her watch. "Let's go. Don't want to be late to the party."

Upstairs, Vivian greeted me with a warm hug. We assembled in the study, and Vivian sat at the desk, facing the computer screen. Mom, Dad, and I perched on the couch, out of the camera's view. Woody parked himself next to Vivian. Carl tried to climb in her lap, but I snatched him up and threatened him with exile if he didn't behave.

At the appointed time, the Zoom invite flashed on the screen. Vivian took a deep breath, glanced at us, and pressed the Join button on the computer, along with the Record button on Mom's phone.

Donovan appeared on the screen. If I'd been expecting a Robert DeNiro mobster type, I was disappointed. Vivian's brother was a small, feeble-looking man with frizzy white hair. The moment he saw Vivian, tears streaked down his sagging cheeks.

"Val. I can't believe I'm laying eyes on you after all these years. It's nothing short of a miracle."

Vivian reached a quivering hand toward the screen, as if she might be able to touch her brother through the glass. "Oh, Van. How I've missed you."

They spent twenty minutes crying and laughing and catching up. Donovan spoke of his daughters and grand-kids, avoiding any mention of his only son, Eugene. Vivian told him about her past in Rock Creek Village and the brief marriage she'd been compelled to end. Van began leaking tears again and urged his sister to fill him in on the years since she'd left the village. I leaned forward. This was the part none of us had yet heard.

"The Marshals Service moved me to a small town north of San Francisco," she began. "I chose Vanessa Snow as my new name—Snow for the place I'd left behind, and Vanessa...well...for the brother I loved and missed."

Van lowered his eyes, and Vivian grabbed a tissue and dabbed at hers. "I got a degree in library sciences and became a librarian. My mother had a heart attack and died soon after I moved away from Rock Creek Village. The Marshals Service sent me word."

"I heard," Donovan said. "I'm so sorry."

It took a moment for Vivian to compose herself enough to continue. "It was horrible not seeing her again. And not to be able to even attend her funeral..." She wiped her eyes and took a breath. "Anyway, I led a quiet life—a few casual friends. But it was hard for me to get close to anyone. After George...and Mom...well, I never knew when I might have to leave someone I loved. So, I chose not to love anyone."

It was a heart-wrenching tale, and all at once, I understood Vivian's choice to stop running.

Donovan reached a hand toward the camera. "I can't find the words to express how sorry I am, Val. For everything. I implored Jack to back down, but he refused. He said he wouldn't rest until you'd begged for his forgiveness. If he had to track you down and drag you back to get that apology, so be it. When he died, I told the family we were through searching for you, that we'd leave you in peace."

Vivian shook her head. "If you called off the search, Van, how did Eugene find me here?"

Donovan sighed. "It might be hard to believe, but it had to be pure coincidence. He was in the village with that Lydia woman..."

I wrinkled my nose at the distaste in his voice. He apparently thought as highly of Gene's choice of paramour as Tonya had of Lydia's.

"How did he recognize me?" Vivian asked. "He hadn't even been born when I...when I left."

He bit his lip. "I'm afraid that's my fault. A couple of years ago, I ran into some health problems..."

Vivian sucked in a breath. "Health problems?"

He raised his hand. "We can talk about that later. Suffice it to say, it left me longing to see you again, Val. To make things right between us. So I took the last photo I had of you..." He grabbed a frame from his desk and turned it toward the screen. In it, a young woman in her twenties stood next to a dashing younger version of Donovan Murray. The two of them had their arms around each other's shoulders, and they smiled with genuine glee.

Vivian leaned in and stared at the photo, her current smile bittersweet.

"I took the photo to one of those age progression services," he said. "They created this."

Now he brandished what appeared to be a portrait studio image of Vivian at her current age. As to be expected, there were minor discrepancies—the white of her hair wasn't exactly right, the curve of her eyebrows off a bit —but overall, the likeness was uncanny.

"Gene saw the photo. Everyone in the family did. I can only speculate that he recognized you from that. I can't be certain since...well, since I can't ask him."

He choked on the last words and looked away. Vivian covered her heart with both hands. "Oh, Van. What happened to Eugene...it's awful. I hope you can believe me when I tell you I had nothing to do with his death. The doctor says I may never regain my memories of those moments, but I know in my heart I would never hurt anyone, especially not your son."

Donovan wiped away his tears and locked eyes with his sister. "I know that, Val. Tommy tried to convince me otherwise, but I assured him there'd never been a mean bone in my sister's body. You used to rescue bugs that got trapped in the house, cupping them in your little hands and setting them free outside, remember?"

The image of Vivian smashing her knee into Tommy's nose flashed into my mind. Maybe Donovan didn't know everything there was to know about his sister's capabilities.

Donovan smiled at his own memory, then continued. "Tommy has always held a grudge against you. He rants about how you were responsible for sending his father to prison. I told him you only testified against Jack because you had a conscience the size of Las Vegas."

"And I wanted to save you from Jack's fate," Vivian whispered.

"Yes. You saved me. I've never forgotten that, Valerie. We have an unbreakable bond." He shook his head. "Tommy, though...I don't know how much you remember about him..."

"He was sixteen during the trial," Vivian said. "He'd just gotten his driver's license. The boy was a wild one back then."

"He only got worse," Donovan said. "From the day he was born, that child felt entitled. No desire to work for anything. When Jack died, I tried numerous times to take the business legitimate. To a large extent, I succeeded. But Tommy continually undermined my efforts, to the point of pulling Gene into his illegal activities. He's a degenerate, possibly even a sociopath."

He took a moment to drink some water, then cleared his throat and continued. "When Gene went to Rock

Creek Village last week, Tommy headed out there, too. Said he wanted to make sure Gene wasn't pussyfooting around with the local business owners. Then Gene died, and Tommy contacted me to tell me you were in Rock Creek Village. Since that moment, I've lived in terror that he might harm you. I warned him and threatened him, but nothing I said got through to him. Losing my only son was bad enough. If I'd lost you, too...I didn't know what to do."

Well, you could've phoned the Rock Creek Village police and expressed your concerns, I thought. *You could've driven here and warned your sister in person.* But when I looked at the man on the screen—his stooped shoulders, his sickly countenance—I almost sympathized. Everyone had a story, as I'd learned during my years as a journalist. Everyone got the way they were through the totality of their experiences. It didn't excuse bad behavior, but it might at least explain it.

Vivian took a deep breath. "Van, about Eugene. If Tommy was in town at the time of his murder, do you think it might've been Tommy who—?"

Donovan held up a trembling hand to stop her. "I know you have people there with you, Val. And I expect you're recording this conversation. It's the smart thing to do, and you've always been smart as a whip. But I won't speculate aloud on anything concerning Tommy. I'll leave law enforcement to figure it out."

She nodded. "I understand."

"And just for the record, the Murray family business exists no more—even the legitimate parts. I'm an old man, and with my son dead and Tommy in jail, I've terminated it. Forever."

"I think that's for the best," Vivian said.

Donovan blotted a handkerchief across his brow. His

energy appeared to be waning, but he wasn't ready to end the conversation quite yet.

"I want to assure you that you're safe, Valerie. I swear on my dear mother's grave. You have no reason to go back into hiding. No one in this family will ever pose a threat to you again."

He paused and frowned. "I mentioned my health earlier, Val. It's...well, it's been declining for a while now. Parkinson's, I'm told. No one can say how much longer I have—months, maybe. A year if I'm lucky. But...I'd love to see you in person one last time. To put my arms around you. I understand you might feel wary of coming back to Vegas, so I'd come to you. Anywhere you want. Just...please say you'll consider it."

"I will," she promised. "Until then, we can talk online whenever you'd like. I'm happy we've reconnected. You're my dear brother. The only one in the world who shares a history with me. Memories of my childhood."

After that, talk shifted back to nostalgia and reminiscences. Disinterested in the trip down memory lane, Carl curled up in my lap and began to snore. I tuned out as well, turning my focus to the ramifications of the conversation. I was fully on team Vivian/Valerie/Vanessa now. There was no way she'd killed Gene. But did that mean Tommy had done the deed? Even his own uncle seemed to think so, though he wasn't willing to go on the record.

I shook my head. How could a family get so dysfunctional? I thought of Tonya and Lydia and their strange love-hate relationship. For the umpteenth time, I thanked my lucky stars I'd been dealt the parents I'd gotten. Family could be a blessing and a burden, all at the same time. Vivian had lived with the burden of her family for forty years. Maybe now, getting back in touch with her brother, she'd be able to capture a smidgen of blessing.

Chapter Forty-Five

It was Thursday morning, ten days after Gene's murder, and my mother and I were en route to the scene of the crime—Western Pioneer Cemetery. Mrs. Barney had requested additional tombstone photos for her upcoming book, and Mom wanted to add a few more grave rubbings to her collection, so we were on our way to capture a few more graven images.

As soon as she got in the car, Mom warned me she was enacting a moratorium against any discussion of murder and mayhem. "Let's just enjoy a pleasant morning," she said.

"At the cemetery," I quipped.

"Yes, darling. The cemetery can be a peaceful, contemplative setting."

"Unless the dead bodies are lying on top of the graves rather than beneath them."

As she shooshed me, I pulled out of the Knotty Pine lot and onto Evergreen Way, content to let her win this round. After all, the murder had been solved. At least, so they told me.

I had to admit I hadn't entirely quieted the niggle of doubt in my brain, but since it was my nature to be forever unsatisfied, I told myself to let it go. There were other topics in the world besides crime, right?

But when we were a half mile from our destination, a herd of elk decided it was the perfect time to hold a family meeting in the middle of the road. As we waited for their conference to end, I drummed my fingers on the steering wheel and shot a sidelong glance at my mother. "About the Murrays—"

She raised an eyebrow. "Callahan Maureen Cassidy, I know you understand the definition of moratorium." She huffed. "Besides, there's nothing left to say."

"So, I guess you don't want me to give you the latest on Lydia..."

Interest gleamed in her eyes. I watched her face as she wrestled with the angel and devil on her own shoulders. Finally, the devil won, as she so often did. Mom threw her hands in the air. "All right, all right. What's going on with Lydia?"

I resisted the urge to crow. "I had coffee with Tonya this morning. Mrs. Finney joined us, of course, and Monika..."

Mom sighed. "Get to the point, darling."

"Lydia called Tonya last night from an unknown number. For some reason, she's still using a burner phone."

"Caught up in the intrigue, no doubt," Mom said. "Drama always was her way."

"Anyway, Tonya told her the danger was over and she could come back, but Lydia said in the interest of safety, she and her 'friend' are off to Asia."

"The continent?"

"She wouldn't be more specific. She said the less Tonya knows, the safer she'll be."

Mom shook her head. "That woman truly baffles me. How's Tonya handling it?"

I shrugged. "She's used to her mother's antics. I think she's relieved she won't have to deal with her for a while. Her biggest worry revolves around inevitably having to meet boyfriend number three hundred and ten, or whatever he is."

The conversation paused when one of the elk lowered his antlers and prodded his brother. Was the family meeting turning into a rumble? I placed a hand on the gearshift, ready to reverse if necessary. This time of year, elk were unpredictable, and I didn't want my Honda becoming a casualty of family dysfunction. From the backseat, Woody uttered a low growl, as if offering to handle the herd. Carl barely bothered to lift his head.

Eventually, the two elk settled their differences, and the herd completed its trek across the road. I put the car in drive and took off toward the cemetery.

"So," I said tentatively, wondering if we'd officially concluded the moratorium. "Did you ever discover how Vivian got to Rock Creek Village?"

Mom sighed in surrender. "She still doesn't remember any of that. But Frank told your father their working theory is that she took a bus to Boulder and caught a rideshare from there to the village."

"Any evidence to support that theory?" I asked.

"No, darling. It's a question to which we may never have a definitive answer."

I wrinkled my nose. Unanswered questions were the bane of my existence. One of them, anyway.

"I've been thinking about Jamal," Mom said, changing the subject. "Dad said he's back to work."

"Yes. The doctor says there's no lung damage, and his

burns are almost healed. He's back to normal, and so is Snow Plow Chow."

"Good to hear." A smile played at her lips. "Speaking of the Chow…"

Uh oh. I had an idea where this conversation was headed.

"I'm told Sam has planned an outing for the two of you," she said. "Monday, isn't it?"

I nodded but didn't speak.

"Are you ready?" she asked.

"Ready for what?"

She gave me a look. "Angelface, it's no secret that boy has been itching to propose. Now that you and his parents have mended old wounds, the writing is on the wall. I'm your mother. I want to know how you feel about it."

I chewed on a cuticle as I pondered the question. When Sam had suggested a romantic afternoon in the mountains, I, too, suspected a proposal might be in the works, and I'd been giving it a lot of thought. In fact, some people—like my therapist—might characterize it as obsessing. Though the prospect of marriage still provoked an internal battle between anxiety and excitement, anxiety was losing its footing. When I thought of Sam these days, the word "forever" floated through my mind—and my heart. I wanted him. I wanted us.

"I love him, Mom. I think I'm ready for a future with him."

She clapped her hands. "Oh, darling. How wonderful!"

"Listen, don't get ahead of yourself. We don't know that he's planning to propose. Maybe he just wants to take me on a hike."

She emitted a chortle.

"I'm serious," I said. "I'm not prepared to plan the wedding."

"Yet," she said with a knowing smile.

To my relief—and thanks in large part to my lead foot on the accelerator—we pulled into the cemetery parking lot, putting an end to further speculation. After I hopped out of the car and looped my camera around my neck, I placed Carl in his carrier and snapped Woody's leash onto his collar—all the while casting a righteous glance toward Mr. Fallow's cottage. Mom retrieved her supplies from the trunk, and we took off down the path.

On cue, Mr. Fallow stepped onto his front porch and crossed his arms. "See that you keep those animals restrained."

"Good morning, Cedric," my mother sang out. "Hope you have a lovely day. Looks like we might get an early snowfall. Stay warm."

He pursed his lips and grunted. I tried to swallow a giggle but only managed to mute it.

We walked through the canopy of trees and into the heart of the cemetery. I lifted my face to the sky. Mom was right—from the look of the puffy gray clouds overhead and the escalating breeze tickling the aspens, snow seemed imminent. Though it was only October, it wasn't unusual to get a dusting this time of year. If so, it would likely be gone in a day and wouldn't put a damper on the big date Sam had planned.

As my thoughts returned to rings and promises, a loud screech came from the carrier on my back. Carl began scratching at the mesh. Then he turned his fury to my back. I yelped, dropped Woody's leash, and wriggled the cat off my back. Though Carl was known for his petulance, this level of agitation was unusual. The second I unzipped the carrier to explore the issue, he clawed his way out and darted down the path. Woody ignored my "stay" command and ran after him.

"Something's wrong," I said. Captain Obvious.

I took off after them and heard Mom pattering behind me. It didn't take long to reach them. When I spied the two golden creatures at George Corwin's grave, I experienced a wave of déjà vu—one that deepened when I spotted a figure crumpled on the ground.

Not again.

Carl emitted a fierce yowl designed to break my paralysis. It worked. I stepped forward. I could see that the figure was a man. Then I got a glimpse of his face, and my heart dropped.

It was Ken Pearly.

His eyes were closed, and his mouth drooped open. Was he...? I couldn't see his chest rising and falling with breath.

When I leaned over to put my fingers to his neck, I noticed a toothpick on the ground near his mouth. No surprise. It was Mr. Pearly's habit to chew on a toothpick. But it triggered a memory, an image in my mind. At that moment, the curtain in my brain opened, and I understood it all: Vivian's injury, Gene's murder—even the fire at the restaurant.

I touched the camera hanging from its strap around my neck. A scroll through my saved photos would confirm my theory. But not now. I needed to tend to the man lying at the foot of George Corwin's grave.

As I reached out to check for a pulse, Mr. Pearly stirred. He was alive. Barely alive, it seemed, but there was hope.

Mom reached us then, her eyes widening as she saw him lying there. "It's Ken. What happened to him?"

His eyes fluttered open, finding first me, then Mom. A

faint smile crossed his face, followed by a flash of regret. "I'm sorry," he said, his words slurring. "So very sorry. I wish you hadn't found me. Not yet."

Mom crouched beside him and touched his forehead. "Ken, you're so cold." She shrugged out of her jacket and covered him with it. She turned to me, her expression anxious. "He needs an ambulance."

I nodded, pulled out my phone, and grimaced when I looked at the screen. No service.

"I'll be right back." I sprinted back up the path far enough to find a signal and called 9-1-1. In less than two minutes, I gave the dispatcher details and disconnected without answering questions. I was back at the scene in a flash, breathing hard.

My mother knelt on the ground beside Mr. Pearly, and the creatures sat at attention nearby, as if holding vigil. Mr. Pearly's lips were blue and his breathing ragged. If help didn't arrive soon, I feared we'd lose him.

"Mr. Pearly, where are you hurt?" I asked.

With great effort, he lifted his hand and pointed to his chest. "In here, my friend. I'm hurt in here. But it's not a wound you'll see. It's in my soul."

He looked at my mother then, affection filling his glassy eyes. "Don't fret, Maggie. I'm going to a better place."

He struggled to free an envelope from his pocket. "The answers are here. I pray you will forgive me. That everyone will."

"For what?" I asked, though I thought I knew.

My mother held up a hand to silence me. She leaned toward Mr. Pearly and laid a gentle hand on his cheek. "Of course, Ken. You're forgiven. Be at peace."

Tiny snowflakes began to fall. Mr. Pearly turned his

gaze to them and smiled. "So beautiful," he said. His eyelids drifted shut, and his breathing stopped.

I nudged Mom aside and rolled Mr. Pearly onto his back, ready to begin CPR.

"It's no use," Mom whispered. "He's gone, darling." She held up a pill bottle. "I found this beside him. He's overdosed."

"Still, I have to try."

As I positioned my hands on the man's chest, Woody barked. Footsteps pounded down the path, and I turned to see the paramedics. I got to my feet and moved aside, letting them do their thing. Mr. Pearly was limp and unresponsive beneath their touch.

Mom was right. Mr. Pearly was dead.

Chapter Forty-Six

My mother and I stood a few feet away as the EMTs did their best to reverse fate. Woody and Carl sat quietly at our feet. When all hope was lost, the medics busied themselves with analysis while they waited for the police to arrive.

Mom hugged me tight, then held up the envelope. "Should we hand this over to the detectives, or...?"

She trailed off, but I didn't hesitate. "I say we do both. Read it first, then turn it over to Raul and Lynn." She seemed uncertain, but selfish as it sounded, I wanted a look at that letter. "Mr. Pearly gave it to you, Mom. He meant for you to read it."

She started to remove the letter from the envelope, but I stopped her. "Before you open it, let me check something." I turned on my camera and scrolled through photos until I reached one of Gene's body lying on this very spot days earlier. I leaned in, squinted, and...yes, there it was. That small shard of wood near Gene's body. A toothpick.

"What is it?" Mom asked.

"Evidence I overlooked. We all did."

I explained my hypothesis, and Mom nodded thoughtfully. "I'm sorry to say it makes perfect sense. Let's see if Ken's letter verifies your theory."

She removed a piece of cream-colored stationery from the envelope and unfolded it, positioning it so we could both read it.

To my Rock Creek Village family:

Time is running out for me, so I'll keep this brief. But I want—need—to explain my transgressions and beg forgiveness.

Here's my story. I've been known to be wordy, so I hope you'll bear with me.

I always loved cooking and running my restaurant, but I was never especially skilled at the financial aspects. Still, I made ends meet and even profited most years— until recently. The past couple of years, my debt outpaced my earnings so significantly that I was on the brink of losing my business. The restaurant I'd loved for so long. My life.

So, when Gene Murray approached me last year with a proposition to launder Murray family money, I viewed it as a way out. It was an unsavory alliance, but I rationalized it was a victimless crime. I couldn't come up with any other way to save my restaurant. I vowed to myself that I would partner with him only until I'd repaid my loans. After that, I'd break ties.

You've probably guessed by now that it didn't work out that way.

When I told Gene I wanted out, he laughed at me and said I no longer had a choice, that I was in bed with his family forever.

I didn't know what to do. I couldn't involve the police—I'd broken the law. I'd lose everything.

Never have I experienced the depth of panic and despair that filled me in those days. But I nurtured a spark of hope that everything would turn out all right. When I saw Gene jogging into the cemetery that terrible morning, I followed him. Foolish man that I am, I believed I might find the words that would make him see reason.

I don't know what impulse caused me to snatch up the pickaxe I tripped over as I wove through the cemetery. I dearly wish I hadn't. Moments later, I heard angry voices. I followed the sound to George Corwin's grave, where I witnessed Gene grabbing an older woman's arm. As I watched, she pulled away from him, stumbled, and fell. I heard the thwack of her head as it hit the tombstone. Then she lay still. Gene bent over her, and I thought he meant to kill her...if she wasn't dead already.

Instinct took over. I ran from the trees and shouted at him to leave her alone. When he saw it was me, he laughed at me. Again. He took out his phone and began tapping at the screen, as if my presence was inconsequential. As if he hadn't just injured, or possibly killed, a woman.

I snatched the phone from his hand. When he clawed at my arm, trying to retrieve it, I swung the pickaxe at him. I felt its sharp tip sink into his flesh. Blood spurted from his neck. That image has haunted me every day since.

Coward that I am, I ran.

I left Gene to die. Even worse, I left that poor woman behind, not knowing if she was dead or alive.

I threw Gene's phone into the waters of Rock Creek. After that, I tried to act as if everything was normal. I opened the restaurant, cooked steaks, greeted customers. I didn't think, just acted. Muscle memory, they call it.

The next night, Tommy Murray came to the steakhouse with Tonya Stephens' mother. A loud argument flared up between them. When I came out of the kitchen to deal with them, Tommy laughed at me, just as Gene had. I walked away and shut myself inside my office. My entire body shook with rage and fear. I had just managed to calm myself when Tommy entered, without even bothering to knock. It was as if he owned the place. Owned me. With a cocky smirk on his face, he assured me his cousin's death didn't end my alliance with his family. I knew then there was no way out for me.

That's the moment when I decided to destroy my own restaurant. The place was my life's work, my passion, but I refused to let evil scumbags like the Murrays control it. With the insurance money, I thought I might even start fresh in another town.

I told my employees we were experiencing equipment malfunctions and would need to close the restaurant until repairs were made. Once the place was empty, I lit a few matches, tossed them into the grease trap, and left, knowing it would only be a matter of time.

But as my father used to say, if I didn't have bad luck, I'd have no luck at all. Jamal happened by just as the flames began to spread. In his valiant effort to save my restaurant, the young man sustained injuries. I'll never forgive myself for that.

What an idiot I'd been. I hadn't stopped to think that my selfish acts might harm someone else. If Jamal hadn't extinguished the fire, it could have damaged neighboring businesses—or worse, killed someone. When had I turned into such a monster?

That brings me to today. I find I cannot live with my guilt and anguish. I have no family anymore—except you, my Rock Creek Village family. And I have failed you.

You'll find my will in an unlocked safe in my bedroom closet, along with a copy of this letter.
May those I've hurt find it in their hearts to forgive me.
Regretfully, Ken Pearly

I TOOK the letter from my mother's trembling hands and tucked it back into the envelope just as Raul and Lynn came running toward us. Tears poured down Mom's cheeks, and I realized I was crying, too. Lynn headed straight toward Mr. Pearly and the EMTs, while Raul stopped in front of Mom and me. I held out the letter.

"Ken Pearly killed Gene Murray," I said. "This is his confession."

Mom snuffled and swiped at her cheeks. "This proves Vivian didn't kill Gene," she said. "Tommy Murray is innocent, too."

"The letter clears Tommy in Gene's death, that's true," I said. "But he's far from innocent. Thankfully, he's facing a mountain of other serious charges. Hopefully, he'll still go to jail for a long time."

Raul glanced at the envelope, then his eyes flicked to Mr. Pearly. Lynn caught his eye and shook her head.

He turned back to us wearing a concerned expression. "Are the two of you all right?"

We both nodded. Raul studied us for a moment, then headed over off to confer with Lynn and the paramedics.

A sob escaped Mom, and I reached for her. We held each other tight, letting the tears fall as the creatures nestled against us.

I glanced toward Mr. Pearly. He was just a bulky figure beneath a blanket now, not an inch of him visible. He was gone, and his death would leave a void in the village. The man had made mistakes, that was certain. And those mistakes had caused grief, worry, and heartache for many people—both guilty and innocent. But his letter had been his final gift.

The murder investigation was closed.

Chapter Forty-Seven

The sun gleamed across the mountain peaks, and pine trees swayed in the soft breeze as Sam and I drove through the Rocky Mountain National Park. Though an inch of snow had fallen days earlier, the predictable unpredictability of Colorado weather brought unseasonably warm temperatures today, perfect for a picnic in the park.

On the drive, we spotted elk roaming in a meadow, as well as a few deer. The scenery bordered on perfection—a picture postcard I should be itching to photograph.

But circumstances rendered me too distracted to appreciate nature's beauty. It was Date Day, and if my mother's prophecy was correct, it might mean an enormous change in my life.

Sam glanced at my hands twisting in my lap. "You seem preoccupied."

"Hmm? No."

"What are you thinking about, then?"

I gave myself a shake, trying to bring myself back to the

present moment. "Just that last time we attempted a picnic, it didn't go so well."

"I'm hoping this one will have a better result," he said.

I swiveled in my seat to look at him, and the smile I'd been faking turned genuine. Sam gazed out the windshield, his hands resting lightly on the steering wheel. He'd rolled up the cuffs on his shirt, revealing his forearms. I could almost feel those arms wrapped around me, pulling me into his chest. With a happy sigh, I put a hand on his knee, causing his blue eyes to twinkle and his smile to broaden.

I loved this man with all my heart. What did I have to be nervous about?

Sam shot me a devious look. "Guess what? I am currently in possession of insider information that even master snoop Callahan Cassidy does not possess."

I frowned. "Master snoop?"

"Consider it a compliment. But let's not get side-tracked. Do you want to know what I know?"

I squeezed his knee. "You'd better believe I do."

He waggled his eyebrows. "What's it worth to you?"

I took his hand, kissed each fingertip, then let my lips rest on his palm. "How's that for starters?"

"I'm definitely getting the better end of this bargain. But we should save the rest of the payment for later. These windy roads require my attention."

I laughed and leaned back in my seat. "All right, enough with the intrigue. Tell me what supposedly tasty tidbit you've acquired before me."

"Remember you told me Pearly left a will?" he asked.

My eyebrows shot up. "Yes...?"

"Well, in it he left his restaurant to Jamal."

"What? You're kidding. That's not just a tidbit. That's huge!"

Sam grinned. "Figured you'd be interested."

The smile fell from my face as I thought of poor Ken Pearly, tortured by the Murrays and then by his own demons. Yet his ultimate acts had been ones of kindness—his confession letter and now the bequest of his restaurant to the young man who had been injured saving it.

"I assume he wrote the will after the fire," I said.

Sam nodded. "Had it notarized the day before he…"

He trailed off, but I knew. The day before he'd overdosed.

We drove without speaking for a minute or two, both paying our silent respects to the man. Then, a thought occurred to me, and I cocked my head. "If Jamal owns a restaurant, that means he'll be leaving Snow Plow Chow."

Sam shrugged. "At least he's not leaving the village."

"Can you handle the competition?" I teased.

"Ha. We won't be competing. As you know, the Chow has transitioned to serving only breakfast and lunch. Jamal's talking about creating an upscale dinner venue."

"In Rock Creek Village? Even with tourism, it doesn't seem as if there'd be enough of a customer base to keep him afloat long."

"He's researching a concept called 'destination dining.'" I made a face, and Sam caught it. "I hadn't heard of it either. Apparently, it's a millennial thing. Very exclusive. People will come from all over for a chance to eat at a place like that."

"Interesting." I touched a finger to my lips. "Sounds like the kind of thing social influencers like Bradley and Tim would be into. Bet we could get them to help with promotion."

"Good thinking," Sam said.

I smiled to myself, happy to discover a pebble of joy amidst the painful rubble of the Murray scandal.

"What will you do when he leaves?" I asked. "Go back to cooking, or hire another chef?"

"Well, Jamal will still be with me for a while. The will has to go through probate, which takes time. Then he'll have to tackle restoration and renovation. After that, I don't know...maybe I'll hire my parents."

I chuckled. "They seemed to enjoy themselves the day they pitched in."

"They did, but not enough to return to the snowy weather. Florida climate is way too appealing for them. They're excited for us to visit, though. I told them possibly February."

I pictured Sam and Elyse lying on the beach with Conrad and Lila and sighed, a little envious. But wait—wouldn't Elyse be in school in February?

Then it hit me. "When you say *us*, do you mean you and me?"

He laughed. "Yes. You and me."

I grinned. I guess his parents still liked me.

Sam pulled into the Moraine Lake parking lot, and I felt a flash of dismay. The place was fine for families, but it didn't brim with romantic vibes. On the plus side, cars were sparse and there wasn't a school bus in sight. I liked kids, but I didn't need a cluster of them witnessing Sam's proposal.

He carried the picnic basket, spread out a nice feast, and we ate. That was it. No candles, no wine...I was beginning to think my mother had been wrong.

But when we finished the last brownie, Sam smiled across the table at me. "I have something for you. A gift."

My heart rate accelerated. My palms started to sweat. Sam handed me a box.

A long, rectangular box.

This must be some oddly shaped ring.

I tore off the wrapping paper, opened the lid, and stared at the contents. "A watch?"

"An Apple watch." He smiled. "You said you wanted one. Do you like it?"

"I...uh...of course I do. I love it. Thank you. That's very thoughtful."

My disappointment surprised me. A few weeks ago, I wasn't sure I was ready to get engaged. But now that it hadn't happened, I was experiencing an emotion akin to sadness.

Apparently oblivious to my internal turmoil, Sam packed up the lunch things and held out his hand. "Ready to go? I was hoping to get in a hike. Your new watch can track our steps."

"Sure. That sounds great."

We stashed the picnic basket in the trunk and left the parking lot. Ten minutes later, we turned onto a small side road. I perked up when I realized he was taking us to the Alluvial Fan. The trails there were among our favorites.

Surprisingly, the parking lot was empty. This time of year, the place was rarely packed, but normally we'd find at least a few hikers on the trails. I pointed to a large blue tent at the far side of the lot. "What's up with that?"

"Rocky Mountain National Park Marathon this weekend, remember? This will be the finish line. Guess they're getting things set up."

He took me by the hand, and we headed across the bridge leading to the hiking trail. When we reached the center of the bridge, Sam stopped and rested his elbows on the railing, gazing up at the fan. I leaned on the railing beside him, tucking my arm through his. "You've always loved this place," I murmured.

"Fitting, since I've also always loved you."

He kissed me, and I melted into him. He gestured to

the water and the stones. "Do you know the history of the Alluvial Fan?"

I swatted his arm. "Of course I do. I grew up here, too. Back in…what? 1982?…a breach in the earthen dam at Lawn Lake sent a wall of water and debris sweeping down the mountainside. It demolished the existing landscape."

He lifted his chin to the scene. "Look at it now."

I did. A rush of water cascaded across the boulders. I closed my eyes and listened to the soothing babbling sound. "Beautiful," I murmured.

"More than beautiful. Symbolic. See the bushes and trees growing among the boulders? It's life rising from destruction. Renewal. Like us."

I turned and looked into his eyes. They were shining, and it was the glow of pure love.

He dropped to one knee. My hands flew to my mouth. Unlike the Apple watch box, the one he held now was small and square and velvet.

"You're my renewal, Callie. Every day we're together, I feel reborn. I want to feel that way for the rest of my life. And I want to give you that same happiness." He opened the box, and the ring inside glittered in the light. "Callahan Maureen Cassidy, will you marry me?"

Hot tears flowed down my cheeks. Happy tears.

Sam cupped his ear. "I can't hear you…"

"Yes, Sam. The answer is yes. Yes to forever. Yes to never letting you go again. Yes, yes, yes!"

He let out a whoop and jumped to his feet, folding me in his arms. Then he kissed me, and the world was right.

After a moment, I pushed him away. "Enough of the mushiness. Let's see that ring."

He laughed and reached into the box, plucking out the most perfect piece of jewelry I could have imagined. Once he'd slipped it on my finger, I held it up and studied it. "I've never seen anything like this."

"It's called a grey spinel. I wanted something unique, something…you." A worried expression crossed his face. "If you don't like it, we can exchange it."

I wrapped my arms around his neck. "Sam, I love it. And I love you."

We kissed again, but the sound of barking interrupted us. It was a bark I recognized, and it was coming from nearby.

Sam cringed. "Oops. Guess I forgot something."

He reached inside his jacket pocket and pulled out a cylindrical device with a string hanging from the bottom. Holding it over our heads, he pulled the string. The device emitted a loud popping noise and a shower of silver confetti.

I looked over his shoulder at the canopy in the parking lot. The fold opened, and Woody dashed out, running toward us at warp speed. Behind him, people erupted through the opening. First Mom, then Dad, holding Carl. Then Elyse. Tonya and David. Summer, Jessica, Renata, Ethan, Zoe, Raul, Lynn. And bringing up the rear, Mrs. Finney and Mr. Purdy.

"You planned all this? And managed to keep it a secret?" I said in wonder.

"Even the master snoop didn't figure it out," he said proudly.

I gave him a side eye. "Well, genius, what if I'd said no?"

He reached into his other pocket and pulled out a similar device, this one black. "It whistles instead of pops. If they heard a whistle, they were instructed to stay in the tent. Would have been really embarrassing. Glad you didn't make me use it."

Woody made it to the bridge first. He leapt up on his hind legs, stretching to full height and resting one front paw on my shoulder and the other on Sam's. Mom and Dad arrived next and pulled Sam and me in for a squeeze. In keeping with his nature, Carl rolled his eyes at all the fuss but then graced us with a favorable purr.

Elyse trotted onto the bridge, bouncing on the balls of her feet. She held out her phone to show us Lila and Conrad clapping their approval.

The rest of our friends converged around us, and there was so much hugging and laughing and chattering. I hoped the bridge could sustain the weight of all these people who loved us so much. A surge of joy bubbled through me. It was so all-encompassing I almost couldn't bear it. My gaze drifted to the Alluvial Fan, and I remembered what Sam had said about renewal. About new life rising from what appeared to be destruction. I stared at my ring. I felt Sam's eyes on me, then his arm around my shoulders. I smiled up at my boyfriend. My fiancé. Soon to be my husband.

And I felt renewed.

Become a Subscriber

Ready for a trip back in time to meet Callie and her friends in their younger years? Subscribe today to receive two free prequel short stories.

It's free to sign up, and you'll never be spammed by me. You can opt out at any time.

www.lorirobertsherbst.com

Acknowledgments

I'd intended this book, number six in the Callie Cassidy series, to be released six months earlier than it actually was. As the song "Beautiful Boy" says, "Life is what happens while you're busy making other plans." But I'm glad the book is finally here, and I know it wouldn't have been born at all without the support and encouragement of some exceptional people. Thanks and appreciation go out to the following:

My Sisters in Crime friends and colleagues who helped push the story across the finish line. I doubt I'd be an author today without this incredible group. The friendships I've made, the mentors I've found, and the resources they've made available have enhanced my career in ways I never imagined possible.

My exceptional group of beta readers for GRAVEN IMAGES: Lynda Allen, Syrl Kazlo, Jane Meyers, Mary Rosewood, Debra Shaw, Grace Topping, and Cheryl Wilson. You improved the story and the structure of this novel tenfold, and I'm so appreciative.

My editor and friend, Lisa Q. Mathews of Kill Your Darlings Editing Services. How lucky I am to have found an editor who has grown to be a dear friend. Thank you for always making time for me, even when your own life is crazy busy.

My cover designer, Molly Burton, at Cozy Cover Designs. This amazingly talented woman always manages to provide a tangible vision for my stories. I so enjoy working with her.

Readers, readers, readers. I can't say thank you enough to the people who tell me they are impatiently waiting for the next book. You keep me motivated and driven.

As always, my wonderful family for grounding me, making me laugh, and giving me purpose.

And especially my husband, Paul, always my first and most loyal reader. I'm grateful for the space you give me to pursue my writing and for the light you've given my life.

About the Author

Silver Falchion and CIBA Murder & Mayhem award-winning author Lori Roberts Herbst writes the Callie Cassidy Mystery series. A former journalism teacher and counselor, Lori serves as Board Secretary for Sisters in Crime. She is a member of Mystery Writers of America, as well as the SinC Colorado chapter, the SinC North Dallas chapter, and the Guppy chapter, where she moderates the Cozy Gup group. Lori spent most of her life as a Texan but recently moved to Colorado Springs. She is a wife, mother of two, and (gasp!) grandmother of four. You can follow Lori on Facebook, Instagram, Goodreads, Amazon, and BookBub.

Subscribe to Lori's newsletter for updates and other fun stuff (including FREE Callie Cassidy prequel stories) at www.lorirobertsherbst.com

www.ingramcontent.com/pod-product-compliance
Lightning Source LLC
Chambersburg PA
CBHW022014310726
48972CB00006B/1648